THE INN at EAGLE HILL

A Novel

SUZANNE WOODS FISHER

Revell
a division of Baker Publishing Group
Grand Rapids, Michigan

Published by Revell
a division of Baker Publishing Group
P.O. Box 6287, Grand Rapids, MI 49516-6287
www.revellbooks.com

Mass market edition published 2017
ISBN 978-0-8007-2921-9

Printed in the United States of America

Most Scripture used in this book, whether quoted or paraphrased by the characters, is taken from the King James Version of the Bible.

This book is a work of fiction. Names, characters, places, and incidents are the product of the author's imagination or are used fictitiously. Any resemblance to actual events, locales, or persons, living or dead, is coincidental.

Published in association with Joyce Hart of the Hartline Literary Agency, LLC.

17 18 19 20 21 22 23 7 6 5 4 3 2 1

Praise for *The Calling*

"Fisher is an amazing author. She has written a believable story about those who embrace their flaws."

—*RT Book Reviews*

"Fisher's new romance novel has enough twists and turns to satisfy any reader, but those who want to see the special world of Amish culture and family will be rewarded too."

—*Literary Scene*

Praise for The Inn at Eagle Hill

"Fans will cheer at this latest offering from the popular Amish romance specialist."

—*Publishers Weekly* on *The Letters*

"We get a glimpse of life few outsiders are privileged to see, with some surprises, twists and turns."

—*RT Book Reviews* on *The Letters*

"Woods Fisher brings together every tantalizing thread in this bold conclusion to The Inn at Eagle Hill series, perfectly weaving revelations and romance."

—CBA Retailers on *The Revealing*

"Readers can expect to be chuckling one minute and getting misty eyed over the sweetly written romance the next minute. This book has it all, and is highly recommended for all readers."

—Family Fiction on *The Revealing*

Books by Suzanne Woods Fisher

Amish Peace: Simple Wisdom for a Complicated World

Amish Proverbs: Words of Wisdom from the Simple Life

Amish Values for Your Family: What We Can Learn from the Simple Life

A Lancaster County Christmas

Christmas at Rose Hill Farm

The Heart of the Amish

AMISH BEGINNINGS

Anna's Crossing

The Newcomer

LANCASTER COUNTY SERIES

The Choice

The Waiting

The Search

SEASONS OF STONEY RIDGE

The Keeper

The Haven

The Lesson

THE INN AT EAGLE HILL

The Letters

The Calling

The Revealing

THE BISHOP'S FAMILY

The Imposter

The Quieting

The Devoted

Dedicated to
my youngest son, Tad,
who spent days during Christmas 2012 reading
through the messy first draft of this manuscript,
and nights walking and rock-
ing his newborn niece to sleep.

1

As far as Bethany Schrock was concerned, this summer was hotter than a firecracker lit on both ends. A little rain would certainly be welcome, she thought, as she untied her stiff prayer cap strings and tossed them over her shoulders, but the heat wave held Stoney Ridge tightly in its grip. All the more reason to set to work in the cool of the basement of the Sisters' House.

At the bottom of the basement stairs, she held the lantern up to gaze around the dusty, cobwebby basement, and blew out a puff of air. If it were even possible, there was more clutter down here than in the rest of the house. She'd been steadily trying to organize the Sisters' House for weeks now and had barely made a dent. Sylvia, the youngest of the five elderly sisters of the Sisters' House, had told her she was doing a fine job and they didn't know how she worked so quickly. "You are a doggedly determined young lady," Sylvia had said.

Bethany had smiled, pleased that Sylvia was so pleased. She had always considered doggedness to be a rather unappealing characteristic, but it had been valuable at the Sisters' House. "Thank you," she told Sylvia. "It's easy when you know how to organize things."

The sisters, on the other hand, did not know how. They were in desperate need of someone with dogged determination after the deacon had gently reminded them they were overdue in taking a turn to host church. Overdue by years and years. They needed to get their house tidied up first, they told him, giving him their sweetest smiles. And that's where Bethany came in.

Jimmy Fisher had done the sisters a very great favor by suggesting they hire Bethany to organize their house. If it wouldn't cause his big head to swell even bigger, she might even tell him so one day.

But she wouldn't tell him how much she needed to work, to keep busy, to get her mind off the near shipwreck she had made of her life. It still galled her to think that just four weeks ago she was *this* close to running away with Jake Hertzler, only to find out he wasn't the man he said he was. Not even close. He was a no-good, low-life skunk, that's what he was.

In the end, as her stepmother Rose often reminded her, she hadn't run off with Jake. Something deep down in her knew better, Rose insisted. Her grandmother, less forgiving in nature, had left a 1948 edition of *A Young Woman's Guide to Virtue* on Bethany's pillow, a not-so-subtle poke about her disastrous judgment in men. Bethany thought she might use it to start a fire.

Bethany carefully pushed and pulled boxes so she could carve a path to the small window. She needed fresh air in this stuffy, musty basement. Hands on her hips, she looked around and wondered where to begin.

The sisters had left for a quilting at Naomi King's house this afternoon, which suited Bethany just fine. She much preferred working without them anywhere nearby. Just this morning, her younger sister Mim had asked if she minded working for such ancient ladies.

Mim was right about them being old. Ella, the eldest, was in her nineties. Sylvia, the youngest, was in her early eighties. Fannie, Lena, and Ada fell somewhere in between. But they were lovable sisters, spinsters, who had lived together all their lives.

No, Bethany didn't mind their ages. What she minded was that they were so extraordinarily messy. Yes, it gave her a job to do and, yes, the sisters paid her well. But it was not an easy job. These old sisters saved everything. Everything!

The cleanout and organizing of the Sisters' House could have gone faster but for two reasons. First was the sisters' involvement. They were constantly rummaging through Bethany's system of three boxes: keep, throw, give away. The sisters were particularly interested in the giveaway box. Somehow, nearly everything Bethany tossed into it was quietly removed and slipped into the keep box.

The second reason the cleanout job moved slowly was Bethany's doing. There was prowling to be done, especially in the basement. Being her share of nosy, she took her time examining wondrous things she had never seen the likes of—treasure chests overflowing with fancy old clothes, ruffled parasols, lacy unmentionables. Who knew that these ancient sisters had an exotic past? How thrilling! How worrisome.

She took care to hide the unmentionables in the

bottom of giveaway boxes. It would never do to have such things end up at a Sisters' House yard sale. Word might get out that the sisters were fallen women. Unrepentant jack-a-dandies. She could just imagine the dour look on her grandmother's face, sorting through a box of ladies' whale-boned corsets. Next thing you knew, the old sisters would end up on the front row of church, kneeling for confession before the entire congregation, promising to mend their ways. How awful!

Well, never mind. The old sisters' secrets would stay safe with her.

It was fascinating to sift through the lives of these eighty-plus-year-old women. There were old newspapers and musty books, boxes of clothing, old quilts, even an old diary. One box held little bottles filled with liquid. Bethany hoped the bottles might be perfume, that she had found another delightful secret about the fallen sisters. But when she opened one, it smelled like medicine. Evil smelling, strong and sickly sweet.

She came upon a soft black leather trunk, packed underneath other boxes at the bottom in a corner of the basement. It looked like it hadn't been touched in years. The leather straps were cracked and dry, the brass nails that held it together were black with tarnish. She tried to open it but the latch was jammed, so she found an old iron fireplace poker and pried the lid open. Bethany peered into the trunk and stood with a start. A coppery cold moved along her spine, and the perspiration on her skin turned to ice. She'd never had a sensitive bone in her body, unlike her friend and neighbor Naomi King, who'd imagined seeing ghosts and angels and demons her whole life. But this . . . this!

Shootfire!

She backed toward the stairs, trembling. It would take a raging river to wash from her mind the sight of what was in that trunk. Human bones, including two skulls with their empty sockets looking back at her. She hurried up the basement stairs, thinking of all the things she had to say to Jimmy Fisher to singe his tail feathers.

The day was so hot that Jimmy Fisher waited until the sun wasn't directly overhead to do some needed training exercises out on the road with Galen King's newly purchased sorrel gelding. The blacktop was hot enough to fry an egg, and they wouldn't last long out here, but he wanted to expose this gelding to a few passing cars or trucks.

In the afternoons, his employer and partner, Galen King, gave Jimmy conditioning exercises to do with a few of the horses. At first Jimmy was nervous when Galen watched him work a horse. Galen's silences had a way of making him lose track of his thoughts—some of which were perfectly good thoughts, in their way. He felt Galen might be watching because he was doing something that needed correcting. But one afternoon after another passed by, and Galen merely observed.

Today, Galen had left him with instructions to walk the gelding onto the road to start conditioning him to traffic. Most of the racehorses were accustomed to the unexpected—loud noises, distracting movements—but their response was to run, hard and fast, to the finish line. That wouldn't do for a buggy horse, which was Galen's and Jimmy's main objective: take young and retired racehorses and train them to become buggy horses. Today was the first time Galen wasn't hovering and Jimmy didn't want to mess up. He walked the gelding up and down the road for nearly half an hour, hoping a car or truck would come by. Naturally, there was nothing. Just as he thought about heading to a busier road, he saw Bethany Schrock come zooming toward him on her scooter, mad as a wet hen.

As she drew close to him, she jumped off the scooter and let it drop to the ground with a thud, startling the sorrel gelding. She came at Jimmy with a pointed finger aimed at his chest. "I should have known! Whenever someone talks fast and fancy like you do, I should have known better than to listen. You were just trying to pass off a skunk as a swan."

Beautiful. She was beautiful. She might be the prettiest thing he'd ever seen. With that crazy tumble of pitch-black hair, as shiny as a child's, that never stayed put for long under that pinned and starched prayer cap. She had high, wide cheekbones and a dainty, pointed chin that gave her face a Valentine's shape. Her skin was like freshly skimmed cream. Her body was lean and long-limbed, but not at all delicate. She exuded confidence and strength, even arrogance.

After a pause, Jimmy spoke. "Okay. I'm not following."

"Those sisters! They're nuttier than loons! They have a box of bones down in the basement. Human bones! Are they killing people and stuffing them in trunks? Why would you get me a job at a crazy house? It was pure meanness on your part. Is this your idea of a big joke?

Because it's not funny, Jimmy Fisher!" Her hands were on her hips, her brows knitted in a fierce frown.

Jimmy tried to make sense of what she was saying, but he kept getting distracted by sinful thoughts that would require some confession on his part before the day ended, stirrings in places he shouldn't even be thinking about.

Bethany Schrock intrigued him. Quite a bit. But there were plenty of attractive girls around Stoney Ridge. If that was what appealed to him, all he had to do was show up at a youth gathering. Any number of good-looking girls were eager for his attention.

Why her? Why this feisty, hot-tempered girl? Why now?

He didn't have the answers to those questions any more than he knew how to draw traffic along the road right now to condition this horse to unexpected noise.

It was something in her eyes, he decided. Deep, dark, intense. Yes, she was attractive, but it was the intensity in her eyes that spoke to him. There was some kind of fathomless depth to those eyes, and in them, something vulnerable. It quivered around the edges of her all the time, something a bit lost, lonely. Confused, maybe.

It wasn't as if Jimmy didn't have a few reservations about pursuing Bethany. He had plenty. Mainly—she'd been planning to run off with Jake the Snake, and though Jimmy had a quick-to-forgive nature, he wasn't about to let himself be runner-up in any girl's estimation. It was true—Bethany did refuse Jake—but Jimmy wanted a girl's whole heart. Not the leftovers.

"Simmer down, now," he said, his voice what's-the-weather-today calm, trying not to stare at her rosy lips and deep blush. "I'm sure whatever is bothering you is just a misunderstanding."

That made her all the more upset. For just an instant, he pressed his fingers against her mouth, but she pushed him away, furious. "I am not one of your horses! You can't speak to me with soft words and think you'll win me over, just like that!" She stamped her foot fiercely and that set the gelding dancing on its lead.

Jimmy held tight to the lead and stroked the horse's back, whispering sweet words to it. After the gelding settled, he turned his attention back to Bethany. "Calm down and start from the beginning." He tried to keep his voice even sounding, yet firm. The same way he spoke to this skittish gelding.

She had been watching the gelding, but with those words, she swung around on him so fast her capstrings bounced. She flashed her dark eyes at him with one single, pointed glance, a glance that managed to be both accusatory and frightening. "You try calming down after opening up a trunk and finding a skeleton staring back at you! With *two* skulls. *Four* empty eye sockets!"

The gelding pinned its ears back at Bethany's loud voice and Jimmy tightened his hold, keeping one eye on that horse. One more shout from her and his horse would bolt to kingdom come.

Bethany shuddered. "I will never sleep again." She was furious, shoulders rigid, chin tilted at that arrogant angle.

But at least she wasn't shouting anymore. "Maybe there's a reasonable explanation. Did you ask the sisters about the trunk?"

"No, of course not. They weren't home." She crossed

her arms. “They’re hardly ever home. I don’t know what they do with their time, but it sure isn’t spent cleaning their house.” A little laugh bubbled up in her throat. “Besides, why would I want them to know that I knew they were killing people and stuffing them in trunks? I’m not stupid.” She gave him one last look of utter disgust and marched back to her scooter.

The gelding pointed its ears at Jimmy. He stroked the horse along its neck and spoke to it softly. “Did you understand a word of that?” The horse stood as if planted to the ground. “Me either. Well, Bethany may not have been a passing truck, but she does have a way of creating a maelstrom. I think she took care of your conditioning exercises for today.”

For the past three summers, Miriam Schrock’s twice-removed third cousin from York County had invited her to come along on a vacation to visit relatives in Maine with them, and each time she thanked them and thanked them, then said no.

Her older sister, Bethany (her half sister—same father, different mothers—to be precise, and Mim valued being precise), couldn’t get over this. A free trip to Maine! Weeks of swimming and lobsters and hiking and fir trees. No chickens to feed. No stalls to muck. No goat to stir up trouble. All that sounded nice, but Mim didn’t want to go. She just wanted to spend the summer in Stoney Ridge—to watch Galen King and Jimmy Fisher train Thoroughbreds, play with her younger brothers if and when she felt like it, and read piles of library books.

What if she were to get sick while she was away? She had never been away from home without her mother, and she wasn't about to start now. Her mom needed her. Ever since her father had died suddenly in a drowning accident last year, Mim just wanted things to be safe and familiar.

Besides, who would visit with Ella at the Sisters' House? Ella was the oldest of the five ancient sisters who lived together in an even more ancient house. Mim tagged along now and then when Bethany worked at the Sisters' House trying to organize their enormous accumulation of clutter. Mim did odd jobs for the sisters and had become rather fond of Ella. She was round and short, warm and steamy like a little teapot. She always smelled of fresh-baked gingerbread. Whenever Mim would stop in at the Sisters' House, Ella would look up from her crocheting or quilting or newspaper reading, pat the chair next to her so Mim would sit down beside her, and say, "So tell me everything."

Ella said she considered Mim to be the granddaughter she never had. Mim wished Ella *were* her grandmother. That had to be a private wish, though, since she already had a grandmother. Mammi Vera. Well, Mammi Vera was just Mammi Vera. Mim thought she was born old and cranky.

Yesterday, Mammi Vera said that Luke, Mim's brother, who would soon be eleven, was full of the devil. He had memorized a Bible verse to a snappy tune and taught it to Mammi Vera. It was one of those tunes that got stuck in your head. A neighbor named Hank Lapp stopped by to say hello and heard her humming it. He asked her about it, so she sang the Bible verse. Then Hank laughed so hard tears rolled down his leathery cheeks. Turned out Luke had been singing Bible verses to a radio jingle for fine-tasting filter cigarettes. That was when Mammi Vera said Luke was full of the devil.

The devil seemed to be lurking around Eagle Hill on a regular basis, in Mammi Vera's mind, and she was often warning Mim, Luke, and their eight-year-old brother Sammy with strange proverbs from the Old Country: "Speak of the devil and he will flee."

Awhile ago, Mammi Vera caught Mim peering into a mirror. In a loud voice she said, "Wammer nachts in der Schpiggel guckt, gucket der Deiwel raus." *When you look into the mirror at night, the devil peers out.*

The thought scared Mim so much she didn't look in a mirror for an entire month. She even took down the mirror in her room, just in case she happened to forget and glance at it during the night. Finally, she discussed Mammi Vera's saying with her very good friend Danny Riehl and he thought it didn't sound at all logical. Why would the devil only look at you in the night? That's the kind of thinker Danny was. Logical. He made everything easier to understand.

Mim was so touched that Ella thought of her as a granddaughter that she nearly confided in her about her great devotion for Danny Riehl. In her diary, she had filled the margins with versions of her name connected to Danny Riehl: Mrs. Daniel Riehl, Miriam Riehl, and her very favorite, Danny's Mim.

Mim had never told a soul how she felt about Danny. Although she shared almost everything with her sister Bethany, she had never mentioned Danny to her, because sometimes, oftentimes, her sister could be a little insensitive. If Danny found out, even accidentally, about Mim's deep feelings for him, it would be the most humiliating thing she could ever imagine.

Today, as Mim ran to get the mail, she was glad she had turned down her York County cousin's invitation and for an entirely different reason than Danny or Ella. Nearly every day, there was a letter in the Inn at Eagle Hill mailbox addressed to Mrs. Miracle from someone who direly needed an answer to a problem.

A few months ago, when Mim's mother, Rose, had first opened the Inn at Eagle Hill, she had asked Mim to paint a sign for the inn. Mim was known far and wide for her excellent penmanship. Excellent. She worked long and hard on the large wooden sign, penciling the letters, painting them in black with a fine-tipped paintbrush. At the bottom of the sign, Mim had added a little Latin phrase she had found in a book and liked the way it rolled off her tongue: *Miracula fieri hic*. At the time, she didn't realize what it meant: Miracles occur here.

A newspaper reporter, who happened to have taken five years of high school Latin, he said, translated the phrase and said *this* was the story he'd been looking for. There was a human-interest angle to spin from the Latin phrase—it spoke to a longing in everyone for a place that fed their soul and spirit. He wrote up an article, weaving in truth and mistruths, about the miracles that occurred at the Inn at Eagle Hill. The article was picked up by the Pennsylvania newspapers, then the internet, and so on and so forth. Soon, the inn was considered to be a place where people could practically order up a custom-made miracle like a hamburger. And then people started to write letters to Mrs. Miracle. Buckets and buckets of letters. They kept pouring in. Mim's mother, overwhelmed by the quantity, was relieved when Mim offered to answer the letters. But she told Mim what to say: "The Inn at Eagle Hill couldn't solve their problems. Only God could provide miracles."

Mim believed that part about God and miracles, but after reading a few letters, she thought she could help the people solve their problems. Most of the problems were pretty simple: injured feelings, sibling rivalry, how to cook and clean. All of that she had plenty of experience with, especially with the sibling rivalry. Her two little brothers couldn't be in the same room without some kind of fuss and tussle. So she decided to answer a few letters, offering advice, posing as Mrs. Miracle. Then a few more and a few more, until she finished the big pile. She knew she hadn't done what her mom had expected her to do, but it was just a small disobedience, a slight adjustment to the truth, and for the best of reasons. She was helping people, and hadn't she been taught to help others? Plus, Mim was sure the letters from people seeking advice would dwindle down as the Inn at Eagle Hill miracle story blew over. After all, with this heat wave they'd been having, the inn had been getting cancellations for reservations as soon as people discovered there was no air-conditioning. If they really thought the inn could dish out miracles, they wouldn't let a little hot weather stop them, would they?

Maybe, maybe not. But letters addressed to Mrs. Miracle kept coming. Mim made a point of meeting the mailman each day so her mom wasn't made aware of this interesting development. Each afternoon, she listened for the squeaky mail truck to come down their road and bolted to the mailbox when she heard it. So far, so good. The letters continued to arrive, stealthily, and the problems in the letters were still pretty simple to solve. She hadn't been stumped yet.

In today's mail was a letter from the local newspaper, asking Mrs. Miracle if she would like to have a regular column in the *Stoney Ridge Times*. Mrs. Miracle would be paid five dollars each time the column ran. Five whole dollars! Mim would be rich!

There was just one glitch. The letter from the newspaper stated she needed to be over eighteen and they wanted her signature and birth date on the W-2 form. Mim was only fourteen. She didn't mind bending the rules for a good cause, and this was definitely a worthy cause. But she would need help. First, she thought about asking Naomi King, her friend and neighbor, who had turned eighteen recently. But then she dismissed that notion. Naomi followed rules the way she quilted: even, straight, tiny, perfect stitches. No mistakes. Keeping a secret like Mrs. Miracle's true identity might cause Naomi to unravel.

Then she thought of her sister Bethany, who had just turned twenty and didn't mind bending rules at all. But the tricky part was catching Bethany in just the right mood to ask for a favor. It all depended on if Bethany was feeling friendly or not. Anticipating Bethany's moods lately took skill—often, she seemed pensive and just wanted to be left alone. It was all because of Jake Hertzler. He was Bethany's ex-boyfriend, a charming fellow who had worked for her father at his investment company. When Schrock Investments went belly up, Jake

Hertzler, along with Mim's oldest brother Tobe (again, to be precise, Tobe was her half brother), went missing.

On a cheerier note, this newspaper column was a wonderful opportunity for Mrs. Miracle. It was disappointing that Mim needed to keep this opportunity top secret—her mother, and *especially* her grandmother, must never find out! The way Mim rationalized it, it was only a tiny breaking of all the rules her church was so fond of and she was helping all kinds of people and that was worth keeping a secret or two. But if her grandmother found out—oh my! Then Mim would be full of the devil.

As soon as Geena Spencer arrived at her church office this morning, the elder board of the New Life Church of Ardmore, Pennsylvania, had called her into a meeting and told her, gently and firmly, that they were very sorry but things weren't working out the way they had hoped and they had to let her go. They had already found another interim youth pastor, an enthusiastic young man fresh out of seminary, to fill in for her. Starting today. They thanked her for her service, said they'd provide a glowing letter of recommendation, and asked if she needed any help cleaning out her office.

Stung and ashamed, Geena bent her head and went to her office.

Objectively, she could see that they were right. The elder board had wanted a youth pastor who could preach the paint off the wall and act like a magnet for the youth of Ardmore. They had a plan to triple the size of the youth group, thereby drawing parents into the main sanctuary. Geena had a way with people, especially teens, as long as it was one-on-one, but as hard as she tried, she was a terrible public speaker. That was why she'd been passed over for so many positions. She only received the church in Ardmore because her favorite seminary professor, who happened to be her uncle and a good friend of the head elder, had called in a few favors and promised Geena would improve with time and practice.

Also, no other candidate accepted the call.

It had been an opportunity for Geena to prove herself, but after only six weeks, the elders started to pay her Monday morning visits with what they considered to be helpful suggestions: "Don't read your notes. Make eye contact. Speak up. Slow down. Speed up." Their feedback only made her all the more nervous. During youth group each Wednesday night, a handful of elders would come and sit in the back of the room. She would glance out at the sea of young faces, then at the back row of old faces, and feel a startled jolt, a deer in headlights, as if she were preaching to a room full of dour seminary professors.

Geena knew she wasn't a gifted orator, but she thought by now the church might have developed an appreciation for all she did do well: She'd been told she was a "2:00 a.m. pastor"—the kind families wouldn't hesitate to call in a crisis. During spring break, she organized a youth group trip to help on a Habitat for Humanity building project in Kentucky. She started weekly Bible studies—one for the boys and one for the girls. While the youth group wasn't exactly tripling—not by a long shot—she was discipling a core of committed teens. She tried to equip them so they could influence their peers in any situation—at school, in sports, or just hanging out. She never forgot anyone's name. And she loved them, every single one of them.

But obviously, all that wasn't enough.

It was humiliating to suddenly be let go, released. Fired. As she took books off the shelves and placed them in boxes, she kept telling herself to pull it together, to find a way to get over this, to stop being a big baby. But it wasn't working.

She felt sorry for herself. It was hard not to. She thought this was "it"—the job she'd been waiting for all her life. At long last she could set down roots. She'd been Head of Children's Ministry for five different churches since she graduated from seminary—hoping one or the other might turn into a youth pastor position. Each opportunity seemed promising, until the Sunday morning came when Geena was given a chance to fill in for the senior pastor. It was customary for the ordained staffers to preach on low attendance Sundays—after Christmas, after Easter. When the congregation heard her preach, everything went south.

No call ever came, not until the one from this church in Ardmore.

The call to ministry was a strange thing. It was exactly that—a calling, a thing you responded to not because you wanted to but because you had to.

Stranger still to have the call and not get a call.

As Geena opened her top desk drawer, her eyes fell on a gift certificate from grateful parishioners, a quirky, big-hearted couple named Lois and Tony. They had given it to her a month ago, after she had come to the hospital when their granddaughter had been involved in a car accident. She stood vigil with them until the doctor brought good news, and they were appreciative of Geena's calming presence during those troubling hours. The gift certificate was for two nights' stay at an Amish bed-and-breakfast in Lancaster County.

Impulsively, Geena called the Inn at Eagle Hill and asked if there was an opening for tonight. A woman answered the phone, her voice as soft as chocolate. "Actually, I happen to have a week's opening because of a cancellation," she said. "The heat wave we're having is discouraging fair-weather visitors. I have to warn you, we don't have any air-conditioning."

Geena jumped at the chance to leave town. "I don't mind the heat. I just need . . . a place to take a break and do some serious thinking for a few days. I'll take the whole week." Boy, did she ever have thinking to do. Like, her entire future.

"Well, then, it sounds like you'll be coming to the right place."

Two hours and one stop at Sonic for a double cheeseburger and fries later, Geena had exited I-76, driven along the Philadelphia Pike, then followed her GPS to the country road that wound to Stoney Ridge. She noticed a siren in her rearview mirror. She pulled over, hoping the police officer just needed to pass by. Her heart sank as he stopped his patrol car behind hers. He walked to her passenger window, leaned over, and growled, "License and registration."

Geena handed him the paperwork and waited while he returned to his car. After a few more long moments, the officer reappeared at her window. "What brings you to Stoney Ridge, Ms. Spencer?"

"Reverend. Reverend Spencer. I'm a minister." She was slightly ashamed to play that minister card, but . . . it often worked in the clutch.

He didn't bat an eye.

"What brings me here? Just a whim." She shrugged. "I needed a little vacation."

He nodded slowly. "Well, I'm sorry your vacation is starting off on a sour note," he said as he scribbled on his pad, "but as fast as you were going, I really don't have a choice." He tore the ticket off the pad and handed it to her. "You'd better start slowing down, Reverend Spencer. You're in another world."

2

It was the silence that woke Geena on the first morning after her arrival at the Inn at Eagle Hill. She had never heard such silence. Now and then, a horse would neigh to another horse, an owl would hoot, or she'd hear the clip-clop of a horse and buggy travel along the road. Mostly, though, all was still. Utter quiet.

She tried to go back to sleep—after all, how many times in her life could she sleep in?—but finally gave up and decided to take a long walk into the hills that lined the back of the farmhouse. Rose Schrock, the Amish woman who ran the inn, the one with the voice as soft as chocolate, checked her in last night and told her about a trail that would take her to the top of the ridge.

Rose also mentioned that breakfast would be delivered at her door at seven in the morning and hinted at something about blueberry cornbread. Geena had heard glowing stories about Amish cooks and wasn't about to miss breakfast. Her father always said she had the appetite of a professional football player—unusually impressive for a five-foot-one, one hundred-and-seven-pound woman.

Yesterday, as Geena got out of her car at Eagle Hill, the sour manure smell from the cornfields, mingled with the humidity of a prolonged heat wave, pinched her lungs hard enough that she coughed like an old lady to get air. Today, her nose felt a little more accustomed to the unique aroma of an Amish farm. She walked to the middle of the front lawn and turned in a slow circle, taking in a full panorama: the red barn, the mare and her colt in a fenced pasture, a goat sticking his head through to another pasture to find better grass, the soft green canopy of shade trees, the four little sheep down by the creek. Her heart missed a beat when she caught sight of an eagle pair soaring over the ridge. Eagle Hill, she decided, looked exactly as an Amish farm should. Pristine, cared for, safe for all creatures, peaceful.

It was good that she had come.

It was bad that she had been fired.

What hurt her most about being let go was that she had tried so hard to meet the needs of the congregation. Once she even returned from a vacation when she learned that a fire swept through the home of a teen in her youth group. She dropped everything and helped organize a donation drive to provide for this family. How could the church turn its back on her?

She shook her head. *No wallowing, Geena.*

She had come to Eagle Hill to stop, take a breather, absorb the blow, and think about what to do next.

The first fingers of sunlight tipped over the eastern edge of the ridge that framed the farm. The light was a delicate pale butter, washing the hills with a soft brush, hazing the edges of the trees. The very top leaves of the trees were illuminated, almost glowing. Birds whirred and whistled. A pair of squirrels chased each other around a tree trunk.

When had she last stopped and noticed the delights of God's handiwork in nature? Really, truly noticed?

There was *something* about this farmland. It was so drastically different from the city. Not a freeway or high-rise in sight—only wide open rolling hills that whispered history and serenity. Rose had told her that by mid-August, the land would look entirely different. The farmers' corn, now ankle high, would tower above any man. "You won't be able to see the hills like you can now," she told Geena. "You'll have to just come back and see for yourself how this area changes through the months." Geena wondered where she would be, come mid-August, when that corn grew taller than her.

For the first time since she was a teenager, she questioned herself. What if she wasn't meant to be a youth pastor after all? Maybe she'd misunderstood the call. What was that old joke her father used to tell? "If you get the call, you have to answer. But then again . . . you might just let it ring."

Geena's father was a well-known, beloved pastor, a leader of one of the largest congregations on the East Coast, and particularly revered for the delivery and punch of his sermons. Her uncle, too, was the dean of a highly regarded seminary. They were so proud of Geena for finally getting a call to a position. How could she tell them she'd been fired?

No wallowing, Geena. And maybe, for just a little while, no thinking about your future.

She forked off on a trail that ran behind the hill, pondering how she wanted to spend the rest of her day. Yesterday, as she drove through the small downtown section of Stoney Ridge, she was glad to see there wasn't a tourist shop in sight. Not an inch of neon on Stoney Ridge's main street. Not a single billboard. This was a place where you could walk to town, where you could buy a quart of milk or a packet of shoelaces in the village. It was easy to completely forget she was only two hours away from Philadelphia, to forget that society even existed, let alone a society brimming with traffic, hustle and bustle, and stress. She felt her soul start to settle, relax, let go.

She had always loved to hike—had loved the feeling of being alive under the sky, feet touching the earth, being wholly herself. Thinking. Walking. Praying. On the trail, she had always been able to leave her troubles behind. Here there was only room for wind and sky and sun and communing with God.

The early morning silence, broken only by the faintest of crickets somewhere out in the fields and the crow of a rooster, fell on her like a quilt. It had texture and depth, a velvety weight to ease her jangled nerves, her weary brain. *Everything will be all right*, was what she heard.

She knew that nearly audible voice. Knew it well. It came to her when she least expected but when she most prayed for it. The words were always short and to the point; clear, concise directives. Nothing confusing, nothing vague. And the message was always accompanied with peace. Bone-deep peace that couldn't be explained and wasn't dependent on circumstances.

She turned around and headed down the trail back

to the farm. As she neared the farmhouse, the smoky scent of frying bacon reached her nose and she picked up her pace. She made a shortcut through the yard, along the side of the henhouse, then stopped abruptly. A man emerged through the privet bushes that ran between Eagle Hill and the neighboring farm.

Geena had never seen an Amish man before; she had imagined them to be portly, flush-cheeked, ragged old hippies. But the man who came striding across the yard from the neighbor's farm was tall and fit, young and very deeply tanned, weathered in the way of an outdoorsman. And the look on his face as he saw Rose come out of the kitchen door with an overflowing laundry basket in her arms, well, it was a sight to behold.

Geena leaned against the henhouse. She knew she should turn around and leave—good heavens, she was a grown woman—but she found herself mesmerized by what was going on between them. The man's eyes met with Rose's, a quiet greeting that lasted a good long minute.

Rose's face was bright, as if with happiness. She set the laundry basket on the ground and waved. "Good morning, Galen."

A big golden retriever spotted Geena and bounded toward her. She was sure he'd bark and give her away, but when he reached her, he sat in front of her, shifting from paw to paw, considering her. It was as if he was asking, "Well, now, who are you?" and regarded her with the gentle expectation of a wise old teacher waiting for a student to come up with the answer. Geena bent down and stroked his thick fur through her fingers, eyes again glued to the Amish couple.

The man—Galen—walked over to the clothesline. As Rose's gaze settled fully on him, her eyebrows drew together in a slight frown. "What's the matter?"

Galen hesitated for a moment, as if he was gathering his thoughts. "Rose, I want to tell you something," he said, "only I don't really know how to say it properly. Words can't—" and he made a small, helpless gesture.

"Well, try."

"I love you, Rose. I love you. That's all. That's all I have to say."

From where Geena squatted, against the side of the henhouse, absently stroking the big dog, she could see Rose's face go blank, utterly expressionless. She wondered why the man had felt the need to express his feelings like that, right now, on a summer morning. The silence became painful—he was getting nothing back from her. Nothing. Poor guy.

Then a smile began, starting in Rose's eyes, until it covered her entire face. "I'm taking the boys for a swim later today, at Blue Lake Pond. Would you like to join us?"

Suddenly, the mood lifted, as real as if sun had broken through gray skies, and the two grinned foolishly at each other. "I'd like that." He touched the edge of his hat and strode back to the hole in the privet, slipping through and disappearing. The golden retriever bolted after him, tail feathers wagging like a flag.

Hiding like a schoolgirl, eavesdropping on an Amish couple, Geena knew she should be ashamed of herself. And yet, it was such a charming moment! So unexpected. She felt a delight at such a surprise—who would have thought she'd stumble upon a tender moment of expressed love on an Amish farm? She grinned.

Such surprises were good. A tiny glimmer of well-being wisped through Geena, the first she'd felt since arriving at the church office yesterday morning. Coming here had been a good idea.

Everything would be all right.

After Mim had taken a breakfast tray down to the new guest in the guest flat, she looked everywhere for Bethany and finally found her outside, beside the henhouse, tossing cornmeal from a tin pie plate to a flock of hens pecking the ground. "For a tiny little lady, that preacher sure does like to eat. I asked her how many pancakes she wanted and she said six. Even Luke can only down five."

Bethany flung her arm out wide, and the wind caught the cornmeal and sent it swirling in a yellow cloud. "I like a girl who's not afraid to admit she's hungry."

A good sign. Bethany seemed to be in a good mood. Mim tiptoed across the chicken yard, carefully as she was barefooted, and stood closer to her sister. "I need your help with something."

Bethany tossed another handful of meal at the hens. "If the goat has wandered off again, I'm not going after it. If he doesn't have enough sense to get himself home, I say good riddance."

"No. It's not the goat. It's something personal. But first I need your promise that you'll keep it to yourself, even if you decide not to help me."

She scattered the last of the cornmeal for the hens. "All right."

"You promise?"

"I told you all right, didn't I?"

"Do you remember the letters that came to the house after I had put that Latin phrase on the bottom of the Inn at Eagle Hill sign?"

Bethany squinted her eyes, trying to remember.

"The newspaper reporter translated it to mean 'Miracles occur here.' Then he wrote a newspaper story saying that our inn handed out miracles."

Bethany shrugged. "I don't remember."

Was she serious? How could Bethany not remember *that*? Because she was mooning over Jake Hertzler, that's why. Just like she was now. Mim tried not to look as disappointed as she felt. "Well, it was a news story that other newspapers picked up, then it was on the internet . . . then Bishop Elmo came by and asked us to paint over the Latin phrase."

Bethany let out a laugh. "That doesn't surprise me." She turned completely around. "That's the problem with being—"

"Funny you should mention that, because it underlines my need for secrecy." Mim had to cut Bethany off, straightaway, and reroute her back to the topic at hand. She knew just where her sister was going with this. Ever since Jake Hertzler had come and gone, she'd been complaining about being Amish. Everything started with "That's the problem with being Amish . . ." as if there was just one thing. Bethany had a long list of complaints: she thought she should be able to have print fabric for her dresses, shorter church services, telephones in the house, a computer might be nice. On and on and on. *Blah blah blah.*

Mostly, Bethany was just "in a mood." The moods

changed—sad, teary, angry, snappish—but rarely happy, like she used to be. It seemed to Mim that Jake Hertzler stole something from everybody: he stole a horse from Jimmy Fisher and he stole happiness from Bethany. She wasn't sure, but she had a feeling that her brother Tobe's running away had to do with Jake Hertzler. So, in a way, Jake stole her brother away from them too. How could one person hold so much power over others?

"I haven't got all day," Bethany said.

"Letters started coming to the inn. Addressed to Mrs. Miracle. Asking for help with their problems. Lots of them."

Bethany tilted her head, mildly intrigued.

"Mom didn't have time to answer them. It happened around the time when Mammi Vera was ailing, then she ended up having brain surgery. So Mom let me answer the letters. She told me to say that only God makes miracles and that we couldn't solve their problems . . . but . . ." She hesitated.

"So . . ." Bethany urged, surprisingly interested.

Mim tried to sound nonchalant. "I didn't exactly do what she said to do. I wrote the people back and solved their problems."

"You *what*?"

"I pretended I was Mrs. Miracle and solved their problems. Most of their problems were pretty easy to solve. And the ones that weren't—I think those were people who just wanted to be listened to." She bit her lip. "You won't say anything to anyone, will you?"

"Verzaehl net alles as du weescht?" *Tell not all you know?*

"Something like that."

"And Rose doesn't know about this?"

Mim shook her head. "The letters kept coming. More and more and more. It hasn't stopped. I hurry to the mailbox every day so I get the letters first. So . . ."

"So . . ."

"The features editor from the *Stoney Ridge Times* wrote and asked if Mrs. Miracle would write a weekly column for the newspaper. But he thinks Mrs. Miracle is an old lady."

Bethany's eyes went wide with astonishment, then she burst into laughter. That tears-rolling-down-her-face kind of laughter.

Mim was horrified. She hadn't confided in Bethany to be laughed at. She took her role as Mrs. Miracle very, very seriously.

"Oh Mim!" Bethany finally said, gasping for air. "This is the funniest thing I've heard in a long time."

Mim was crushed. She had made a serious mistake and now Mrs. Miracle's future was in jeopardy. What if Bethany told her mom?

Bethany wiped tears from her face. "Well, it's a humdinger of a chance for Mrs. Miracle, and it sure beats feeding chickens. Just tell me what you want me to do." She grinned. "But remember this, Mim: Loss dich net verwische, is es elft Gebot." *Don't get caught is the eleventh commandment.*

The afternoon sun's piercing glare gave Naomi King a headache, making her feel as if a red-hot poker had been stuck through her head. She had woken with a mild headache and tried to ignore it, hoping it would ease up as the day went on. She even went to her quilting, since she was good for little else. It soothed her head a little, and the soul, as well, freeing her of self-pity. She loved quilting more than just about anything, and the twice-a-month quilting bee was an event she looked forward to.

She wouldn't have missed the Sisters' Bee for all the tea in China, and she loved tea. She'd rather quilt than eat, any day of the week. The Sisters' Bee was named because it was originally the quilting group of the five sisters from the Sisters' House. They added Edith Fisher, Jimmy's mother, and years later, they invited Naomi to join. Naomi wasn't really sure why she was included in the Sisters' Bee but on the day she turned fifteen, she was swept into the circle. It happened to be the year the group had volunteered a quilt to be auctioned off to help the Clinic for Special Children in Strasburg and Edith Fisher had chosen a pattern that was beyond anyone's piecing skills. Suddenly, Naomi found herself to be a highly valued member of the group.

Last night, she had stayed up late to finish a quilt top for today's bee: it was a Sunshine and Shadow pattern—bright reds and yellows and shiny gold.

As the women nibbled on Naomi's lemon cookies, they oohed and aahed over the quilt top. "This is the best you've done yet, Naomi!" And she agreed.

Which wasn't vanity. She had made her first quilt, a doll blanket, when she was seven, and she'd been making them ever since. She was a devoted gardener, a cheerful cook, but only a true expert at this one thing. When it came to fine, intricate stitches, she couldn't be beat. She took twelve stitches to the inch whereas most of the women took eight. She had a talent for working out complicated patterns, and an eye for piecing colorful swatches together in surprising ways.

Naomi thought her gift at piecing might be because of her headaches—they gave her plenty of time to quilt and think and dream. And sometimes, those strange bright lights that flashed in her head, those disturbing auras, gave her ideas for color and pattern variations. Sometimes, she saw strange things. Or rather . . . she *felt* them. Warnings, hunches, presentiments. The old sisters called it a gift. Naomi didn't consider it a gift. To her, it felt more like a burden. And she was of a mind that everyone had such intuition, but few paid attention to it.

Today, the quilting bee was held at Naomi's house. They were welcoming back Edith Fisher, who had just returned to Stoney Ridge after the untimely and unfortunate passing of her brand-new husband. It was true that no one was overly fond of Edith Fisher, but Naomi always felt her bark was worse than her bite. Edith had never said a mean word to Naomi, though she had never said anything kind, either. She was a big sturdy woman without much softness.

Earlier this morning, Naomi had dropped off a loaf of banana bread to Eagle Hill and mentioned that Edith Fisher had returned to Stoney Ridge. As Vera Schrock took a slice of banana bread, she said, between bites, "Edith can be as sour as bad cider when she wants to be, that one. Words out of that woman's mouth fade like snow in a fry pan."

Those observations struck Naomi as ironic, seeing as they came from a woman who was more than a little cold and sour herself.

"Say what you will about Edith," Rose Schrock said, "but her son Jimmy Fisher is a credit to her."

Even Vera didn't dispute that, and she disputed nearly everything her daughter-in-law Rose had to say.

Jimmy had been working for Naomi's older brother, Galen, for a few months now and considered himself a partner in the horse-training business. Galen rolled his eyes at that, but Naomi thought he was quietly pleased by Jimmy's dedication. His hard work too. If Galen wasn't pleased, Naomi supposed, he would have sent Jimmy packing. He could be like that—once he made up his mind about a person, that was that.

Most girls in her church were green with envy that Naomi got to see Jimmy Fisher nearly every day. For breakfast and lunch and often dinner, which he showed up for on a regular basis. Naomi liked Jimmy. She liked him quite a bit. But she wasn't in love with him and knew she never would be. Jimmy was a fine-looking man, of a good build and height—not tall, but he held himself very straight as if to make the most of what he had—with hair like the stubble left in the fields after haying, and eyes as luminously blue as agates. When he smiled, the right side of his mouth curved up more than the left. He was fun-loving and lighthearted and charming and downright adorable. But she wasn't in love with him, nor he with her. They weren't at all right for each other.

Naomi had a sense about these kinds of things. She had predicted her brother Galen's romance with Rose Schrock long before it was obvious to others. She saw how her brother stilled whenever Rose was nearby, or the way his eyes lingered after her. She was hoping Jimmy might have those same sweet feelings for Bethany, though it was true that Jimmy Fisher liked most girls and even more girls liked Jimmy Fisher. But maybe it was finally time for Jimmy to settle on someone. At least, his mother thought it was high time.

Since Edith Fisher had returned to Stoney Ridge, her first objective, she made clear, was to get Jimmy married. Paul, her older son, had tied the knot during Edith's brief marriage and then surprised everyone by moving off to Canada with his bride right after Edith, unexpectedly widowed, returned to Stoney Ridge.

Edith was indignant! She was counting on localized grandchildren, she said, and now it was all up to Jimmy. And she made it no secret that she had selected Naomi King for him. No thank you! Jimmy Fisher might be adorable in every way that mattered, but he was not right for Naomi. Besides, her heart belonged to another, but that was a secret she guarded carefully.

Naomi had a hope that once her friend Bethany was done with her melancholia for Jake Hertzler, she might wake up to the fact that Jimmy Fisher was perfectly suited to her.

Naomi adored Bethany. She was fond of Mim, the younger sister, but being with her was like looking into a mirror. Naomi and Mim did things exactly alike, and sometimes Naomi knew what Mim was going to say before she said it. Bethany was a real live wire, and it was exciting to be around her. She made life interesting.

Naomi knew Bethany was hurting after the Jake Hertzler disaster, and she had a plan to help. She was sure that if she could bring Bethany into the quilting group, gently nudging her toward Jimmy Fisher while wooing over his mother, those wounds would heal.

Naomi stopped to examine the seam she was stitching. She picked up a pair of scissors and trimmed a loose thread. She was waiting for just the right moment to bring up Bethany's name, to test the waters and see how Edith Fisher would react. Anyone wanting to marry Jimmy Fisher was going to have to win over Edith Fisher. Wasn't there a saying for that very thing? Wann'd der Sohn hawwe witt, muscht dich mit der Mudder halde. *She that would the son win must with the mother first begin.*

Not that Bethany was interested in Jimmy. Not yet. But Naomi was going to do her best to light that spark between them she was sure was there. Almost sure.

When there was a lull in the conversation, Naomi casually said that she thought it would be nice to include her friend Bethany in the quilting bee. Naomi finished her stitch at the instant she looked up at Edith and caught the look of disapproval on her face, which made her run the needle into her finger. When she glanced down, she saw a little drop of blood on the place she was stitching around and put her finger into her mouth.

The five elderly sisters stopped their sewing but kept their heads bowed, the edges of their capstrings dancing on the quilt top. They didn't say a word. Not a peep. Naomi glanced nervously around the circle.

Unfortunately, whenever Naomi felt nervous, she babbled. Her brother Galen grew quieter and she grew more talkative. Their mother used to say they evened each other out. As she realized the women were staring at her, she started a long tale about how she had known Bethany for years and years, and what a fine cook she was, and how she was sure they'd all enjoy having her in the circle. She spoke faster and faster, jumping from topic to topic, making very little sense, all the while wishing her mouth would just snap shut. She sped right on: "And Bethany said she doesn't like to sew." She cringed and clamped her mouth shut.

What possessed her to say *that* when she was trying to snag an invitation for Bethany to a sewing group? It was true, but why did she have to say so? Just yesterday, Naomi had mentioned to Bethany that she quilted because it was the most comforting thing to do. Bethany said the reason she quilted was because it kept her from biting her fingernails.

Edith Fisher squinted at Naomi through her thick spectacles until Naomi blushed and looked down at her piecing. "I've never met a woman who didn't like to sew."

Sylvia, the youngest of the elderly sisters, finally spoke. "Bethany's a more modern girl, Edith. She has other things to do besides sew with old ladies."

Sylvia forgot that Naomi wasn't an old lady. All the women forgot. There were times when Naomi wanted to point out that she wasn't a spinster quite yet, not at eighteen. They'd never thought to wonder if Naomi King had feelings, dreams, desires of her own. She knew they considered her to be a frail thing, someone to be pitied and fussed over. That might be how she seemed on the outside, but on the inside, Naomi felt strong and brave. At least, that was how she thought of herself when she wasn't plagued with one of those dreadful headaches.

Then Edith Fisher cleared her throat, determined to take charge, and Naomi wondered what everyone was in for. "Speaking of modern and worldly ways, I understand those Schrocks have a preacher staying in their guest flat now." She pursed her lips as if tasting a sour lemon. "A lady preacher."

"A youth pastor," Naomi said quietly but firmly.

"Same thing," Edith said.

"Now, Edith," Fannie said, a smile wobbling at the edges of her mouth, "your halo always did fit a little too tight." Fannie was second from the bottom of the five sisters, the polar opposite of her younger sibling, as full figured as Sylvia was petite and as opinionated as Sylvia was soft-spoken.

"How did you hear that, Edith?" Sylvia asked.

Edith paused while she threaded her needle. "Oh, well, people talk. You know."

People do talk; Edith certainly did.

"Mark my words. Those Schrocks attract trouble like molasses draws flies. They're just like those Amos Lapps over at Windmill Farm. No difference at all. And I don't mind telling them so right to their faces."

Something out the window caught Naomi's eye. Up the walk came Hank Lapp, former suitor to Edith before she spurned him for her now-dead brand-new husband. And that was when Naomi's headache took a turn for the worse.

Jimmy was in the cool of the barn, wrapping his prize horse Lodestar's leg before he exercised him so the horse wouldn't knick his forelegs with his hoofs.

"JIMMY FISHER? WHERE ARE YOU?" The horses in the barn stirred and lifted their heads at the sound of Hank Lapp's bellow.

Jimmy popped his head up over the stall. "Hank, how many times do I have to tell you to keep your voice low and calm around these Thoroughbreds?"

Hank Lapp was a one-of-a-kind older Plain man in looks and personality. Wiry white hair that stuck out in all directions, a wandering eye that made a person unsure of which eye to look at, a fellow with his own way of thinking about things. Most folks had trouble tolerating him for a multitude of reasons, all reasonable, but Jimmy was fond of him. For all his bluster, Hank had a good heart.

"Well, you could have warned me that house was filled with cackling hens."

"And just how was I supposed to know you were looking for me?" Jimmy bent down to finish wrapping Lodestar's foreleg. "How was Ohio?"

"It was fine. Just fine. Julia and Rome are trying to talk us into moving there with them."

"No kidding? Is Amos considering it?"

Hank shrugged. "All depends on Fern. She's from there, you know." He picked up a currycomb and examined it. "Women run the world," he muttered. "You could have warned me that Naomi had her quilting bee today."

"Now, how could I have warned you when I didn't even know you were back in Stoney Ridge?"

"Well, you should tack a sign up on the front door. Give a fellow a little heads-up." He lifted his hands in the air, drawing a sign: "ENTER AT YOUR OWN RISK."

"When did you get back?"

"Yesterday. Thought I'd better grab you for some afternoon fishing before someone beats us to all the good ones."

"I'd like to, Hank, but Galen's at an auction and I need to get a few things done before he gets back."

"Now, see? Galen had enough sense to go missing from the farm on quilting days." Hank scratched his neck. "Did you know your mother is up there in that henhouse?"

So *that's* what was nettling Hank. "Yup. She returned to Stoney Ridge a few weeks ago. You probably hadn't heard since you were in Ohio. Her new husband passed."

Hank took off his hat. "Well, I'm sorry to hear that." He put his hat back on. "Not too terrible sorry, though. I never did understand why she up and married him so fast after she spurned me." He leaned against the stall wall. "Women are a mystery."

"They are at that." As Jimmy wrapped Lodestar's other foreleg, he made sure the wrap would stay tied. Galen was always chiding him for babying this horse, but Lodestar wasn't just any horse. Jimmy didn't want a single scar on his forelegs to mar his appearance. He had plans for Lodestar—this horse was going to be the anchor of his breeding business. He checked the ends one more time, then straightened up.

Hank picked up a piece of straw and chewed on it. "You still trying to get Bethany Schrock to pay you any mind?"

Jimmy frowned. "Getting girls' attention has never been hard."

"No, not most. Just hers."

"If I really wanted Bethany Schrock, I could get her."

Hank let out a rusty laugh. "Well, I never thought I'd see the day when a Fisher boy couldn't get a girl!"

Hank Lapp had just sailed past friendly and arrived at annoying.

"You're just like your brother. Always shopping, never buying."

"Paul *did* get married," Jimmy said, teeth gritted. The Fisher boys' reluctance to settle down was a constant source of amusement for Hank—ironic commentary from a dedicated bachelor. It deeply annoyed Jimmy to be compared to Paul. He wasn't like him. He wasn't. "I will, too, when I'm ready to pick the girl."

"Unless that girl happens to be Bethany Schrock!" Hank roared. "You'll have to chase her till she catches you!"

What irked Jimmy was that Hank spoke the truth. He wasn't accustomed to not being taken seriously by a woman. Most girls loved any attention Jimmy threw their way. Bethany acted as if she could take him or leave him. For example, if they happened to be talking, she was always the first to say goodbye. That bothered him. He liked to be the first to say goodbye. He thought it left a girl wanting more.

But it was time to change the subject. "Hank, why would you suppose someone might have a trunk of human bones hidden in a basement?"

Hank pulled off his hat and turned it in a circle, thinking hard. "Well, there could be all kinds of explanations."

Now, that was just one of the reasons Jimmy tolerated Hank Lapp better than most. When Hank grew irritating, which he inevitably did, Jimmy could steer him off in a different direction. Hank didn't mind exploring odd trails of conversation. His entire life was a giant trail of loose ends.

"Could be a real simple reason." Hank scratched his wooly white hair. "Not sure what it might be, though."

Jimmy thought about that for a long moment. "You just gave me an idea." He closed Lodestar's stall, locked both sections of the door with a keyed lock, and hung the key on the wall. This beautiful stallion had escape on his mind at all times. "Coming with me?"

"Where are we going?"

"Just up to the house." Jimmy grabbed his hat. "I have a question or two I need to ask the sisters from the Sisters' House."

"NO SIR! I'm not going back up there. The way your mother glared at me—I felt as doomed as a chicken laying its head down on the chopping block." He scowled at Jimmy with his good eye. "I'm going fishing."

"Suit yourself," Jimmy said, grinning.

◊

Bethany sat in the air-conditioned waiting room of the *Stoney Ridge Times* office, holding a paper cup of amber-colored lukewarm tea. She'd been waiting over thirty-five minutes for the features editor to get out of a meeting so she could hand him the signed paperwork to set up Mrs. Miracle's new column. She glanced at the wall clock again. Forty-five minutes.

Shootfire! She was already tired of the newspaper business.

Bethany leaned back in her chair and took in a deep breath, then let it go. Offices had a unique smell: ink and paper and waxed floors. A wisp of yearning wove through her chest. The scent reminded her of her father's office at Schrock Investments, and that reminded her of Jake Hertzler. She felt very unsettled today, almost like a storm was heading in, but it wasn't.

Time. Things took time to heal.

Rose had reminded her of that very thing after Jake's abrupt departure. Maybe she should write it on an index card and stick it in her dress pocket.

How could it still sting so much, even as the weeks flew by? It was embarrassing how much she thought she had loved Jake. Humiliating how she had played right into his hands, swept along by his charm. Horrifying when she learned he had tried to cheat Jimmy Fisher out of that pretty horse with the flaxen mane.

Where would Bethany be right now if she had run off with Jake like they had planned? Most likely, he never intended to marry her.

She knew she should feel grateful that she had enough sense to have refused, in the end, to go with him. In a way, she was grateful. But she was also steaming mad at Jake. It wasn't easy to be steaming mad at a person who had vanished . . . where did all that madness go? Stuffed down deep, that's where it went.

Most everyone thought Jake had broken her heart in two when he left, and she let them think whatever they wanted to think. She doubted Jake's heart was broken when she refused to go—but then, she wasn't even sure he had much of a heart. No, breaking up with Jake wasn't the cause of the lingering sting she couldn't shake off.

She still couldn't get her head around that piece of information that Jake had told her months ago when he appeared suddenly in Stoney Ridge—that her brother Tobe, who had gone missing, was with their mother. A fresh wave of anger washed over her. *Bethany* wanted to be with their mother. *She* wanted to know her, to find out why she had left. She knew so little about this mysterious woman who had given Bethany life, then vanished.

Her father would never discuss their mother. Mammi Vera would turn red in the face with rage if the subject came up. And so it didn't.

Why had her mother left? Why? Bethany would never understand. As long as she lived, she'd never understand it. How could a mother desert her children? How did her mother walk away, knowing it would mean she would never see them sing at a Christmas program or wear a wedding dress or hold her grandbaby? Whenever Bethany looked back on all the moments of her life, both trivial and wondrous, her mother was always missing.

Rose was a wonderful stepmother, a truly caring, loving surrogate. But how could anyone take the place of a mother? Why was finding her mother so important to her? It was all she could think about since Jake had told her about Tobe. Bethany could hardly remember her, except in the barest fragments.

She swirled the tepid tea in the cup, mesmerized by the whirlpool it created. Something floated up from the back of her mind, a wisp of a memory—

She closed her eyes, a rush of water swirled around her. Then there was a woman's scream and someone lifted her up. Bethany opened her eyes and saw a woman, dressed in blue. "Don't be afraid, Bethany," the woman said.

Jolted by the sudden blast of memories, Bethany put the cup down and shook her head slightly, as if to shake off that image. What was happening to her lately?

Strange, disjointed memories kept floating through her head, like steam from this teacup.

Someone cleared his throat. "Mrs. Miracle, I presume?"

Bethany snapped her head up to discover a heavyset man leaning on the doorjamb, looking at her with a very bored look on his face. She rose to her feet and tossed the paper cup into the trash can, giving him her most charming smile. "I'm as close as you'll ever get."

3

Mim rode her scooter to the Bent N' Dent to buy some baking soda for Mammi Vera, who preferred it to toothpaste. She had hoped Bethany would go, seeing as she had a surfeit of free time on her hands now that she wasn't going back to the Sisters' House because of the risk of getting murdered. But Bethany said it was too hot to go anywhere and Mammi Vera said she agreed with that. But Mammi Vera didn't think it was too hot for Mim to go.

As she was searching on the shelves for baking soda in aisle four, she heard a deep voice whisper her name. "Hello there, Mim."

Mim looked up to catch Danny Riehl peering down at her, and for a moment she felt absolutely bewildered. She hadn't seen him in well over a month and he had grown a foot or two. His shoulders were wide, and if she wasn't mistaken, there was some peach fuzz on his cheeks and under his nose. Why, he hardly looked like the same boy who finished eighth grade in May. He was on the old side for his grade, but still. He practically looked and sounded like a grown man.

Mim pushed her glasses up on the bridge of her nose at the exact same moment that Danny did. "Hello," she said, trying to sound casual and nonchalant, but everything inside her was on tiptoes. "Are you back from visiting your cousins in Alabama?"

He nodded. "We got back last week. I've been meaning to stop by, but . . ."

"I've been very busy," Mim said. "Hardly home." That wasn't at all true. She was home 97 percent of the time, but Danny didn't need to know that.

"Did you get my postcard from NASA?"

Did she ever! She floated on air for a week after receiving it. And now it was tucked under her pillow. "Yes. Thank you. Did you see any moon rocks?"

A big grin creased Danny's face. "I did. I saw rocket ships and moon rocks and an astronaut suit."

Mim wondered what Mammi Vera might say if she overheard Danny's excitement. Her grandmother was always pointing out the dangers of too much book learning. Je gelehrter, no verkehrter, she would say. *The more learning, the less wisdom.*

Mim didn't agree with Mammi Vera about book learning, and she definitely didn't think Danny was losing wisdom. Just the opposite. Danny's mother was Mattie Zook Riehl, and everyone knew those Zooks were overly blessed with wisdom. Danny's mother was the most respected woman in their church. Everyone went to her with problems. Mim liked to think that someday she would be thought of just like Mattie Zook Riehl. It was one of the reasons she took her job as Mrs. Miracle so seriously. Training for the future, she hoped. Training to be Danny's Mim.

"I was just getting a few things for my mother," Danny said, holding up a small basket filled with some spices. He cleared his throat. "Are you heading home?"

Mim snatched the baking soda off the shelf. "Yes."

After paying at the cash register, they walked down the road and Danny told her about a special chart his father bought him at NASA that displayed the constellations. Once Mim's father had taught her how to identify the Milky Way—like a swirl of milk in a cup of black coffee. "I used to think that the Milky Way was like a big curtain in the sky," she said. "If you pulled it back, you could see Heaven." She felt her cheeks grow warm. "Not logical, I know."

"Not logical, but a nice thought," Danny said.

"Do you think logic can always find answers?"

"No. Some things are just mysteries. Like Heaven." He slowed down a little so she could keep up with him. "I saw your sister in town yesterday. She didn't see me. She was heading into the newspaper office."

"Oh?" A stain rose on Mim's cheeks. Most of the Amish didn't read the *Stoney Ridge Times* because they thought it was too liberal, which was a relief to Mim. She wasn't sure how many might have even heard about the story claiming there were miracles to be had at the Inn at Eagle Hill, but the fewer Amish who knew of Mrs. Miracle, the better.

Danny was waiting for an answer from her. About why Bethany was in the newspaper office.

Diversion. That was how Mim handled topics she'd rather not discuss. "My sister has a mystery. She was cleaning out the basement at the Sisters' House. She opened a trunk and found human bones. Skulls, too. She thinks the sisters might be killing people and stuffing them in the basement. She thinks she is next on their list. She's afraid to go back to work."

Taking a moment to adjust his eyeglasses, Danny seemed in deep thought. "The old sisters don't strike me as ruthless murderers."

"That's just what I told Bethany."

"Why would she think the *Stoney Ridge Times* could help explain a trunk full of bones?"

Oh, boy. So much for trying to derail Danny. "That's an excellent question."

"Has Bethany asked the sisters about the bones?"

"Of course not. She's not very logical."

"That seems like the best place to start. Certainly better than the newspaper."

Mim nodded. *Phew.*

"Let's go ask."

"Really? Now?" She never liked to miss opportunities to talk to the sisters, especially Ella. If it was a good, clear day for Ella, Mim found she often gained insights to use in her important role as Mrs. Miracle.

Danny nodded. "We're not far from the Sisters' House. Let's go."

So Mim and Danny turned down a road that led to the Sisters' House and asked to speak with them about a very private concern. All five sisters came to the door, curious looks on their wrinkled faces. They invited Mim and Danny to come in for tea. That did slow down the investigation considerably, but Danny didn't seem to be in a hurry. “It’s best not to alarm them,” he whispered to Mim. “Just in case they *are* murderers.”

Mim had been going to the Sisters’ House with Bethany since school let out in May, but she was still amazed by the clutter. Every horizontal surface was covered with . . . stuff. Bethany could have a job here until she was an old lady herself, which was good news because she had said those sisters paid well.

When the tea was finally served, all five sisters sat on the living room sofa and waited for the very private concern to be explained. Mim decided she would try to keep her eyes open for what didn’t sound right, to see things from the sides of her eyes.

“Go ahead, Mim,” Danny said.

What? She thought he was going to be the one to talk. She took a deep breath. All five sisters smiled serenely at Mim, capstrings bouncing.

“Of course you know that my sister Bethany has been cleaning out your house.”

More smiles.

“Two days ago, she was down in the basement and opened a trunk and found . . .” Mim squinted her eyes shut.

“My thimble?” Ella said. “I’ve been looking everywhere for my thimble.”

“Now, Ella dear,” Sylvia said. “Your thimble would not have been in the basement.”

A confused look covered Ella’s face.

“You have plenty of thimbles,” Fannie said, mildly irritated.

“I’m looking for the thimble Mama gave me,” Ella said. “It had a band of roses around the base.”

Fannie rolled her eyes.

"Honey, we'll get you a new thimble," Sylvia said.

Danny nudged Mim with his elbow and whispered, "Better say something or we'll be here all day."

"Bones! Skulls!" Mim blurted out. "Human bones and human skulls. That's what Bethany found in the trunk."

The sisters looked at each other, startled, eyes wide. "Glory be!" Lena, the middle sister, said.

"Oh mercy!" said another.

"Is that why she didn't come to work today?" Sylvia asked.

Mim nodded. "She's frightened. She thinks you're planning to kill her."

"Oh my goodness," Ada, the second oldest sister, said. "That poor child."

The sisters assured them that they had no intention of killing Bethany and hoped Mim and Danny would agree, which they did. But none of the sisters had any idea what a trunk filled with human bones was doing in their basement. And could Mim please ask Jimmy Fisher to come over immediately?

The sun was coming up hot again on a new day when Jimmy knocked on the kitchen door of Eagle Hill. He breathed the fresh morning air deeply, happy to be alive and not at home where he was subject to his mother's relentless henpecking. He grinned when Bethany answered the door—he was hoping she would. "You can unglue that scowl from your face, Bethany. I know you're not happy to see me. But you will be, when you hear my news."

"What news is that, Jimmy Fisher?"

He tried not to get distracted by the blue-black ringlets that escaped from her tightly pinned bun and framed the nape of her neck. He diverted his eyes and noticed that she held an empty egg basket in her hands. "Hey," he said. "If you need eggs, all you gotta do is sing out. That's one thing I have plenty of. Fisher Hatchery at your service, ma'am."

She glanced down at the basket. "Usually, we have plenty. But Luke and Sammy started tossing them at each other and then the day's supply was scattered over the lawn. They're spending the morning in their room, contemplating their actions, in case you wonder why they're not over at Galen's."

Those two little brothers of hers were a passel of trouble, especially Luke. Sammy was less impulsive by nature, but Luke talked him into all kinds of mischief. Luke reminded Jimmy of himself, back in the day when he was young and immature. *Not so long ago*, echoed Galen's voice in his head, *like last week*. Jimmy frowned. Wasn't it enough that he worked alongside Galen every livelong day? Did the man have to fill his head with advice and warnings? He shook off that thought and focused his attention back on Bethany. He tried not to grin at the sassy look on her heart-shaped face.

"So what news are you talking about?"

"The mystery. I solved it."

She tipped her head to the side. "What particular mystery are *you* talking about?"

"The bones in the trunk."

She narrowed her eyes. "What about them?"

"I've been back and forth to the Sisters' House lately, asking them a few questions. More than a few. It takes quite a lot of work to keep them on task. Especially Ella. Have you noticed?"

She gave him a look that made him realize he had gone off track just like Ella. Maybe it was contagious.

"Just what are you getting at? Did you tell them about those bones, because if you did—"

Jimmy erased that in midair. "Actually, Mim and Danny Riehl had already told them." Bethany's eyes went wide and her mouth became a round O, then settled into a tight line. Jimmy hurried to his main point. "I'd been going about it in a gentle way, asking them roundabout questions without actually saying they had a trunk full of bones in their basement. Then your sister pays a visit and just bursts out with it—telling them you think they're murderers. Scared those sweet little ladies to the hereafter and back again."

"Shootfire! How could Mim do such a thing!" Bethany spun around to go find Mim and give her the what for, but Jimmy grabbed her arm.

"Hold on. Before you go off half-cocked, there's more to the story."

Bethany gave him a suspicious look, but she did stay put.

"It occurred to me that those old bones might belong to the previous owner of the house. The sisters have only lived in the house for some sixty-odd years." He snapped his fingers. "Bingo! As usual, I made a clever deduction."

Bethany rolled her eyes heavenward.

"A doctor used to live there. In fact, his office was in

the basement—which, by the way, the sisters want you to finish cleaning out as soon as you have recovered from your shock."

Bethany shuddered.

"One of the sisters remembered the doctor. They said he taught anatomy over at the college in Lancaster. They think he probably used the bones for his classes and forgot all about them." He grinned, pleased with himself. It had not been bad work, thanks to his quick thinking and even quicker logic. He believed in giving credit where credit was due, and he was due some. "Well?"

She shielded her eyes against the glare of the morning sun. "Well, what?"

"Aren't you going to thank me for solving this mystery? Now you can go back to work and not worry about getting murdered by five frail and wobbly eighty-year-old women." He took the hem of her sleeve and held it gently between his thumb and forefinger and didn't let go. A quiet spun out between them. She tried to look outraged, but he could see the smile tugging at her lips.

"I'll thank you once you get rid of that trunk with the bones in it."

He let her sleeve slide from his fingers. "Done. Took care of it last night. The sisters want you to come back as soon as your nerves have settled, they said, so you can all have a good laugh about it." He held her gaze until she looked away, a stain of pink rising in her cheeks, and flounced back inside the house in that unique Bethany-flouncing way. As he slipped through the privet to Galen's, he noticed the eagle pair that nested at Eagle Hill soaring high in the sky, in tandem, and his buoyant spirits lifted even higher, if that was possible.

Bethany had stopped by Naomi's to ask her how to fit together some tricky quilt pieces and discovered, to her dismay, Edith Fisher in the kitchen. It was a small kitchen with little in it, and Edith Fisher's large presence made it seem far smaller.

"Naomi," Edith said, "has a little headache and shouldn't be disturbed." She proceeded to show Bethany what she had done wrong with the quilt pieces.

That woman surely needed some castor oil. There wasn't a thing Bethany could put her hands to that she didn't have a hard word about. It befuddled her how a sharp-tongued woman like her reared a son like Jimmy.

Despite all Jimmy Fisher's faults, plus his bad character, he had been kind to her and to her family. Far too patient with her little brothers who buzzed around him like horseflies. Sweet as whipped cream to Mammi Vera, and Bethany knew her grandmother was no Sunday picnic to be around. Helpful to Rose, attentive to Naomi, a hard worker to Galen. It was a shame that his reputation was so low and irreparable. And why did he have to be so handsome?

As Bethany walked through the privet, she saw a woman in jeans and a jacket and a bandana heading to the porch of Eagle Hill with a tray in her hands.

"Hello," the woman said. "You must be Bethany, right?"

"Yes. That's me. I'm Bethany Schrock." She took the breakfast tray out of her hands. "And you must be the lady preacher."

"Not much of a preacher, actually. More like a youth

pastor. Not much of a youth pastor, either." She waved a hand in the air to dismiss the topic. "Just call me Geena."

Bethany looked into the pleasant, beaming face of a small woman with olive skin, brown hair, and chocolate brown eyes. "Are you comfortable in the guest flat?"

"It's fine."

"Hot, though. We're having a terrible heat wave."

"The flat stays pretty cool."

"Rose said you were from the Philadelphia area. Are you planning on staying long?"

Geena looked up at the sky. "I'm not sure. I . . . well . . . to be perfectly honest, I was fired from my church."

"Fired?" Bethany asked, amazed. "For the Amish, only God fires ministers. And that only happens when they pass."

Geena smiled. "I guess you could say that's true for the non-Amish too. But the day jobs might switch up a little more often."

"It must be hard to be a preacher. Preachers make me nervous. Whenever I'm around them, I always think about things I shouldn't have done but did and things I should do but haven't."

Geena's eyes went wide for a second, then she burst out laughing.

Why was that so funny? Sometimes, the sense of humor of English people struck Bethany as very odd.

◊

Geena spent the morning walking around the farm, watching the sheep in the pasture, the horses grazing in the field. A field of white linen draped across the yard—

sheets on a clothesline wafting in the summer sun. It was so peaceful here, so quiet . . . until a high-pitched shriek came from the direction of the barn. The door slid open and two little boys burst out of it, little one chasing the bigger one, with the golden retriever at his heels. The little boy was hollering in a language Geena couldn't understand and running so hard to catch up with the bigger boy that he lost his hat. But both boys stopped abruptly at the sight of Geena.

"You're the lady preacher!" the big boy said. He had dark hair, nearly black, and twinkling eyes, and she knew this cute boy was going to be trouble in a few years. "I'm Luke Schrock and this is my brother Sammy." The younger boy resembled his mother, Rose. Softer, with round cheeks, a headful of wavy curls, and rather sizable ears.

"I'm Geena." Two sets of brown eyes gawked at her curiously. "Something going on, boys?"

"We've never met a lady preacher before," Sammy said.

Geena laughed. "I'm a youth pastor, not a preacher. But I didn't mean me—I meant, whatever caused you both to come flying out of the barn like it was on fire."

"Oh, that," Sammy said.

Luke gave his brother a warning frown, but too late. Sammy, oblivious to undercurrents, blurted out, "Luke bet me a dollar to ride the goat backwards and I did, and now he won't pay up."

Luke jabbed him with his elbow. "You didn't stay on it longer than five seconds! I bet you for a full minute."

"That backwards stuff is harder than it looks!" Sammy complained.

"Luke made a bet?" someone said stonily.

The boys whirled around to discover their grandmother, Vera Schrock, had appeared on the porch steps and overheard Luke's bravado. Geena watched the boys exchange a glance. She knew boys well enough to know their instinct was to bolt and run, but these two knew better. They turned to face their accuser.

Quick as a whip, Luke said, "Why, Mammi Vera, your hearing must be going bad. Sammy and I were just introducing ourselves to the new guest and telling her to be careful of the goat."

That drew a stern look right out of the book of grandmothers. She wasn't buying this boy's wide-eyed, butter-wouldn't-melt look for a minute. "Wer eemol liegt, dem glaabt mer net wann era a die Waahret secht." She glared at Luke and pointed to the house. Head hanging low, he trudged inside. Sammy, wisely, stayed behind. Before Luke went into the house, he turned and balled his fist to pantomime an uppercut at his brother.

"What did your grandmother say to him?" Geena whispered to Sammy.

"He who lies once is not believed when he speaks the truth." The kitchen door slammed shut. "And about now she's getting warmed up for a long lecture about the devil and lies."

Sammy turned and headed to the barn—a sanctuary from lectures and grandmothers and bullying brothers. Geena grinned. Set aside the buggies and bonnets and beards, and she could have been observing any family in America.

4

Bethany arrived at the Sisters' House with a new plan of attack. She tucked a strand of curly dark hair behind her ears as she continued to shuffle through things, sorting them into three piles: keep, give away, throw away.

Books and magazines: give away.

Two sets of binoculars with broken lenses: throw away.

Bags and bags of fabric scraps: give to Naomi for her quilting group, which, by the way, Bethany still didn't want to join.

Threadbare rugs: throw away.

The keep pile was empty . . . until one sister after another would wander into the room and pull things out of the give away and throw away piles and move them into the keep pile.

Since there wasn't any rain on the horizon, Bethany planned to empty out the living room so she could wash the windows and sweep and scrub the floors. She sighed, gazing around the cluttered room. Most every Amish family in Stoney Ridge practiced upkeep. The sisters practiced downkeep. Spiderwebs clung to the corners; a thick layer of dust covered every horizontal surface. There was collective clutter and then there was individual clutter. The sisters called it all functional clutter.

Bethany had created a mental list of considerable length. She had noticed that whenever she started to push the sisters to make decisions about getting rid of things, they would send her off to another room. So far, she had made a dent in practically every room, but not much more than a dent. Well, this house was in for the cleaning of its life, no matter how long it took. The deacon had asked them to take a turn hosting church, but fortunately, he hadn't given them an actual date. Cleaning out this house might take over a year.

Bethany had gone back to work at the Sisters' House today, as soon as Jimmy Fisher had come by to let her know the trunk of human bones mystery was sorted out—and she and the sisters and Jimmy actually did have a good laugh over it. Jimmy, especially, but she thought he found most everything amusing. Especially when she looked to be the fool. She did her best not to get riled at him for laughing at her and she didn't say anything about his bad character. Hardly much at all, anyway.

But Jimmy Fisher was a man of his word. He had hauled the trunk of bones away and donated them to the college in Lancaster.

This morning, to her surprise, the sisters asked her to stop working inside and start on the outbuilding that once housed the buggies. They were heading off for the day—and after the bones in the basement fiasco, they didn't want to leave her alone in the main house. She wasn't sure if they were worried she would find more creepy things, or if she would toss out too much without their knowledge. Both, she presumed.

She didn't mind working outside for a while, especially on such a hot summer morning, and hoped the carriage house would be cooler than the house. At least she'd get some fresh air. She needed to air out her brain too—her thoughts felt all jumbled up.

She wished she could talk to her brother Tobe. Where was he, anyway? Was he still with their mother? How had he found her? Where had she been living all these years?

Bethany mulled over all the questions she'd harbored about her mother. What was she like? Did she ever ask Tobe about Bethany? Then there was the biggest question of all . . . why did she leave in the first place?

All those thoughts were scrambling through Bethany's head instead of the one thought that should have been there: *Get to work!*

She opened the door to the carriage house and took a deep breath. There was barely room to walk. The sisters didn't keep horses any longer, but there was a dusty old buggy, leaning against the wall. "I don't know where to begin."

"It is a bit of a pickle." Sylvia, the youngest sister, had come up behind her and stood by the doorjamb. Ella joined her, then Fannie and Ada. The women peered into the cluttered space, hands on their hips, taking it all in. "It's all Lena's doing," Fannie said. "She's crazy about tag sales. Brings home all kinds of worthless junk."

That wasn't the whole truth, Bethany knew. So far, Fannie blamed the clutter problem on Ella, who blamed Ada, who blamed Lena, who blamed Sylvia, who blamed

Fannie. Bethany thought all the ladies had clutter problems, but who was she to say? She was paid handsomely for sifting through all kinds of interesting things. Even the trunk full of bones was interesting. Frightening, creepy . . . but interesting.

"Mim, maybe you can keep a look out for my thimble," Ella said.

Fannie drew in a chest-heaving sigh. "This is Bethany, Ella. Mim's sister."

Ella gave her head that little shake. "Where's Mim?"

"She had something she had to do." Something to do with Mrs. Miracle. Bethany had brought a cardboard box from the house and set it in the shade of the carriage house. "What would you like me to do with all the things in the discard boxes?" She was trying to be as diplomatic as possible. "I thought we might plan on having a yard sale of your own."

"What a good idea!" Sylvia said. "But we'll have to discuss it first."

Of course, of course. Everything was decided by committee in this household. A long, endless committee of indecision.

Ella and Fannie and Ada walked over to join Lena by the front door. They were heading off somewhere—they always had places to go and Bethany didn't know where.

Only Sylvia remained. "It will be nice to have this place cleaned out. Papa would have been so pleased. He always intended to clean out this carriage house."

Oh, great. That's just great. That meant this carriage house hadn't been cleaned out in at least thirty years. What might be crawling around in here? Several generations of mice and snakes and spiders. Bethany looked around the dusty carriage house, at the thick cobwebs clinging to the corners, at the smudged windows. She shuddered.

"We're off, then," Sylvia said. "Won't be back until after three. Ella needs her afternoon nap."

Ella, the eldest sister, was ninety-two and never without a sweet smile on her face. Sylvia said she put her love in things beyond herself, and that kept her spirits high.

Bethany nodded. "Have a good day."

Then Sylvia leaned close to Bethany and placed her wrinkled hands on her arms, peering at her with mortal seriousness. The top of her head only reached the tip of Bethany's chin, but there was no shortage of stature in Sylvia's tone when she spoke up like this. "You mustn't blame yourself or look back—not any longer than it takes to learn what you must learn. After that, let it go. The past is past. But you're still here," she whispered urgently and exerted a gentle pressure on Bethany's arms. "And I'm glad. You be glad too."

Tears sprang in Bethany's eyes. How did Sylvia know how troubled she'd been feeling this summer? She'd never said a word.

Sylvia gave the carriage house one more look-over and waved her hand. "Oh goodness—this old carriage house can wait another week. What would you think about helping us today? We could always use an extra pair of hands, especially at the end of the month."

Bethany wiped away a tear. "I'm all yours."

"Excellent!" Sylvia said. "The more the merrier for this project." She pointed to two little red children's wagons, filled with food, waiting on the front walk. "You can help us pull those wagons."

"Where are we going?"

"To the Grange Hall. To make lunch."

Bethany was about to ask why but decided against it. She'd find out soon enough.

Like any town, Stoney Ridge had good areas and not-so-good areas. The Sisters' House, one of the oldest in the area, was in the not-so-good area. As the town grew, the original area became run-down and neglected. The Sisters' House was only a block from the main road. The Grange Hall stood at the corner. On one side of the Grange was a vacant lot. On the other side of the Grange was a group home for wayward teenage girls. The entire block looked tired and worn-out and neglected.

As the women pulled the wagons past the Group Home, Bethany looked at the house more carefully than she ever had. No one tended the grass. There were no flowers in pots, no curtains on the windows. A television screen, always on, could be seen from the road.

Hopeless. That's what the house looked and felt like. It seemed a little disturbing to Bethany, as if the house had a personality of its own—which was ridiculous—but the sisters just waved to the wayward girls and walked right on by it. Only one of the wayward girls waved back.

When they got to the Grange Hall, they went around back and parked the wagons by the kitchen door. "We'll need to take a few trips to get all that food inside."

"That's an awful lot of food for lunch for you," Bethany said.

"It's not for us." Sylvia walked up the three steps and unlocked the kitchen door. "We run a soup kitchen for the folks in Stoney Ridge who are a little down on their luck."

Fannie put a large bottle of Dr Pepper at the base of the door to hold it open. "A few years back, when the recession hit head-on, we sisters kept seeing a need in this town. So we talked to the fellow who had the keys for the Grange and he told us we could use the kitchen to serve the hungry. Once a week, everybody in Stoney Ridge who's in need gets a hot meal."

That, Bethany thought, *would be a very small group*. She didn't know a soul in Stoney Ridge who was in need.

Lena read her mind. "Child, look out the window."

Bethany turned to see what she was talking about. She could see into the backyard of the Group Home. Five or six girls sat at a picnic bench, a few of them smoking. "You mean, you feed *them*?"

"That home is for girls who are in trouble, or their parents are. There's a woman whose job is housemother. She does her best with what the county gives, but it's not enough to stretch the week."

"So how many people come for a lunch?" Bethany asked. "Those five?"

"Anywhere from twenty to thirty-five," Fannie said. "Busier at the end of the month when food stamps run out."

Ada handed Bethany a bag of onions. "And we send out five meals to the homebound. Can't forget them."

Bethany was shocked.

"We cook most things from scratch," Fannie added.

"A good cook starts from scratch and keeps on scratching." Ella chuckled at her own joke while Fannie gave her a look like she was sun-touched.

"We haul the wagons over here and do the cooking and serve it up," Lena said.

"You pull those wagons all the way here and cook all those meals?" How had Bethany never noticed? She'd been working for the sisters, three days a week, for over two months. She had no idea this was where the sisters went on other weekdays. You'd think she would have noticed something. Or asked. She felt ashamed of herself. And yet it was baffling to Bethany too. How could the sisters live in a home of such clutter and chaos yet have the wherewithal to plan and execute such a purposeful event, once a week, week after week?

Sylvia read the look on her face and answered her question as if she had asked it. "We'd rather be out, doing things for others, than fussing with a silly house."

"Sometimes, it takes two trips to get the wagons to the Grange Hall kitchen," Sylvia said. "But it's good exercise for us. It's a long day. We usually get here by nine and spend the morning chopping and cutting and cooking. The kitchen opens up from twelve to one, then there's cleanup."

"But why hasn't anyone been helping you?" It was the Plain way for neighbor to help neighbor. It was what they did best.

From the look on Sylvia's face, the thought never crossed her mind. "It started small enough that we could manage ourselves. And then, as it got bigger, we kept finding new ways to manage. Besides, it's summertime and farming families are busy."

"Where do you get the food?" Bethany asked.

"We get most from the Lancaster County Food Bank," Sylvia explained. "Some things, like this pork butt, are donated by the butcher on Main Street. The Bent N' Dent gives us their canned goods that are too bent and dented to sell. The Sweet Tooth Bakery gives us their day-old pastries. Some things are from our own garden."

The sisters had a system for getting things in the kitchen from the wagon. They lined up along the stairs like an assembly line and passed items along. Ella had a little canvas chair and put things in the chair, then dragged the chair with her cane across the threshold and into the kitchen. She used her cane to prop open the refrigerator. Remarkably resourceful, these ladies were.

Today, Bethany took care of the lifting. The Grange Hall kitchen was starkly clean. A whiff of Clorox lingered in the air—Bethany could see the tile floor had been recently swabbed. Utensils were neatly hung on hooks. The pots and pans, battered and sturdy, in every imaginable variety, were stacked below the countertop and on the shelves around the room.

Sylvia had a system for everything. She had gone through a certification process with the Board of Health so she knew what she should serve and how to keep the kitchen sanitary. Bethany realized that she must've started this soup kitchen when she was in her late seventies. Amazing! Mammi Vera was only in her mid-sixties and acted like she needed full-time tending.

Soon, the kitchen was humming. On the stove in big pots were sautéed onions and green peppers. In another pot was the pork butt in a braising liquid. As Bethany chopped onions, she glanced out the window now and then at the girls from the Group Home, sitting in the shade at the picnic table. They seemed so . . . apathetic.

By noon, they had set tables with plastic spoons and forks and napkins, stirred up the sugary punch the sisters had created and added Dr Pepper to it, and Sylvia opened the doors.

In walked the girls from next door, the five from the picnic bench and four more. The two knots of girls sat far apart from each other. A handful of old men walked in, a few families, and a single mother with three toddlers. There were the homeless, of course, wearing too many layers of clothes, none too clean, and young drifters and runaways, pierced and tattooed, their eyes hungry.

Bethany had no idea there were so many down-and-outers in need in Stoney Ridge. How had she not noticed? It wasn't easy for her to see them or to smell them. The musty scent of unwashed bodies nearly choked her. After a while, she grew used to it, though now and then a whiff of someone sorely in need of a bath and a bar of soap hit her hard, and she turned away by faking a cough. It shamed her, but it was the truth. She wished for hot showers and soft beds for them.

After everyone found a seat, Sylvia insisted on a word from the Lord. "Jesus gave you this day," she said. "He didn't have to do that, but he did. So now we are going to hear his words." Everyone bowed their heads as she read a few verses from the Sermon on the Mount.

"Amen!" an older black man shouted out after she read that the poor would be blessed. "Amen for that blessing, Sister Sylvia! Praise the Lord!"

Accustomed to the man's enthusiasm, Sylvia gave a nod to Bethany to start serving the paper plates. She liked to control the portions, so each plate received the same amount of food: two slices of pork, mashed potatoes, green beans, a slice of watermelon. People could have seconds, she said, if they asked.

Bethany took plates to the table of girls from the Group Home. They looked at her with blank stares and took the plates without even a thank-you. *Do you realize how hard these old sisters are working?* she wanted to ask them. *Do you even care?*

Bethany felt the eyes of someone on her. She turned and was startled by one girl at the end of a table, staring at her. Her fiery red hair was long and tangled, as if she had not combed it at all, and she eyed Bethany with a hard-edged hostility. Angry eyes. Bethany looked back, and even from this distance she could feel the radiating resentment, so fierce and terrible.

By three o'clock, Bethany was exhausted. The five sisters kept at it, making sure everything was spick-and-span in their careful, deliberate way. Each pot had been scrubbed, rinsed, and returned to the shelf. The kitchen was spotless, just the way it had looked when they arrived. And nothing at all like the kitchen in their own home.

◊

It was Sunday morning. The summer heat lay heavy over the barn, blending the air with barn smells of horse and cow and hay, along with Sunday smells of soap and starch and brewing coffee. Seated on hard backless benches on one side of the large barn were the men and boys. Across from them sat the women and girls.

As much as Jimmy Fisher tried to keep his mind on the sermon, his gaze swept across the room to a checkerboard of pleated white and black prayer caps. Seated along a row of young women, white shawls and white aprons and crisp black prayer caps to mark their maiden status, with them, and yet somehow apart from them, was Bethany Schrock.

She sat with her shoulders pulled back and a look on her face as if she was supremely interested in the minister's lengthy description of the plagues of Exodus. She appeared utterly pious but Jimmy knew better. His gaze fell to her lap, where she was gripping and releasing, gripping and releasing, small handfuls of apron.

Bethany Schrock didn't have the hands of a typical Amish girl, Jimmy noticed, not big, blunt-fingered hands. They were slender, delicate hands. He tried to push those thoughts away, to keep his mind on the suffering of the Israelites, but one thought kept intruding—what was Bethany thinking about that made her hands so tense? What was running through her mind?

It was unfortunate that Katie Zook happened to be seated next to Bethany. Each time Jimmy chanced a look at Bethany, whose eyes stayed straight ahead, Katie assumed he was making eyes at her and she would start to brazenly blink her eyes rapidly and her lips curled into a pleased smile. His interest in Katie Zook had come and gone like a summer rain burst, but her interest in him was more like a coal miner staking a claim. He would have to give some thought as to how to go about dropping her kindly. Katie was the persistent type, cute but clueless.

He listened to the chickens cluck and scratch outside the open barn door, to the horses moving around in the straw in their stalls, to the bleats of the sheep out in the pasture. The minister was preaching now of how persecuted the Israelites had been as slaves to the Egyptians, how many hardships they suffered. The familiar words rose and fell, rose and fell, like gusts of wind. This was the first of two sermons preached, testimony given, prayers and Scripture read, more ancient hymns sung—and the whole of it would last for over three hours.

Plenty of time to ponder how to face Katie Zook's blinking eyes and let her down easy, so gently she'd think it was her own idea. Plenty of time to ponder how to capture and hold Bethany Schrock's interest.

Bethany had perfected the art of appearing deeply attentive during church while her mind drifted off in a thousand directions, especially during the long and silent moments between sermons and testimony and Scripture reading. The only part she could say she enjoyed was the last five minutes. If there was any exciting news, that's when it would be announced. The grim and somber hymns that told the stories of the martyrs through the ages were her least favorite part of the service. Most of these hymns were written in dark and damp prison cells, four hundred years ago, and while she did have a healthy respect for what her ancestors had endured—what Plain person wouldn't?—it was hard to fully appreciate it all on a beautiful summer day.

After the benediction, the church sat and waited. Bishop Elmo rose to his feet in the middle of the barn, straightening his hunched back. He raised his head and his gentle gaze moved slowly, carefully, over each man, woman, and child. First he faced the women; slowly he turned to face the men. Then he began to speak. "Two of our young people want to get married."

Instantly, Bethany came back to the world. Among the Lancaster Amish, weddings didn't usually happen until the fall when the harvest was in. She wondered which couple might be getting engaged. This was the most exciting moment in a woman's life. She searched the rows of prayer caps, trying to see which of the girls might be blushing—giving away the secret. She wasn't alone in her curiosity. All the women were looking up and down the rows. All but one.

Mary Kate Lapp had her head bowed, chin tucked against her chest.

Bishop Elmo cleared his throat. "The couple is Mary Kate Lapp and Chris Yoder. The wedding will take place in late August so they can move out to Ohio. The church there is in dire need of a buggy shop and Chris Yoder has been asked to come." Then Bishop Elmo sat down and the song leader announced the last song. Everyone reached for their hymnbook and opened it to the page, singing a mournful hymn as if nothing unusual or thrilling had just happened.

As soon as the song ended, Mary Kate and Chris rose and walked outside. By the time church was dismissed, they had driven away in Chris's buggy. They were off to address invitations to their wedding.

Bethany felt a combination of delight for her friend, sorrow that M.K. was moving away, and, if she were truly honest, jealousy. M.K. and Chris seemed to have it so easy. They met, fell in love, were getting married, and would live happily ever after. End of story.

That's what Bethany had wanted too. But she had the bad luck of falling for that crooked lowlife Jake Hertzler, who had everybody fooled with his easy charm and winning smile. She shuddered. She would never let herself fall in love with anyone, not ever again.

As she put the hymnal back under the bench, her sister Mim slipped over and stood in front of her, her face filled with worry. "Who is going to teach school next term? When Teacher M.K. gets married, who will take her place?"

Bethany lifted one shoulder in a half shrug. "I don't know, Mim. But they'll find someone. They always do. Some poor unsuspecting soul who has no idea what's about to hit her."

On Sunday afternoon, Mim suggested a picnic out at Blue Lake Pond to escape the stuffy house, and Mim's mother was delighted. Naomi, Mammi Vera, and Bethany were invited, but Naomi needed to rest and Mammi Vera said it was too hot and Bethany said she was in no mood for mosquitos. Mim thought that mosquitos or not, Bethany always seemed to be in a touchy mood lately, but she was disappointed not to have her company, touchy mood and all. Her little brothers caused chaos and turmoil, even if they just stood still.

Those boys wouldn't be doing any standing still at Blue Lake Pond. It was their favorite place to be on a summer afternoon. The buggy hadn't even come to a stop before the boys jumped out and hightailed it for the blackberry vines drooping with ripe fruit. Galen lifted old Chase out of the buggy as he was getting too arthritic to jump, though not too old to run after the boys. He loped behind them, tail wagging so fast it looked like a whirligig. Galen tied the horse's reins together and fastened them to a tree so it could graze while they picnicked.

Mim inhaled a deep breath. So sweet. The summer air smelled of sunbaked pine needles and lake water and freshness. She spread a blanket under the shade of a tree and set up the picnic.

Her mom pointed to those blackberry vines and said, "Mim, we could have great fun making jam."

Oh, boy. Mim knew what the week ahead was going to look like: picking berries, pricking fingers, scratches on arms from thorns, followed by hours in a hot and steamy kitchen with pectin, Mason jars, wax, sugar, cheesecloth. *Fun?*

Galen sat with his back against the tree and tipped his hat brim over his eyes. Mim liked that Galen was the kind of person who could sit and not fill every second with chatter the way Mammi Vera did. Sometimes, her head hurt from Mammi Vera's ongoing commentary of Mim and her brothers. Of course, it was always critical. Her grandmother would stand tall and draw in a deep breath and pucker her lips like she was sucking on a lemon and . . . watch out! So unlike Galen, whose words were few and soft, in that deep, gravelly voice, and when he spoke, others always listened.

Her mom nudged her gently with her elbow and whispered, "Now there's a sight you don't see too often." She pointed to Galen. His hat cast his face in a shadow, and his whole body looked relaxed and lazy. He was the hardest working person they knew, and that was saying a lot for a Plain man in Stoney Ridge. Mim pushed her glasses up on the bridge of her nose and smiled at her mom. It was a peaceful moment and she was glad she'd thought of coming to Blue Lake Pond.

Then suddenly the boys were upon them, jerking Galen out of his all-too-brief nap. Juice ran down their faces and onto their shirts.

"You're more the color of berries than boys," her mom said. Sammy smiled, his teeth white in his purple face. She gave him a cake of Ivory soap. "Get in the lake and scrub the stains off. Luke, watch your brother."

The boys dove into the lake in their berry-stained shirts. When Luke came to the surface, he let out a whoop that echoed off the trees. He went under again and stayed down a long time before coming up in the middle of the lake. Sammy, not as skilled a swimmer, stayed in shallow water with the bar of soap in his hand and watched his brother rise up and down in the water like a whale.

"I don't think Luke's got stain scrubbing on his mind," Galen said.

The three of them sat side by side in the quiet, watching the boys as they swam. "Jimmy Fisher's been teaching the boys to swim this summer," her mother said. "Trying, anyway. They exasperate Jimmy. Luke, especially."

Galen glanced over at Mim. "Notice anything different about Jimmy lately?"

"Like what?"

"He's . . . distracted. Off his feed." Galen stretched one ankle over the other. "The kind of work we're doing with Thoroughbreds—he has to keep his mind on the job." He looked directly at Mim. "Anything you're aware of going on with Jimmy? A new girlfriend?"

Mim had a pretty good idea what was nettling Jimmy. "Naomi said his mother's back in town."

Galen's dark eyebrows lifted. "I hadn't thought of that. I saw her at church this morning. She came to visit Naomi last week."

"She's moved back," Mim's mom said, brushing some leaves off her dress. "Her new husband passed and she decided to return to Stoney Ridge. And her older son Paul moved with his new bride to her family's home."

"That's awful sudden," Galen said.

"Quite," Mim added, though her mother raised an eyebrow at her. It was true, though. Tongues had been wagging about it all week. "I heard that the last straw was when Edith Fisher starched and ironed Paul's underwear. The next day, they said they were moving."

"Mim, don't tell tales."

Galen stretched out his legs. "I suppose I'd move on too, real quick, if someone were to starch and iron my underwear."

"When it comes to a mother-in-law and a daughter-in-law, it's never just about the starched underwear."

Mim's head popped up like it was on a spring. For days, she'd been puzzling how to answer a letter to Mrs. Miracle. Her mom had just crafted her the perfect response.

Galen's mouth lifted in a slight smile. "Edith Fisher always did cast quite a shadow on her boys." Then he became silent again and their attention turned to the boys splashing around in the water. After a while, her mother insisted they come out of the water and dry off.

"Are you hungry?" Mim's mother asked, spreading a feast out on the blanket.

"Always," Galen said.

Out of a basket, she pulled fried chicken, deviled eggs,

macaroni salad, watermelon, and her special blueberry buckle for dessert. The boys, wrapped in towels, pinned down the edges. Chase was banished to the outer perimeter, watching hopefully for any scraps that might be dropped.

A few hours later, after they had returned home and the remains of the picnic basket were put away, Mim slipped up to her room and pulled out the typewriter. She took out the manila envelope of letters to Mrs. Miracle that she kept hidden under her mattress.

Dear Mrs. Miracle,

Last night, my husband and I had our first fight. It was over the silliest thing: whether to have eggs scrambled or fried. It's been four days and we still can't agree.

What should I do?

Thanks to her mother's keen insight, Mim knew just how to answer:

Dear What Should I Do,

It's never about the eggs . . .

Sincerely,
Mrs. Miracle

5

For no reason, between one stride and the next, Jimmy Fisher's prize stallion, Lodestar, suddenly rolled out of his easy gait into a flying buck. Jimmy had been exercising Lodestar on a lead rope, relaxed and calm, but somehow this horse had sensed that he had his mind on other things. He bucked, then reared, and as the rope slipped out of Jimmy's hands, Lodestar took the opportunity to jump the fence and gallop off into the woods.

Aggravating! This horse was conditioned by his former owner, the slippery Jake Hertzler, to be a "runner" and it was taking all of Jimmy's efforts to break him of that habit. In a way, Lodestar's independent streak pleased Jimmy—he had never cared for totally docile horses. He liked an animal that was as alert as he was—or, in this stallion's case, even more alert. Jimmy had been aware of his own preoccupations, whereas he had had no inkling of Lodestar's intentions. He had no doubt the horse would try bolting again and again.

Jimmy jumped the fence and grabbed a bucket of oats he kept handy for Lodestar, then ran into the woods, whistling for him. He knew the horse wouldn't go far from the barn—he always exercised Lodestar right before feeding time for that very reason. That horse may like his freedom, but even he wouldn't pass up a bucket of oats.

As he walked into the woods, his thoughts drifted back to all that filled his mind. The last few days, something was rolling around inside Jimmy Fisher, making him tense and snappish. He could do nothing with Lodestar lately. Horses took on his mood, and Galen had taught him that those weren't the days to do the work of training. Galen's spirit was quiet and calm and the horses sensed that. Jimmy had worked with Galen long enough to know that if he could mirror that calm, the horses calmed too. Those were the days he made progress in training. Especially with Lodestar.

All week, Jimmy Fisher had been working from sunup to sundown at Galen King's and he was happy to do so because he didn't want to go home. His mother had moved back to the family farm at Stoney Ridge and his new sister-in-law lasted only a week. He had overheard the argument between Paul and LaWonna.

"It's been two days," LaWonna was telling Paul, "and your mother has told me I do everything wrong, from the way I fold your shirts to how I spread jam on bread. Every blessed thing! Paul, I can *not* live under your mother's thumb for the rest of my life! I just can't do it. No woman could!"

The following day, Paul told his mother and Jimmy that he'd been given a wonderful opportunity to manage

LaWonna's parents' farm in Canada. And they'd be leaving immediately.

For the first time in his life, Jimmy was the sole focus of his mother. Paul was no longer the buffer between them. She wanted Jimmy to give up the horse breeding business and take over the full management of the hatchery. That hatchery was supposed to be Paul's life's work. Jimmy's life's work was going to be all about horses.

Be a full-time chicken farmer? No thank you.

And then there was his love life. His mother was working overtime to encourage Jimmy to court the girl she had picked out for him: Naomi King. Now, Naomi was a sweet girl, and in a certain light she might be considered pretty, but Jimmy liked fire in a girl. There wasn't even a spark in Naomi. He saw her every day, and she was a good friend to him, but all he knew about her was that she suffered from terrible headaches and she liked to quilt. What kind of life would that be?

His thoughts slipped off to Bethany Schrock, which was happening quite a bit lately. That girl was maddening, hot-tempered, and feisty . . . and entirely fascinating to him. One minute, she would hardly pay him any mind, the next minute she would bat her eyelashes at him and send a look his way that would make his heart turn over. He could never quite tell if she was flirting with him or not. It was a contest . . . and Jimmy loved a challenge.

His mother must have caught wind that he had his eye on Bethany Schrock and she was doing everything she could to redirect his attention to Naomi. She kept dropping by to visit Naomi and inviting her over for meals, cultivating the relationship with her intended future daughter-in-law.

In the distance, Jimmy saw a buggy coming up the road with a horse following behind. In the buggy was Galen. Trailing with a rope was Lodestar, which made Jimmy feel better and humiliated, all at once.

He walked to meet Galen and took the rope from him. "Thanks."

"Wouldn't keep happening if you kept your mind on your work."

Galen headed up the road to the farm. Jimmy and Lodestar followed along. In the barn, Jimmy led Lodestar to his stall and gave him a slap on the rump as the big horse crossed the threshold. He was a magnificent horse but he took every ounce of Jimmy's attention. Jimmy tossed two slices of hay over the top half of the stall door and reached over to grab the water bucket to fill it.

As Jimmy walked down the middle of the barn aisle to fill up the water bucket, he suddenly heard the unmistakable sound of Lodestar's hooves clip-clopping on the concrete and spun around. Lodestar's stall door was wide open and the horse was heading toward the open barn door. "Galen! Close the door!"

In the middle of pitching hay into a wheelbarrow, Galen stabbed the pitchfork into a hay bale and made a lunge for the door. He grabbed Lodestar's halter just as the horse reached the threshold and led him back to his stall, scowling at Jimmy.

"I know, I know." Jimmy lifted the water bucket. "I was filling the bucket."

Galen shut the hinges on both parts of the door. "What is the problem with you lately?"

Jimmy sat down on a trunk and crossed one ankle

over the other. "My mother wants me to give up the horse breeding business."

"Ah," Galen said.

"She wants me working full-time with the chicken business. And she wants me to think about getting married . . . to the girl she's got picked out."

"Who's that?"

Instantly, Jimmy regretted bringing that topic up. There was no way to talk about Galen's sister Naomi and come out on the right side of that discussion. If Jimmy disparaged her—admitting that he could never imagine himself with her—he would find himself tossed out of the barn on his rump. On the other hand, if Jimmy were to compliment Naomi, he would also find himself under Galen's constant surveillance. It was a no-win situation and Jimmy wanted none of it. Galen was very protective of his little sister. Unless a fellow was happily married, Galen didn't want him anywhere near Naomi.

Jimmy pitied the poor fellow who would ever try to court Naomi. Galen would be watching that fellow like a duck watched for waterbugs. He glanced at Galen and realized he was waiting for an answer. "You know my mother. She's got a short list of acceptable females that meet with her approval."

"Someone who'll kowtow to her."

Jimmy nodded. Then he slapped his hands on his knees. "I do not want to be a chicken farmer and I do not want to have my mother pick my bride."

Galen picked up a broom and started sweeping the hay that had dropped from the wheelbarrow. "Didn't Hank Lapp have a fondness for your mother?"

"Yeah, but he courted her for more years than ticks

on a mule. She got tired of him dragging his heels about getting married."

Galen set the broom against the wall and crossed his arms against his chest. "Well, seems as if even your mother might have trouble if she had too many pots boiling on the stove."

"What do you mean?"

Galen closed his eyes briefly, and it seemed to Jimmy that under cover of his lids, he rolled them. "You've got a brain. Use it." He picked up the handles of the wheelbarrow and started for the door. When he slid it open, both Galen and Jimmy saw Bethany Schrock flounce across the yard to head to the house to visit with Naomi. "I doubt Bethany Schrock would be on your mother's short list."

"No. She's got something against those Schrocks. Doesn't matter, though. Bethany doesn't take me seriously. She thinks I'm nothing but a flirt."

"She's right." Galen grinned. "Now, Bethany Schrock is a girl who would go head-to-head with your mother. I sure wouldn't mind having a seat in a tree when those two come together."

"I'm having enough trouble getting Bethany to go out with me. I sincerely doubt having my mother impress her opinions would endear her to me." He gave Galen a sideways glance. Since Galen was courting Rose, he knew Bethany pretty well. "Any suggestions?"

Galen belted out a laugh. "Women have always confused the daylights out of me. Let me know when you figure out how to understand what a woman means when she says something." He strode off to the closest pasture, where five horses hung their heads over the pasture fence, eager for their meal to arrive.

Jimmy leaned against the doorjamb. *Interesting*. Sometimes—often—Galen saw things before he did. Since Jimmy had been promoted to Galen's partner in the horse breeding business, things had become easier between them. More and more it seemed Galen was a man he could have a comfortable word with from time to time. His mother turned every word into an argument about his future. Galen was different. Galen observed things. Rarely would he volunteer advice, but when asked, his advice was always to the point. Jimmy admired him greatly.

Maybe . . . if Jimmy could get Hank Lapp to start buzzing around his mother again, she'd be too distracted to manage Jimmy's life. He took a deep breath, feeling his bounce return to him.

Bethany was coming out of the house and hurrying back across the yard. She had her usual look—the look of a woman whose mind was somewhere else. It gave her a distracted beauty.

"Hey, Bethany," Jimmy called out and jogged over to her. "Wait up for a second."

She stopped and turned, cocking her head in that saucy way, as if to say, "Why should I bother waiting for the likes of you, Jimmy Fisher?" Those vivid eyes were looking straight back into Jimmy's.

"How's about letting me take you home after a Sunday singing sometime?"

She lifted her chin and flashed him a bright smile. "Well, seems to me you might want to take Katie Zook home like you've been doing lately."

It was true—Jimmy had dallied a little with Katie Zook. Just a little. He couldn't help himself. He was a natural dallier. Unfortunately, Katie had misunderstood his dallying and taken it for serious courting. But how in the world had Bethany heard about it? Was there to be no end to the humiliations of this day?

He tried to think of a way to explain about Katie Zook; he tried out what he wanted to say to her in his head, but everything he came up with made it all seem worse. His mouth had suddenly gone dry. Bethany was already slipping away, walking with fast, sure strides toward the privet hole, soon to disappear. He threw his hat on the ground. Was he losing his touch?

Bethany Schrock was as taxing and exasperating as a girl could be.

And yet the feeling made him strangely light-headed, the same way he felt as he dove into Blue Lake Pond on a hot summer day and the cold water gripped him like a fist and pulled him down, down, down.

Bethany put a red-checkered napkin on top of the breakfast tray to keep the food hot while she walked it over to the guest flat. Coffee in a thermos, cream in a small pitcher, six blueberry pancakes, syrup, four strips of bacon, two halves of a grapefruit, one bowl of cereal, and a large glass of orange juice. One thing she had learned quickly about this little lady preacher—she had a sizable appetite. Each morning, the tray was returned empty. Practically licked clean.

Bethany barely knocked on the door and Geena

opened it with a big smile. Bethany set the tray on the little kitchen table. "What are you planning to do today? Most of our guests go over to Bird-in-Hand or Intercourse to shop. Those towns are more touristy than Stoney Ridge."

"Already been. To each and every town along the Philadelphia Pike. I'm kind of tired of being a tourist and thought I'd do more hiking in the hills. I do need better hiking shoes. Any chance there's a shoe store nearby?"

"Only if you happen to be a horse."

Geena turned half around to her and smiled. She poured some cream into her coffee and stirred, took a sip, and got a look on her face like she was instantly transported to Heaven. "I don't know what you do to the coffee, but it is delicious."

"Broken-up eggshells. I add them to the grounds. Takes the bitterness out."

"Everything is so good, Bethany. You and Rose are excellent cooks."

Bethany was pleased. Not all the guests were easy to delight. A few were fussier than Mammi Vera and that was saying a lot. Last week a man stayed at Eagle Hill and knocked on the kitchen door one morning. He told Mammi Vera he'd like to show her the proper way to make a poached egg. She scolded him in a rapid stream of Penn Dutch and thoroughly confused him so that he tucked tail and hurried off to the guest flat.

"Well, I'm due at the Grange Hall soon. Serving lunch to the down-and-out of Stoney Ridge," Bethany said as she walked to the door.

"Need any help?"

Bethany spun around. Was Geena serious? "Well,

sure. The sisters who run it could always use an extra pair of hands. But I'm leaving in ten minutes."

Geena was already seated, napkin in her lap, fork in her hand. "I'll be ready."

The sisters were delighted to meet Geena and very curious about her—they had never met a lady preacher before, they said. Geena explained she was a youth pastor, not a preacher, but they didn't seem to think there was a distinction. They were quiet, watching her carefully, but Bethany could see they were itching to ask Geena something. Like an avalanche that began with a pebble, Ella asked one thing first, then Fannie, and soon, all five sisters pummeled her with questions.

What did she preach about? All kinds of topics from the Bible. Did she wear long black robes? No. Were folks nice to her? Mostly. Did they accept having a lady preacher? Again, she explained she was a youth pastor. What did she like best about being a lady preacher? Serving God by caring for the youth. What did she like least? Well, preaching.

It seemed no time at all before they had arrived at the Grange Hall; the kitchen was unlocked and the groceries were stacked on the countertop. Geena seemed to know how to help without being asked. She walked right into the kitchen and pulled open the dishwasher. It was full of clean dishes, so she put them away, opening cupboard doors and quickly getting familiar with the layout of the kitchen. In no time at all, soup was simmering on the stove, the tables were set, bread and butter were on the tables, and the down-and-outers were lining up outside.

Bethany didn't mind making meals for the down-and-outers. She was getting to know each one and understand why they were where they were; each one had a story. She liked keeping busy and she loved to cook, but her pleasure dissipated when the wayward girls from the Group Home arrived. Those girls made her uncomfortable, especially that red-haired girl.

When the red-haired girl walked inside, she looked all around the room like she owned the place, then swaggered over to a table. The other girls followed behind her and sat around her. The red-haired girl stared at Bethany without friendliness. She met that girl's dark eyes, standing her ground. Inside, though, Bethany felt a chill run up her spine.

Geena walked right up to the wayward girls' table and introduced herself. Once, Bethany even heard her laughing—Geena had a very distinctive low-sounding laugh—and she wondered what was so funny. The red-haired girl, she noticed, acted like she didn't care if Geena was there or not.

That was the thing about those girls. None of them seemed to care.

Mid-afternoon, after the kitchen was cleaned up, the women started back down the road that led to the Sisters' House with empty wagons. As they passed the vacant lot between the Group Home and the Grange, Bethany looked at it more carefully. Trash and tumbleweeds blew into the lot, catching on junk of various kinds—discarded tires, plastic grocery bags, sawed-off tree limbs, a couch where two girls sat smoking . . . something small that didn't look like a cigarette. One of those girls was that red-haired girl.

"I just have to say," Bethany said, "that lot is an eyesore and I think something should be done about it. Who owns it, anyway?"

"I think it belongs to the Grange Hall," Sylvia said.

Fannie raised her eyebrows. "Bethany, what would you like to be done with the lot?"

"I don't know," Bethany said. "I haven't thought about that. I wish those girls had something to do besides just sit around and stare at people."

Lena nodded. "They're bored."

"Sylvia, didn't you say there was a housemother at the Group Home? Can't she make those girls do something?"

"Mrs. Green? She does her best but she's old and tired."

Bethany had seen Mrs. Green. She was at least thirty years younger than the sisters. Maybe even younger.

"When school starts in the fall, the girls will be busy during the day," Fannie said.

Bethany glanced at the girls on the abandoned couch. "Seems like they could be gardening on that lot or mowing grass or washing windows at the house. Something."

Geena stopped for a moment to look it over. "Maybe the yard could be turned into—a big garden! Or better still, lots of little garden plots. It gets plenty of daylight, all day long." She turned to Sylvia. "Wouldn't that be something? A community garden."

"It would indeed." Sylvia inclined her head, a quizzical expression on her brow. "Do you think it's possible?"

Geena turned to Bethany. "I'm a city girl. What would it take?"

"I guess we'd have to build raised beds and bring in topsoil. That dirt is no good."

Sylvia nodded. "I think that's a splendid idea, Bethany. You need a project and it needs you."

Bethany stopped. "Wait a minute. I didn't mean *we* as in *me*. I meant it in the generic sense."

Sylvia smiled. "'We' doesn't always mean somebody else."

Oh no. Bethany did *not* need another project. Cleaning out the Sisters' House was more than enough for anyone—and it was not a job for the faint of heart.

"Imagine that!" Fannie said, clasping her hands in delight. "Bethany and the lady preacher want to start a community garden! Plots for each family in need. Maybe a few for the Group Home. That would keep those girls busy and teach them skills too! It's a wonderful idea."

Me? How did one tiny suggestion get carried away? "It's already the end of June," Bethany pointed out. "Too late for planting." The Eagle Hill garden had been planted weeks ago. Same with Naomi's. Strawberries had already come and gone.

"No—not necessarily," Sylvia said. "Amos Lapp has plants in his greenhouse, year-round. He could help us by providing starts. Tomatoes, cucumbers, zucchini, even corn. And then there's fall planting too—swiss chard and spinach and lettuce and carrots. All kinds of things could get in the ground before the first frost hits in October."

Bethany thought of the vacant lot, the hostile girls, and then Sylvia's description of the gardens. In that instant, she caught the vision. She saw the garden in full summer, corn tasseling, pumpkins sprawling, those bored-looking girls plucking tomatoes they'd grown themselves.

She realized she hadn't thought about Jake Hertzler or

her brother Tobe or her mother or father or any other unsolved problem for at least an hour, maybe more. Maybe she did need a project. She turned to Sylvia. "We'll look into it."

Geena woke before dawn and couldn't go back to sleep. Too much was swirling through her mind. She tiptoed to the kitchen to warm some milk for hot chocolate. The milk in the pan frothed and Geena poured it into a chocolate powder she had spooned into the bottom of the mug. She stirred it and took the mug to the sofa, the one by the window, where the soft morning light was just starting to fill the room. Bethany had showed her how to light the stove, but she wasn't quite sure she could manage lighting a kerosene lamp without supervision. She was sure she'd blow up this Amish farmhouse.

Her Bible was in her other hand. Her comfort, her solace. It was leather-bound and well loved, a gift from her father when she graduated from seminary. Its binding had broken and its pages thinned to onionskin. She had always felt that if a fire swept through her belongings, this was the one thing she would grab. Everything else could go, but not this Bible.

Geena burrowed deep in the couch and gently opened the Bible to the center. *Ah. There.* The book of Psalms. They were like old friends, the Psalms, each with a word to address her needs—some for wisdom, some for thanksgiving, some for sorrow. This morning, she sought guidance and direction. She'd been at the Inn at Eagle Hill for eight days now. Rose told her there had been another reservation cancellation and she could stay on through the weekend. She wanted to. But she also knew she had to start facing the inevitable: what to do next.

Psalm 27. She read aloud, softly. "Hear my voice when I call, LORD; be merciful to me and answer me. . . . Do not hide your face from me, do not turn your servant away in anger; you have been my helper."

How audacious. How wonderful! To think David spoke to God in such a familiar way and yet God called David a man after his own heart. The wonder and the mystery of a loving, holy God.

Her finger scrolled down to a verse she had underlined. *Teach me your way, LORD; lead me in a straight path because of my oppressors.*

Who were her oppressors?

Fear. Insecurity. Self-doubt. Anxiety about her future.

Her eyes traveled to the end of the psalm. *Wait for the LORD; be strong and take heart and wait for the LORD.*

Geena leaned her head back and closed her eyes. *Wait for the LORD.* The words swirled around her mind, reminding her, bringing comfort and peace. Surely the God who set the stars in the sky would let her know when and where her next church would be.

Wait for the LORD.

Of course. She would wait.

◊

It was a good thing Edith Fisher slept like a hibernating bear. It gave Jimmy time to sneak out of the house early in the morning and sneak back in late at night. He took his meals at Galen's. He was doing his very best to avoid any confrontation or conflict with his mother, because any interaction with her meant a healthy dose of both. Few would guess that Jimmy disliked conflict, but he did. He never minded stirring things up, but he didn't like to stick around long enough for the aftermath.

Long ago, he had learned that the best way to get along with his mother was to go along with her. At least on the surface. Under the surface, he quietly went about his own business. On this morning, he was tiptoeing down the stairs in his stocking feet when his mother met him at the base of the stairwell, arms akimbo.

"Have you spoken to Galen King yet?"

He stiffened. "About what?"

"About quitting that silly horse business and managing these chickens, full-time. That's what. I've been talking about nothing else for weeks."

And that was the truth. His mother had a way of having one-sided conversations and Jimmy was used to being on the quiet end.

"Now, Mom, we've been over all this. The chickens don't need full-time management."

"Maybe not right now, but that cornfield is going to need cultivating in another month or so. Harvesting a month after that. And if it doesn't get harvested, then it doesn't get ground for meal and then my chickens don't get fed. And Fisher Hatchery goes—" her arms shot up to the ceiling—"belly up."

"Now, now, that's a little dramatic. Don't you think I've been working on a plan? But you see, there's only so many hours in a day. I'm working at Galen's, I'm helping Naomi—" He said that to try to derail his mother's line of thinking and it usually worked. Since she had returned to Stoney Ridge, her favorite topic was the courting of Naomi King.

She cleared her throat, puffing out her cheeks. "Mostly, I hear you're spending time fluttering around Bethany Schrock."

Where did she hear that? It was true, but where had she heard it?

"That's another thing I wanted to talk to you about. Jimmy, you've always been too softhearted for your own good."

He sidled around her to get to the bench by the door. "What are you talking about?"

"You're taking pity on those Schrocks."

He sat down and reached for a boot. First one, then the other. "Now why would I be taking pity on them?"

"Because of all the trouble that family has caused folks. Poor innocent people."

"The women didn't have anything to do with Schrock Investments," he said emphatically. "That had everything to do with Dean Schrock and his son Tobe and that no-good employee of theirs, Jake Hertzler."

"How do you know that? How do you know Rose and Bethany weren't in on it?"

He couldn't explain it to his mother, but some things you just knew.

"Apples don't fall far from the tree."

"Meaning . . ."

"I've never said anything about your flittering around other girls—"

It was too early in the morning for this kind of a conversation. "Well, then, let's just leave well enough alone, all right?"

"—but this time I am stepping in. I'll say it plainly. I don't want you cozying up with Bethany Schrock."

Jimmy bristled like a cat in a lightning storm. "What have you got against Bethany? And don't try to tell me it's about Schrock Investments. You've got something in your craw about her."

"I want someone better for you, that's all. What's so terrible about that?" Her voice was controlled and quiet, but there was an edge of steel in it, the way it got when people tried to talk her down on the price of her eggs.

"I think I'm old enough to make those decisions for myself," he said. "Decisions like becoming a horse trainer."

"Your father—God rest his soul—started this chicken and egg business to pass on to you boys. Paul left. Now it's all up to you. You're all I've got. I'm doing it all alone."

Jimmy sighed. "I know," he said, feeling guilty for snapping at her. His mother really did mean well, but she was so . . . insistent. He softened his tone. "I do agree with you, Mom. About the chickens needing someone part-time."

He stilled, an idea taking shape. *In fact . . . I have just the person in mind!* He jumped off the bench and grabbed his straw hat off the wall peg. Windmill Farm wasn't far from the Fishers' farm, but it would take at least an hour to get Hank Lapp woken up, talked into showering, shaved, changed into fresh, clean clothes, and over to the Fisher farm. "I'll be back soon with our new part-time employee."

He flew out of the house and into the barn to hitch the horse to the buggy before his mother could object.

Fifteen minutes later, he was rapping on Hank's garage apartment above the buggy shop at Windmill Farm. "Open up, Hank! It's Jimmy. Come on, wake up!" He kept knocking until the door finally opened.

Hank squinted at Jimmy with his good eye. "WHERE'S THE DADGUM FIRE?!"

Jimmy winced—both at the loud sound of Hank's voice and his appearance. The sight of Hank Lapp, first thing in the morning, was not for the squeamish. "Hank, my mother asked for your help."

Hank straightened hopefully, then eyed Jimmy suspiciously. "I find that a little hard to swallow. She was awful mad at me when she last spurned me. Then she up and married that other fellow. Then she returned, widowfied, and looked at me like it was all my fault."

"Well, that's water under the bridge. That temporary husband of hers is pushing up daisies on his own accord. A lot has happened since he up and died—no one's blaming you. Paul moved and left me with Mom . . . I mean, left the chicken business to Mom to run. She needs your help, I tell you. Wants to hire you part-time." He clapped his hands twice. "Now. Pronto. Lickety-split."

Hank's good eye lit up. But there were two things in Stoney Ridge that couldn't be rushed: the weather and Hank Lapp. He took his sweet time showering, singing at the top of his lungs—so loud it could break glass. While he showered, Jimmy hunted around the garage apartment for a fresh set of clothes. By the time Hank was done with the shower, Jimmy had a clean shirt and pants waiting for him. "Come on, Hank. You're wasting precious time. Galen's waiting on me."

Hank scowled as he wrapped a towel around his

privates. "You've got me as nervous as a turkey before Thanksgiving. You go on ahead. I'll get there."

"Not a chance. I'm hand delivering you."

Another hour and a half later, Jimmy pulled the buggy into the driveway of the Fisher farm. He jumped out and called to his mother to come outside. "I brought your part-time help, Mom. Someone who has a way with chickens and is eager to please."

Edith came out of the house, wiping her hands on her apron, and stopped short when she saw someone come around the other side of the buggy. Hank took off his hat, held it against his chest, and walked over to Edith.

Their eyes met.

6

On Wednesday, Bethany planned to head to the Sisters' House early in the morning even though they didn't expect her. She packed up the cookies and the buttermilk and most of what else they had left in the refrigerator, telling Mim things were going bad so fast in this heat that giving them to the soup kitchen would save her from having to throw them out later.

She didn't want anyone to think she'd gone soft.

After thinking it over, Bethany had decided to help the sisters serve lunch to the down-and-outers of Stoney Ridge on a weekly basis. She liked most of the down-and-outers and looked forward to seeing them—all except those ungrateful girls from the Group Home. And she worried about the sisters, lugging those little red wagons filled with food under the hot sun and working so hard to make a good meal.

When Mim found out what her plans were for the day, she asked to go along and Bethany agreed. After all, if Bethany could help Mim with the secret of Mrs.

Miracle's true identity, then Mim could help with the soup kitchen. When Bethany picked up the breakfast tray in the guest flat, Geena offered to come too. So the three of them, morning sun blazing hot on their backs, headed over to the Sisters' House.

The five elderly sisters were delighted to see them walk up the front steps. They happily passed off the wagon handles to Bethany and Mim, and the eight of them started up the road to the Grange Hall.

Within the hour, Bethany and Mim sliced and diced big yellow onions on the countertop of the kitchen at the Grange Hall to make a chili soup for lunch. Despite the heat wave, ingredients to make chili soup had been donated by the local Bent N' Dent, so chili soup it was.

Bethany was blinking away onion tears when Jimmy Fisher walked in with his dazzling grin. "Why don't you just admit, Bethany, that I have a powerful effect on you?"

Slicing an onion in half with a big knife, Bethany gave him a look. "Same effect as a pungent onion." But she couldn't help but return his grin. Jimmy's smile was like the sun breaking through the clouds. "Just what brings you to the Grange Hall on this steamy summer morning?"

"I waved him in," Sylvia said, opening a bag of paper napkins. She handed the napkins to Mim to start setting places at the table.

"I was heading to the hardware store in town to pick up some nails for Galen," Jimmy said. "We're fixing a fence that borders Eagle Hill and Galen's back pasture, on account of a certain goat that seems to have a lack of respect for boundaries."

"That goat!" Bethany said. "I wouldn't mind if he wandered off and never returned."

Sylvia walked into the kitchen with something on her mind. "We have a wonderful plan to create a community garden."

Jimmy jumped up to sit on the countertop. "What are you talking about?"

"It was all Bethany's idea," Fannie said, coming over to get a box of plastic forks for the table settings.

Jimmy glanced at Bethany in disbelief. "It was, was it?"

Of course it was. Bethany tried to ignore his look of shock but a blush warmed her chest and rose to her cheeks.

"We're planning on putting the garden over there, in the vacant lot." Fannie pointed out the window.

Bethany did a double take—if she wasn't mistaken, it seemed that Fannie was batting her eyelashes at Jimmy. *That* boy had a strange and particular effect on women of all ages.

Jimmy craned his neck to peer out the window. "The lot between the Grange Hall and the Group Home?"

Sylvia's dark eyes glittered. "That's the one."

Jimmy jumped off the countertop and crossed the room to look out the window. "It'll take a ton of work to clean it up. It's littered with everything from broken glass to old tires."

Sylvia smiled. "That's where you come in, Jimmy."

Swift as anything, he looked at her over his shoulder. "Me?"

"Yes. You. You can gather some of your friends and organize a work frolic to get that lot cleaned up."

Jimmy turned back to look out the window, crossing his arms, thinking. "We're going to need a dumpster for all that trash."

"I thought it would be best to have individual raised beds," Bethany said, still slicing and dicing the onion.

Jimmy gave Bethany a sideways glance. "You did, did you?" But he sounded as if he still couldn't believe she had thought this up on her own.

She gave him her sweetest smile. "You could make those too."

"We could probably use the old fence wood that Galen had me tear down last week. A lot of the boards could be reused to make the beds." He yanked off his hat and worried it in a circle. "Topsoil will have to be brought in. Amos Lapp and Chris Yoder might donate it. I'm sure I can talk Hank Lapp into pitching in."

As he spoke and spun his hat, Bethany took Jimmy's measure. He was a fine-looking young man by anyone's standard. His forearms showed roped muscle, born of a hundred farm tasks he undertook. Then there was his thick blond hair and mesmerizing blue eyes. Those blue, blue eyes, nearly aquamarine. She shook that thought off and tried to replace it with her diced onion. She scooped the onions up with her big knife and dumped them in the big pot to sauté.

"So, you'll help?" Bethany said. "We sure do need it. And you love to be helpful." Sylvia was pretty crafty, she thought. Having Jimmy be a part of this project would ensure any number of young women from the church would be happy to volunteer in the garden.

"It's just dirt, water, and sun," Fannie said.

"And paying attention," Ella pointed out. "Don't forget that part. That's the most important part of all."

"So, then, you'll help?" Bethany repeated. Jimmy flashed one of his charming, easy smiles, and she caught her breath. That grin gave him a dangerous boyish look that she didn't buy for a moment.

He wiggled his dark eyebrows. "What else you got cooking today?"

The onions! Bethany hurried to stir the pot before they burned. The onions were completely translucent. "Chili soup." She scooped up a pile of papery onion skins and dumped them in the trash.

"Save me a bowl, will you? And I'll stop by later to sketch out a plan." He flipped his hat up in the air to land squarely on his head.

"Jimmy . . ." Bethany swallowed and looked at him doubtfully. "You sure?"

"Of what?" he asked with a slow grin. "That you need the help or that you'll have enough chili to spare me a bowl? Answer B is up to you—I love chili, even on a broiling summer day. Answer A is 'absolutely.' You've bitten off a big job, but . . . I'm willing to give it a try." Once again, Jimmy wiggled his eyebrows at her, then headed to the door.

Bethany added ground beef to the big pot and stirred it until it browned. Then she poured in four quarts of beef broth from big cans. She hoped it was beef broth, anyway, because the cans were missing their labels. She added six dented cans of diced tomatoes, stirred, then waited for the liquid to come to a boil. When the soup reached a full, rolling boil, she added four cans of red kidney beans, turned down the heat, added a bay leaf, cumin, chili powder, oregano, salt and pepper, and celery tops.

"Do you think we might be taking on something too big with that community garden?" Bethany asked Sylvia when she came to check on the chili soup.

"It is a big project, but it's a good one. You're the one who realized those children at the Group Home needed a project." The chili soup was so thick that Sylvia added some water to the pot. "It will give them a sense of purpose." She left the kitchen to help Mim and the sisters set the tables.

Bethany stirred the water vigorously into the chili mixture. "I wish I felt that," she said to no one in particular. "A sense of purpose would be nice."

Geena took the empty cans and dumped them in the recycling box. She turned and inclined her head. "You need only ask God for it, Bethany. He is all about purpose."

What would it be like to stumble onto your future and recognize it so clearly? Was it really as simple as opening a door and seeing it before you? Then what? "But then watch out, right? What if I get called to do something like becoming a lady preacher, like you did?" Bethany was joking.

"Youth pastor," Geena corrected. "And I love serving these people." She put a hand on her heart, unaware that Bethany had been teasing her. "Serving gives life meaning, and shape, and purpose. I am honored God would call me to this work. That's how it works." She picked up a knife and grabbed a loaf of day-old bread from the Sweet Tooth Bakery.

Geena sliced the bread and put out sticks of butter on

paper plates while Fannie, Ella, Lena, and Mim poured juice into paper cups. Sylvia stood by the door, waiting for the clock to strike twelve to open the door. A line had gathered, out of thin air, right at noon, and in filed an odd assortment of people.

It was easy for Bethany to ladle up the chili soup for these down-and-outers, feeling something warm like kindness or goodness fill her chest. At least, she did feel a pleasant glow until the teens from the Group Home, filled with bravado, pushing and jabbing each other, came in knots of two and three. Bethany followed Geena's lead and spoke to each one as she brought out the bowls of chili soup on a tray. "Good afternoon" and "How are you?" and "Would you like chili?" Most didn't answer and kept their eyes down, but the angry red-haired girl met her eyes, almost in a hostile challenge—*Do you see me?*

I'm trying, Bethany thought. *But you make it so difficult.*

A few spoke in return. "I don't like onions," said one, holding the chili soup bowl up in the air. "Can you take them out?"

"No," Bethany said in a no-nonsense tone she had learned from Fannie.

"You're new," said another, a girl with hair dyed as black as coal. She looked Bethany up and down. "You in some kind of trouble?"

She was a big girl, at least fifteen or sixteen years old, with arms that were tattooed from wrist to shoulder. Bethany couldn't help but stare. The girl noticed Bethany's gape, laughed, and held out her arms so she could see the drawings. "They're called sleeve tattoos. They tell the story of my life."

Bethany was horrified. Rose called tattoos "permanent evidence of temporary insanity." What kind of permanent story could fill up both arms when you were only fifteen?

There were others, too, whom Bethany would not have expected. There were two painfully young mothers with toddlers on their hips, washed and humble, waiting for bowls of chili soup. Sylvia said to hold on, just wait until the end of July if she really wanted a surprise: Families of all shapes and sizes and colors. She said they were especially busy the last week of each month because people on public assistance had run out of food and money and wouldn't get any more until the first.

In that moment, Bethany realized she hadn't thought about her problems all day long. It was happening each time she helped at the sisters' soup kitchen—she forgot all that troubled her, for a little while anyway. She turned to serve the next girl, a round girl with acne and thick glasses, who smiled at her. This felt . . . good. Really good.

There were three things Mim liked about helping the sisters with the soup kitchen. First, she liked any excuse to be near Ella, the oldest sister. She stuck to Ella like glue. Today, a mouse came running through the Grange Hall kitchen and Mim chased it away with a broom. Afterward, Ella was feeling a little wobbly-kneed so she sat on a chair, pulled a tissue from her dress pocket, and dabbed at her forehead. "There's just something about a mouse," she said, and Mim had to agree.

The second thing she liked was that as soon as the kitchen was cleaned up and the sisters returned home with their empty wagons, Mim and Bethany set off to the *Stoney Ridge Times* office. Bethany went into the building and returned with a large manila envelope of mail for Mrs. Miracle. As soon as they turned the corner, Bethany handed Mim the mail pouch.

"What are you going to do with the money you're making?"

"I'm not sure," Mim said. "It's only five dollars a week." Mostly, she needed to buy paper and envelopes and stamps. She might try to save enough money to buy Danny a new telescope that didn't need to be held together with black electrical tape, but she had no idea how much telescopes cost. Plus, she wouldn't want him to think she was sweet on him. She was, but it was better not to let a boy know such a thing. She had read that very thing in Mammi Vera's book, *A Young Woman's Guide to Virtue*.

The third thing Mim liked about volunteering at the Grange Hall was that she and Bethany passed by Danny Riehl's home on the way home to Eagle Hill from downtown Stoney Ridge. If Mim walked slowly enough—if she had to stop and tie her shoelaces, for instance, like she did today—there was an excellent chance Danny would be doing chores in the barnyard and spot them. And when it happened, he waved and talked to them for a few minutes.

She liked that best of all.

Later that day, Mim sat cross-legged on her bed, unsure of what to do. Mrs. Miracle's response to *What Should I Do* ran in Tuesday's edition, and by this afternoon, Wednesday, when Bethany picked up the mail pouch at the *Stoney Ridge Times* office, there was already a responding letter to Mrs. Miracle's wise and witty wisdom.

Dear Mrs. Miracle,

I showed my husband your column in which you said that our arguing really wasn't about the kind of eggs we have for breakfast. We talked and talked about it . . . racked our brains over it . . . even went to an emergency counseling session with our pastor over it last night . . . but discovered it really was about the eggs!

So our pastor suggested that we compromise: scrambled on Mondays, fried on Wednesdays, sunny-side up on Fridays. He also suggested that I not ask you for marital advice.

Sincerely,
Now I Know
What to Do

Oh, boy.

As usual, life moved faster than Hank Lapp intended it to. Jimmy had hoped that working part-time at the Fisher Hatchery, in close proximity to his mother, might rekindle their on-again, off-again romance. The plan completely backfired. Hank had a love of talking and an aversion to hard work—two qualities his mother had no patience for.

Though loyal and good-hearted, Hank had never displayed the slightest ability to learn from his experience, though his experience was considerable. Time and again he would walk into the yard of the henhouse, knowing there was a protective rooster lurking about, and then look surprised when the rooster came flying at him, claws first.

Young Luke Schrock did the same kind of thing over at Galen's. He would walk up on the wrong side of a horse that was known to kick, and then look surprised when he got kicked.

When Jimmy thought about it, he wondered if there were some people in this world who were destined to make the same mistakes over and over. They simply could not learn from experience. Or maybe they just had no common sense.

Jimmy saw Hank walk up the driveway three hours after he was due for the chickens' first feeding. There was no point in losing any more time. If Hank was not of a mind to be serious, nothing could move him. Jimmy needed to fire Hank before his mother insisted on it.

"HELLO THERE!" Hank hollered when he saw Jimmy in the distance.

Jimmy walked down the hill to meet him. "Hank, you're late. Ridiculously late."

"Not for the fish at Blue Lake Pond! We had a predawn appointment today. My oh my, they practically leapt into my boat, Jimmy. You shoulda been there."

"Hank, you would exasperate a preacher."

"Well, I always figured preachers needed a little exasperating."

Jimmy yanked off his hat and swiped at the drops of sweat that clung to his forehead. "The thing is, Hank, the chickens can't wait until you get back from fishing. They need to eat at a specific time, or they get stressed. If they get stressed, they stop laying eggs. If they stop laying, Fisher Hatchery goes under."

"Good thing them chickens have you looking after them."

"That's the thing, Hank. The very thing. I was hoping *you'd* be looking after them so I could keep my job over at Galen's. You've been late four out of four days this week."

"Now wait just a minute. I was only doing you a favor—minding those squawking hens. I don't even like chickens. And I hate roosters. Always have." Hank stiffened up like wet leather left out in the sun. "You know—you used to be a whole lot more fun. You're turning into a crotchety old schoolmarm."

Jimmy sighed. "I'm sorry, Hank. I shouldn't have pressured you into working here in the first place. I need to let you go."

Edith Fisher came out of the house, hefting a heaped laundry basket on a practiced hip, and crossed the yard to the clothesline.

Hank noticed. In a split second, the expression on his face changed from a frustrated frown to a brilliant smile, like the sun appearing from behind a cloud. "DON'T FRET, BOY!" He winked at Jimmy. "Being in between jobs gives me a little more time to come calling on your sweet mama." He brushed past Jimmy and went up the hill. "LET ME HELP YOU CARRY THAT HEAVY BASKET, MY LITTLE BUTTERCUP!"

What was even more shocking was the mildly pleasant look on his mother's face as she saw Hank approach.

Jimmy shook his head in wonder. Maybe his plan hadn't backfired quite as badly as he thought. Maybe he shouldn't have fired Hank. No . . . that was definitely the right thing to do. His chickens would have perished under Hank's care.

His chickens? Since when did he think of those pesky hens as *his* chickens? Never! He felt just like Hank did about poultry. Couldn't stand them.

What was going on with him lately? Hank was right—he wasn't fun like he used to be, if you considered fun to be stealing a nap by the pond when he should have been at his chores or playing a prank on an unsuspecting someone. Someone like the bishop, who could be easily tricked and was never the wiser for it. Jimmy didn't even tilt his hat at a rakish angle anymore.

But why? Why was he suddenly acting like . . . a man? A responsible man? He never expected such behavior of himself. It wasn't comfortable—making a hard decision like firing his old friend Hank. It felt like he was wearing a pair of stiff new shoes. The newly mature side of him pointed out that maybe the shoes just needed breaking in. But the old side of him asked, why? The old shoes were pretty comfortable.

The thing that made Jimmy least comfortable of all was that, deep down, he knew the reason for his newfound maturity. He never lied to himself. It had to do with Bethany Schrock. He was falling for her.

The feeling had started even before he knew his

mother didn't want him courting Bethany, though he wouldn't deny his mother's vehemence made him all the more determined. He had started falling for Bethany from the first second he'd laid eyes on her, and a little deeper every moment he'd spent in her company since then.

A few weeks back, he took Katie Zook home from a Sunday singing, and even kissed her a few times, just to see if he could be distracted by another girl, if being around another girl made him feel the same way he felt when he was around Bethany. It didn't. It was yet another experiment that backfired on him.

At night he thought of Bethany, and wondered if she ever thought of him. During the day, if he caught sight of her coming or going from Eagle Hill, he watched her, whenever he thought he could do so without her noticing. Her eyes were mysterious to him—often she seemed to be amused by him, at other times irritated. Sometimes her eyes seemed to pierce him, as if she had decided to read his thoughts as she would read a book. It didn't stop the longing he felt for her. He imagined them raising horses and children together. In a strange and wonderful way, he knew she was the girl for him. In a way he couldn't quite explain, even to himself, he knew she needed him.

No one had ever needed Jimmy before, not really. Not the way Bethany did.

7

Shootfire! Not another word of excuses!" Bethany pointed to the house. "You boys get right up to your rooms and think about how you'd you feel if you were that goat!" Sammy and Luke climbed the porch stairs in tandem, with her watching all the way.

To Bethany's annoyance she saw Jimmy watching her from the hole in the privet with an amused grin on his face. "Sorry," she said, trying to make light of it.

"Don't be," Jimmy said. "I'm glad to see that you lose your temper with other people as well as with me." He walked toward her. "What did those two do now?"

"Look for yourself."

Over by the patch of grass along the side of the house was the billy goat with a push lawn mower harnessed behind him. "I told them to mow the lawn and this is what they came up with."

Jimmy grinned. "I tried that once myself. Didn't work. The goat didn't budge." He walked toward her. "You have to give them credit for creativity."

"Lazy. That's the only thing they get credit for. I'm about fed up with those two. If I give them any slack they run headfirst into trouble. You can never guess what may be going on in the minds of boys—"

"Usually not much. Speaking from personal experience."

"—but it doesn't pay to let them out of your sight very long."

"Aw, Bethany, they're just being boys."

"They're savages, I tell you. Savages. They don't give anybody a moment's peace from dawn to dusk."

Right under the open window of the boys' room, Bethany could hear Sammy and Luke arguing about something. She looked up at the house and frowned.

"My father used to say that sometimes there wasn't any better music than two brothers bickering." She looked back at Jimmy. "He should have told that to Mammi Vera. Her favorite saying about those two is 'Buwe uffziehe is so leicht as Eise verdaue.'" *Raising boys is as easy as digesting iron.* "Just this morning, she gave them something to chew over for breakfast: 'Sand and sin are one and the same. Tolerate a little, and soon it'll be a lot.' Then they come up with a trick like roping the goat into mowing the lawn. They can't learn a blessed thing without getting in trouble, those two."

Jimmy stared at her for what seemed like forever. She could almost feel his gaze moving over her, like the touch of the wind, before it shifted to the poor goat stuck with a lawn mower roped to its harness. Then came one of those unexpected and dazzling smiles. "Come with me a minute." He went over to the goat to unbuckle the harness and untie the rope that held it to the push mower.

Then he took hold of the goat's harness and locked the goat in the fenced yard. He led Bethany over to Galen's yard and pointed to a large wagon, where tools and wood were stacked. He jumped easily onto the wagon bed. "Rakes, shovels, chicken wire for the base of the beds, nails, hammers. Everything we need for the community garden. Practically a fully outfitted hardware store."

She walked around the wagon, examining everything inside of it. "This is terrific! Where'd you get all the tools?"

"The hardware store provided nails, Galen King provided wood from a fence he was replacing, Amos Lapp is delivering topsoil. He told Chris Yoder to donate vegetable starts from the Lapp greenhouse. Even the Sweet Tooth Bakery is offering pastries for the frolic." He wiggled his eyebrows. "Day-old, of course." He jumped off the bed and stood beside her.

Her delight amused him, and once again that slow grin claimed his face.

Bethany looked at all the supplies, thought of all the work he'd done, the time he'd spent, and put a hand on his arm. "I don't even know what to say. You've done so much. Thank you, Jimmy. You're really . . ." He looked at her, and Bethany didn't turn away, wondering if something might be blooming between them. "Thank you," she said simply.

He covered her hand with his. "So, then, how about letting me take you home from Sunday's singing?"

The warm wind kissed her face and rustled the ends of her capstrings. A sense of anticipation skittered over the top of her skin, traveling up her arm, brushing her elbow, tickling the back of her neck. His eyes were shaded by the soft brim of his hat, so their color was a simple dark blue, and his mouth was very still. He leaned forward, bringing his face close to hers. Too close, so that she wanted to pull back from him, but she didn't.

"You know you want to say yes," he said, giving her one of his cat-in-cream smiles. "And I know a place we can talk privately." The wind blew between them in a gush of warmth.

She narrowed her eyes. "Said the spider to the fly."

"I mean it. I'd like to get to know you better."

There was such a sweetness in his voice that she almost got lost in the sound of it. Maybe, she thought, this was something possible. The thought made her smile.

Then the kitchen door opened and Naomi came out of the house with Katie Zook at her side, and Jimmy's head jerked in their direction. He waved and gave the girls his best grin.

His best grin. The one she thought he saved just for her. Bethany tried not to let her disappointment in him show, but she knew her eyes would give her away. Her father used to say that her eyes were like a weather vane for her feelings. "Save all your charm for the other girls," she said, sounding a tad more haughty than she intended. She softened, just a little. "I like you just fine without all that embroidery."

He looked surprised. "But I do want to spend time with you! I meant it."

She nodded and started back to Eagle Hill. "I'm sure you always do," she tossed over her shoulder.

◊

Jimmy hurried to catch up with Bethany before she disappeared into the house and before Katie Zook could trap him. She was dropping by more and more often, to see Naomi she said, while cornering him in the barn.

The lady preacher drove in the driveway and Bethany stopped to say hello, giving Jimmy just enough time to reach her. The woman got out of her car and waved. "I saw you at the Grange Hall the other day but I don't think we officially met," she said. "I'm Geena Spencer."

"I know. You're the lady preacher everyone's talking about," he said.

"Actually I'm a youth pastor."

"His name is Jimmy Fisher," Bethany said in a schoolteacher's voice.

Geena shook Jimmy's hand. "What are you two up to?"

Jimmy grabbed his chance. "Bethany and I were just heading over to the Grange Hall with donations for the community garden."

"I never said anything about going with you," Bethany said, frowning at him.

"But you were thinking it."

Flustered, she jerked her gaze away from his.

"Is there room to store everything in the Grange Hall?" the lady preacher asked.

Jimmy half shrugged his shoulders. "Won't need to. Saturday is the day set for the frolic."

"Frolic?" Geena said.

"That's what we call a work party," Bethany said. She glanced over at Jimmy. "Mim and I have started to spread the word."

"Wait a minute," Geena said, confused. "Saturday?

This Saturday? You came up with the idea for the garden on Monday, and you're going to start it on Saturday? Don't you need work permits? Time to coordinate volunteers?"

Bethany and Jimmy exchanged a look. "If there's a need, we just get to it," Jimmy said. "As for volunteers—like Bethany said, we just spread the word around the church. And we're not just starting on Saturday. We're ending on Saturday too. By the end of the day, the gardens should be built and planted."

"But . . . that's so fast!"

"Well, it's already the first week of July," Bethany said. "We can't wait any longer if people want any produce this summer."

Geena tilted her head, amazed. "Count on my help. I'll be staying in the guest flat through Sunday. Longer, if the heat wave continues and someone else cancels their reservation." She went back to her car to unload some groceries.

"I sure hope this hot spell breaks," Jimmy said, trying to keep Bethany's interest. He had spotted Katie Zook, popping her head over the privet, watching, waiting for him, and he wanted to stay clear. "This is one summer I won't miss. Galen and I can't even work the horses like we want to—they get too overheated. I want to get Lodestar out on the roads but the blacktop feels like it's melting." He sidled a half turn to keep Bethany from noticing Katie at the privet.

"How's it going with that horse?"

Jimmy squeezed his eyes shut in disgust. "Bethany, he's not *that* horse. He's one in a million." Lodestar was Jimmy's pride and joy. He was a stallion that Jimmy had bought, several times, off that swindler Jake Hertzler. *Never mind*. Despite how he had ended up with Lodestar, the horse was worth every penny. Jimmy had plans to start using Lodestar as a stud horse, just as soon as he broke him of his bad habit of running off. It would never do to deliver his stud to a mare for a few days' work, only to have him disappear.

"So sorry," she said, feigning her apology. "How is your one-in-a-million horse behaving?"

"We're making progress. Patience is required, you see, when you're a serious horse trainer." And when you're serious about a certain girl. He gave her his most charming grin. "So let's get back to the important matter. What about Sunday's singing? How about letting me take you home?"

She lifted her chin in that saucy way she had. "Well, you'll just have to keep practicing your newly found patience. I haven't decided yet."

He watched her head back to the house. Before she went inside, she turned and gave him a grin. All he could think when she gave him that grin was that he wished he were a better man.

Then his smile faded. Katie Zook was still waiting for him by the privet hole.

Mim bent down and put her eye to the lens. It was a very good telescope, with powerful magnification and a sturdy tripod, even if it was taped together with electrical tape. When she looked through it, the stars popped vividly forward, with one glowing brightly in the middle.

"So majestic," she murmured, then stepped away and looked straight up to the sky, crossing her arms over her chest.

Then Danny came over to bend down and take a look in the telescope. "Amazing, isn't it? I never get over the night sky."

"Do you know the names of those constellations?"

"Some." He straightened up and craned his neck to look at the sky. "That's Cassiopeia, right there," he pointed, "and the Big Dipper, of course, and Gemini."

She tried not to think of how close Danny was standing to her, of how he smelled of bayberry soap, and how good and kind and smart he was. She tried not to think about sneaking out of the house to join Danny tonight and how much trouble she would face if Mammi Vera were to find out where she was and why. Instead, she tried to focus on those beautiful sparkling stars, diamonds on black velvet, and soon she fell into the vastness of the darkness, the far-away-ness of the stars, the possibilities of so many stars lighting so many systems. "So many stars," she murmured. "Millions upon millions."

Danny nodded. "Each star has a place in the sky, a purpose to fulfill."

As usual, whenever she was with Danny, he said something that was so profound, so hard for her to grasp, that she found herself falling in love with him all over again. She tried to rein in her feelings and focus on the stars. Thinking about the stars sent her mind traveling to another baffling letter to Mrs. Miracle from this week's mail pouch. She didn't know how to solve this person's problem:

Dear Mrs. Miracle,

Do you think life is fixed? Like the stars are fixed in the sky? My mother is in jail for shooting my father. I wish I could say I cared but I hardly remember either of them. My mother had all kinds of rage issues and my father was an alcoholic. Will I live the same kind of life that my parents did? It seems I already am. Sometimes, I get so angry . . . I want to hurt someone.

Signed,
Stuck

She had no idea how to answer Stuck's letter. But . . . Danny, with his infinite wisdom, might know. "Do you think a person's life is all his own to live? Or do you think that the way he grows up, or the kinds of DNA he has, shapes a person's life?"

"Nature versus nurture, you mean?"

She nodded.

"That is a conundrum." He glanced at her. "Do you know what that means?"

"Of course. Of course I do!" She had no idea.

"It's an interesting question. Nature certainly does play a role in the way a person thinks or behaves, just the same way your hair is dark and wavy like your mother's."

Mim's hand flew to her prayer cap. He had noticed her hair?

"Certainly, there's a nurture factor. If a person had never received love as a child, how could he grow up to know how to love?"

Maybe that was the problem with Stuck. It seemed as if she had never known love.

"That's what makes it such a conundrum. A difficult problem to solve."

Ah! So that's what conundrum meant.

"But you can't leave out the most important factor: God. The Bible says we become a new creation."

"Where? Where does it say that?"

"Second Corinthians 5:17." He looked up at the sky as if he were reading the words written on the stars: "'Therefore if any man be in Christ, he is a new creature: old things are passed away; behold, all things are become new.'" He started to fold up the telescope. It was time to head home. "So I guess the answer is that while some people might have a harder time than others to break patterns and habits, nothing is impossible for God."

That was just the answer she needed for Stuck! She would write back this very night. She might even say a prayer for Stuck too. It had never occurred to Mim to pray for the letter writers. But Mrs. Miracle had never received a letter like Stuck's, either.

Bethany was checking messages in the phone shanty when a battered old car coughed and sputtered its way up to the house and stopped. She thought it might be someone who was lost and needed directions, so she closed up the phone shanty and walked toward the car.

"Bethany!" the driver hollered.

Then there was her brother Tobe, of all people! Swooping toward her and picking her up in a bear hug.

His face had matured a little in the . . . how long had it been? Ten months? No, closer to a year now.

"Oh Tobe," she said, laughing, "I'm so glad to see you!"

Tobe's attention shifted to the two little boys who were racing each other from the house to greet him. He opened his arms wide and scooped up Luke and Sammy as they barreled into him. "Who are these two giants? What happened to my little brothers?"

The boys squealed and hooted. "We have so much to show you and tell you!" Luke started, then the boys started talking at the same time, both at once, telling him bits and pieces of the news—only the news that pertained to them—the eagle pair that nested on a tree high above the creek, Galen's horses, a new fishing hole Hank Lapp promised to show them before school started in August.

Tobe laughed his deep, hearty laugh, like nothing had happened in the last year. "Where is Mim? And Rose and Mammi Vera?"

Bethany shooed the boys up to the house to find Mim to tell her that Tobe had come home. She filled the short span between the car and the house telling Tobe details about who was where and when and updating him about family news. "Mammi Vera had some surgery a few months ago. She's doing better now. Not one hundred percent, but she's much better than she was before the surgery."

"Did they fix her crankiness?"

Bethany laughed and clapped her hand to her mouth. "Don't say things like that out loud, even if you think it. But no, since you asked, she's as cranky as ever."

They stopped at the porch steps and she took a minute to gaze at her brother. A year of living hand-to-mouth had taken a toll. He was thin, like he needed some good home cooking. A haircut too. His black hair fell in a glossy swath across his forehead. He had large hazel eyes that could be sympathetic or furious or inscrutable. His clothes were English—a washed-out T-shirt, khaki shorts, flip-flops. But when he grinned, he was the same old Tobe: amiable, funny, handsome, charming as ever.

She could hear the chickens fussing in the coop. Mim hadn't fed them yet, Bethany could tell. "Where've you been, anyway?"

"Here and there."

"I heard you were with Mom."

He stopped abruptly, glanced at the house, then lowered his voice. "Where'd you hear that?"

"Jake Hertzler."

Tobe's eyes widened, and Bethany couldn't quite tell what was behind that—curiosity? No . . . no, it was alarm. "Jake is here?"

"Was. Gone now."

So it *was* true. Jake Hertzler, Bethany's ex-boyfriend (and her mind exaggerated the EX part), was the one who had told her Tobe had been with their mother, and he was full of lies. She wanted to know more, and yet she didn't. Not yet. So she changed the subject. "You heard Dad passed, didn't you?"

A flash of anger sparked in his eyes, then he softened. "Of course I heard."

"But you couldn't trouble yourself to come to his funeral?"

He stiffened. “Things aren’t as simple as you’d like to believe, Bethany.”

She let out a short, derisive laugh. “Shootfire! You can say that again. Like you showing up, out of the blue, after disappearing for a year without a trace.” She was pushing him too far and she knew it. She made her voice as gentle as she could manage. “What matters is that you’re home now, Tobe. I’m glad you’re here. I truly am.”

8

When Rose and Mammi Vera arrived home from the Bent N' Dent to find Tobe sitting at the kitchen table like he always had done—one leg stretched out, one elbow resting on the back of the chair—Rose was so stunned she nearly dropped the groceries in her arms. She said she had never stopped praying that he would return home someday, but she didn't know when that someday might ever come.

And Mammi Vera, why, she practically fainted at the sight of her favorite grandson. Wasn't it a tonic for her? To have Tobe home—what better medicine could there be for someone recovering from a major surgery?

It wasn't long before the house was a jumble of noise and confusion and happiness. As Tobe began to settle in to Eagle Hill, he looked more and more like his own rumpled self. Bethany was struck by how much he resembled their father—the same hair, black as starlings' wings, and slender build. So much like their father that Bethany kept getting goosebumps on her arms.

In the midst of the reunion, Galen and Naomi came over to see what the commotion was all about. When Galen saw Tobe, he shook his hand and welcomed him home. Galen's voice was happy sounding, but his face was curious and stunned and then his eyes sought out Rose.

A little later, Bethany was getting butter out of the refrigerator for dinner. As Galen helped get a wooden salad bowl from an overhead kitchen cupboard, she heard him whisper to Rose, "So the prodigal has returned. What do you make of that?"

"I'm not sure what to think," Rose whispered back. She picked up a garden carrot and cut the greens off, then started to peel it. "I really don't."

"Well, his coming will be good for Vera," he said as he set the bowl next to her on the countertop.

Mammi Vera had been pleased to see Tobe, but the excitement exhausted her and Rose had tucked her straight into bed, promising her plenty of time for catch-up talks in the days ahead. She tried to keep everyone quiet, but Vera said not to bother. The sounds of family at the dinner table filled her with happiness.

That, Bethany thought, *was a wonder right there*. Usually, Mammi Vera squawked at the boys to hush up during dinner.

During dinner, Bethany saw the look on Galen's face go from puzzled to amused to wary when he noticed Tobe sit next to Naomi and strike up a conversation. Usually, Naomi was shy as a hummingbird, but she was all lit up as she talked to Tobe, giggly and sparkly. Galen looked at Rose and lifted his eyebrows, and she did the same back.

Later, after Galen and Naomi had gone home and the

boys had been sent to bed, Bethany and Rose put away the last of the dinner dishes and hung the wet dishrag over the faucet to dry. Rose turned and saw Tobe standing by the door, a newspaper tucked under his arm. "I didn't realize you and Naomi had known each other so well."

So, Rose had noticed sparks flying too.

"The three of us—me and Beth and Naomi—we played together when we were younger." Tobe's mouth lifted in a grin. "Ain't she turned into something sweet and fine?"

"Naomi?" Bethany had never thought of her friend like *that*. She'd always been frail, gentle Naomi. But Tobe was right—her gentleness gave her a certain appeal. And tonight, she was positively beaming.

"This inn you've started sure has gotten a lot of attention." Tobe looked up. "Since when have you started calling the farm Eagle Hill?"

"Just a few months ago," Rose said, "after we started the inn. It got its name because an eagle pair has a nest on the property. I'm sure Sammy and Luke will want to show it to you tomorrow."

"First thing, they said." He grinned. "I like the name. And I like the idea of turning the farm into a money-maker." He wandered over to the refrigerator, swung open the door, stood staring into it for a moment, then grabbed the milk, opened the container, and took a few swigs while holding the door open. "I read in the papers some news about miracles on the farm. That a lady's cancer was cured. And someone else's marriage was saved from divorce court. Is any of it true?"

Bethany saw her stepmother stiffen. Rose discouraged the inn's reputation as a miracle maker.

"No, not really," Rose said primly. "It was the same guest, Delia Stoltz. She had surgery for cancer before she arrived, so that was already cured. As for her marriage, well, I do think a miracle saved it. But it wasn't because of the inn. It was God." She turned to Bethany. "I think it's starting to stop—all that nonsense about miracles at the inn. Don't you, Bethany?"

At the sink, Bethany stilled. How could she answer that without lying about Mrs. Miracle? Fortunately, Tobe didn't wait for an answer.

"Rose, you're looking at it all wrong. You can't buy that kind of publicity for any money. You don't want it to stop. That publicity will put the Inn at Eagle Hill on the map. People from all over the country will be coming to Stoney Ridge. Eating, shopping. Why, every business in downtown Stoney Ridge should be thanking you."

Bethany looked at Rose and wondered what she was thinking, why she had such a serious look on her face. His measure of delight in the inn's reputation seemed to push Rose in the other direction. Bethany had nearly forgotten how Tobe had always added some slight, raw element of strain to the family.

"Seems like this is a golden opportunity," Tobe continued. "I think we could be taking better advantage of it."

Rose had been spooning ground coffee into the coffeepot's filter to ready it for tomorrow's breakfast but stopped abruptly at that comment and made an about-face. "You sounded like your father right then. It's something he might have said."

"What's wrong with that?"

She turned back to finish spooning the coffee into

the filter. "Tobe, he was always chasing rainbows." Her voice was gentle, sad, but firm.

Bethany could see Tobe was just about to object when Rose closed the lid of the coffee can and held up a hand. "Son, it's late, and I need to get up early and start breakfast for the guest in the guest flat. We can talk tomorrow." At the doorway, she turned. "It's good you're home."

"Wait. Rose, before you go, I want to ask you one more question."

She leaned a shoulder against the doorjamb.

"From what I've read, it seems like everything is going to work out. With Schrock Investments, I mean. I read in the newspaper that donations from the Amish and Mennonites will reimburse the Plain investors. As for the English investors—they've filed claims with the SEC, so they'll be reimbursed from the liquidated assets."

"That's all true."

"So . . . everything is working out. We've got a fresh start."

Was that why Tobe had returned? He assumed that the slate had been wiped clean? Even Bethany, who didn't know every detail about Schrock Investments' collapse and sure didn't want to, even she was stunned at his naïveté, absolutely stunned.

Rose took a few steps toward him and spoke in a clear voice, gentle but firm. "A lot of people have lost money, Tobe. Families are losing their homes. Parents who scrimped and saved to provide for their children's future are realizing they're going to have to keep working for years to come—"

"I understand that! I do. And I feel terrible about it, but it's not my fault."

Rose shook her head sorrowfully and continued, ignoring his interruption. "It's not over, Tobe. Not even close."

Bethany was afraid Tobe might disappear if Rose told him more. This was his home, where he belonged. She forced herself to smile, hoping it looked natural. "Late at night isn't the time to discuss anything more."

"Bethany's right," Rose said. "There will be time for talk."

But Tobe wasn't ready to drop it. "Rose, you always said that God is in the business of fresh starts."

She hesitated. "And I do believe that. But sometimes the best thing to get off your chest is your chin."

Naomi glanced at the kitchen clock. Galen was out feeding the horses and would come in from the barn soon, hungry for breakfast. She started a pot of coffee brewing and put away some dishes that were drying in the rack. She set a pan of water on the stove to boil, and as soon as the bubbles formed, she stirred in the oats. You couldn't rush oatmeal, just like you couldn't rush a quilt.

Quilting was always on Naomi's mind. She was either working on a quilt pattern or thinking about one. It took a long time to sew a quilt block, to make tiny stitches that would stay tight and secure for years to come, a lifetime even. When she was faced with a pile of scraps, it could be hard to see how it was all going to come together, how each patch would fit with the others and how the colors and patterns would play against one another. She always started with a pattern in mind, but she never really knew how the block would turn out until it was finished. Now and then she had to go back and swap out a color or rip out a seam. More often than not, everything turned out better than she could have imagined.

When she finished a quilt top and held it up, everything looked so right together, the connections so obvious, the points so precise, that she wondered why she hadn't been able to see it from the beginning. But when she started on the next quilt she found that she was just as confounded as she was the time before.

Maybe that's the way it went with life too. Circumstances came into a person's life that were hard to make sense of, like a bag of quilt scraps, but often things ended up turning into something better than anyone could imagine.

When the oatmeal was the perfect consistency, she took it off the stove to cover it and keep it warm for Galen. The brown sugar jar was empty, so she went into the large pantry to refill it. As she scooped, she heard her brother's voice in the kitchen and realized someone was with him. Rose Schrock.

"Galen," she heard Rose say, "I need some advice about Tobe. I'm wrestling with something."

"Hold on," Galen said. "I need to fortify myself with a swig of coffee first."

Naomi froze. Had something happened? She knew quite a bit about the problems of Schrock Investments—she'd followed news reports with great interest. Anything that involved Tobe Schrock was of great interest to her. She was torn between wanting to know more and thinking the right thing to do was to make her presence known. Still . . . Tobe wasn't just a neighbor's son to her, like he was to Galen. This was Tobe. She set down the sugar scoop and carefully closed the door to a crack.

Galen crossed the kitchen and took two coffee cups out of the cupboard. Naomi held her breath. He was just a few feet away from the pantry. She heard him pour the coffee, then add a scoop of sugar to one, just the way Rose liked it. She heard the scrape of two kitchen chairs being pulled out from under the table, then the sound of Rose and Galen sitting at the table, and she let out her breath. Eavesdropping was a terrible thing to do . . . truly terrible . . . and surely revealed an immature character. Now would be the time to come out of the pantry with the sugar jar and no one would think twice about it. Now!

But the moment passed. She couldn't help herself.

"Okay," Galen said to Rose. "Now I'm ready."

Rose sounded pensive. "There's a fellow named Allen Turner from the Securities Exchange Commission who has been looking for Tobe for months now. He wanted me to let him know if I heard from Tobe." She was quiet for a long moment. "I can't stop that inner tussle—should I call him? Or not call him?"

"Why does this SEC lawyer want to talk to Tobe?" he asked.

"He said Tobe adjusted figures at Schrock Investments so that the accounting numbers looked more positive than they really were."

"Do you believe it?"

"I don't want to. I want to believe Tobe would never do such a thing. But what if it's true? What if Dean had known? He didn't tell me everything. When the bank got involved in Schrock Investments—after checks started bouncing and it was apparent there was no money—

Dean was under tremendous pressure. There's a part of me that wonders if they both had been tempted to do something dishonest."

"Even a saint is tempted by an open door," Galen said.

Zing! Naomi cringed. She should definitely reveal her presence and let them know she was eavesdropping.

But then Rose's voice dropped to a whisper and Naomi strained to hear. Ever so carefully, she leaned closer to the open crack of the door.

"Do you think that I should call Allen Turner and let him know that Tobe has returned? How can a mother do such a thing? Even though I'm not his mother, I *am* his mother."

"Rose, if Tobe has nothing to hide, then wouldn't it be better to be up-front about the fact that he's returned?"

Good thinking, Galen! Because Naomi was absolutely, positively sure that Tobe had nothing to hide.

"Yes. No." Rose sighed. "Is everything always so clear to you, so black and white? It seems to me that there are shades of gray worth considering."

"Whenever I'm struggling with a decision, I find it's best to whittle it down to the basic principle. In this instance, the principle is: Do you want the truth?"

"Maybe that's the heart of what I'm struggling with. I still feel such a sense of shame over Schrock Investments. Such a deep shame." The room was quiet for a long moment before Rose added, "I want to find out if or how those records, the ones the SEC confiscated, were falsified. I want to find out if Tobe has done something illegal. I suppose I want to know if Dean had discovered that Tobe had done something, if that knowledge might have driven him to take his own life and drown himself in the pond that day. But even more important than getting answers to those questions, I want Tobe to straighten out and get back on track. By coming home, he's made a step in that direction. It's a start. At least, I hope it is."

Oh, it is, Rose! Naomi thought. *Believe in Tobe! Believe in the best of him.*

"So far," Rose said, "nothing in Tobe's words makes it seem like he's moving forward. So, Galen, what should I do?"

"You're not going to like what I have to say," Galen said.

"Go ahead."

"What you *really* need to do is to tell Tobe about Allen Turner. Then let him make that phone call."

"Maybe I should just talk to Allen Turner first."

"Rose, it doesn't do to sacrifice for people unless they want you to. It's just a waste. As painful as it can be, you have to leave people to their own life."

"I just don't know if Tobe could do it. It would make sense for him to call Allen Turner, but he's . . . never been overly blessed with good sense."

That isn't right! Tobe just has his own way of thinking.

"Sense is wasted on some people," Galen said.

Naomi couldn't argue with that, but she was aware that Galen was hard on people. Maybe too hard. She knew that Galen had never thought highly of Tobe. He had known Tobe since he was a young boy and was convinced he had a lazy streak. Compared to Galen, everybody had a lazy streak. People could change. Tobe could change, if he wanted to. Take Jimmy Fisher. At first, Galen didn't think much of Jimmy Fisher. He only took him on as an apprentice horse trainer because the deacon asked him to. But after a few months, Jimmy had earned Galen's respect and now he hardly flinched much when Jimmy called himself a partner.

"It's time for Tobe to start making his own decisions," Galen said. "The decisions he makes now will determine the person he's going to be. He needs to set his own course."

Until that moment, it hadn't occurred to Naomi that this time—returning home, settling up with his past—was a crossroads for Tobe.

"Rose, you would be robbing that opportunity from him if you overstep now."

She hesitated. "Well, I thought I should give him a little time to get settled."

"Time for what?"

"Meanwhile," Rose said, ignoring Galen's pointed implication, "I was hoping . . . you might ask Tobe to work for you. You don't have to pay him. Just let him help you around the farm."

Naomi practically dropped the lid to the sugar jar. *Oh, what a wonderful idea!*

"No." Then, more softly, Galen added, "He doesn't have the temperament for horses."

"You said similar things about Jimmy Fisher and look how well he has developed into a horseman."

"But Jimmy had the love of horses to begin with. Tobe doesn't love anything."

"You're judging him from how he was as a young teenager."

"There's another reason. I don't want him around my sister."

Naomi straightened like a rod. What did *that* mean?

"Just because he was flirting with her last night? Is that so bad? Maybe Tobe's good for her. I'm sure she'd be a wonderful influence on Tobe."

"What makes you think he'd be any good for Naomi? He's a fence jumper—"

"Galen, that's not fair. If you'd only give him some time . . ."

It was a good thing that Naomi was hiding in the pantry because she was thoroughly flustered.

It took a lot to get Galen riled up, but she could tell by the tenor of her brother's voice that he was annoyed. "And what happens when Tobe finally gets around to calling the SEC lawyer and finds out he's in a little more trouble than he had expected? Have you even told him about the SEC lawyer?"

Silence.

There was a rattle of a cup and saucer, which seemed like Galen's version of ending the conversation. "Rose, you're interfering with that boy's path to adulthood. Like it or not, he has to face consequences. He runs away from too many responsibilities. Once you start running, you can't stop."

A chair clattered. Galen was on his feet, then Rose. Naomi heard their muffled voices as they walked to the door but couldn't make out what they were saying. She waited until she knew they had left the house before she peeked her head out of the pantry. The coast was clear. She took the brown sugar jar and went to the stove to stir the now stiff and pasty oatmeal, pondering all she had learned from overhearing that conversation. No wonder eavesdropping was considered to be a sin—it was dangerously delicious. And so very helpful.

9

Tobe fed hay to Silver Queen and her colt as Bethany filled their buckets with water. Caring for the animals had always been his job when he was growing up. She and Tobe had many good conversations while they worked, side by side. She smiled to herself, thinking how wonderful it was to have him here and how easily they settled into their old routines.

"Tobe, I want to know more about Mom. No, I don't. Yes. I do."

He straightened up, startled by her question.

"You couldn't have taken me with you to see her?"

"It never crossed my mind." He pitched some hay into the stall. "One thing I will tell you, Bethany, she's not what you'd think."

"I don't think anything. I have no idea what she's like. I hardly remember her." She gave him a sideways look. "Do you? Remember her, that is."

Tobe leaned against the stall door. "Probably more than you do. I remember once or twice when she and

Mammi Vera had words. Mom seemed to feel poorly, and slept a lot."

"Tobe, why did she leave?"

He turned and held his hand out to the colt to sniff. "I don't know."

"Yes, you do. Why won't you tell me the truth?"

He didn't look at her. "Some things are best left alone. This is one of them."

"Did you even ask her why she left?"

He shook his head. "We didn't talk much."

"Did she ask about me?"

He shook his head.

"I want to see her. I want to meet her for myself."

He tilted his head, shaking it. "Bethany, I don't think that's a good idea."

"Shootfire! Why not? You got to be with her. How'd you find her, anyway?"

"Jake Hertzler. He knew where she was."

"But . . . how?"

"I guess he poked around Dad's old records. He showed me their divorce certificate, and I copied down the return address on the envelope."

"Was she glad to see you?"

"I wouldn't say . . . glad."

"What would you say?"

"Let's just say it gave me some peace of mind to see her."

"That's what I want too. Peace of mind."

"Bethany . . . you can't unsee a thing once it's seen, or unknow it once it's known."

"What does that mean?"

"Just leave it alone. Remember her the way you want to remember her."

Well, that was the problem right there. She couldn't remember her mother. The images were so mixed up they never made much sense, strange thoughts and feelings that flickered and were gone like moths darting at a lamp. She remembered someone humming a song. She remembered a black-and-white dog sleeping on her bed. She remembered playing checkers with another child—Tobe?—in a room that was dimly lit. She wanted to know more. "Would you at least give me her address?"

He shook his head. "I'm trying to protect you as best as I can."

"I don't need protecting. I need answers." She put the water bucket down. "I just feel so mixed up inside. I'm trying to make peace with things—Jake, Dad's death—but I feel like I can't move forward, not in anything, until I get some things sorted out."

Tobe was silent for a long, long time. "I'm sorry, Bethany. Like I said, some things are just best left alone."

Shootfire! Everybody seemed to think they knew what was best for her.

Mim had responded to Stuck's letter by telling her just what Danny had said—that a life could be transformed by God, if a person were only willing to ask for help. The newspaper didn't want to run something so overtly religious, Bethany said, after a brief meeting with the features editor, whom she thought was small minded and unimaginative, so Mim went ahead and mailed Mrs.

Miracle's response to Stuck to the return address on the envelope.

The features editor did tell Bethany one interesting thing: the column was getting a lot of attention and he was thinking about expanding it from once to twice a week. Bethany said she smiled at him and took full credit. "Here's this week's mail pouch," she said as she tossed the manila envelope on Mim's bed.

It was twice the size of last week's batch.

"I bought more stamps for you while I was downtown." She handed Mim a roll of first-class stamps. "You're not going to make any money if you mail letters to people. Just because the newspaper isn't printing them, it doesn't mean you have to answer them."

"I know. I just want to."

Bethany sat on the bed. "What are these poor saps writing to you?" She put a hand out to reach for the manila envelope, but Mim grabbed it.

"You're being mean. Don't call them poor saps. They're just people. All kinds of people. And you can always read the column in the newspaper. It's not a secret."

Bethany tilted her head. "Isn't it?" She jumped off the bed and crossed the room to the door. "Sure hope you know what you're doing, Mim. You could get into a heap of trouble for this if anyone catches on that you're masquerading as Mrs. Miracle." She closed the door behind her.

Masquerading? How insulting. People needed to write to Mrs. Miracle and she felt compelled to write back. She turned the manila envelope upside down on her bed and let the letters spill out. She picked up a letter and opened it.

Dear Mrs. Miracle,

My name is Peter and I am in the sixth grade. When I talk, I stutter. Yesterday I tried to order a large coke at the movies. I said to the counter guy I would like a llllllllllllllllarge coke. He looked at me as if he thought I was mental. It was very embarrassing. That kind of thing happens a lot to me and I take a lot of teasing.

Sometimes it feels that my mouth is stuck in a traffic jam and nothing can move.

Will my stutter ever go away?

Yours truly,
Peter

Mim remembered a boy with a stutter from her old school. She could still see the pain on his face as he tried to get some words out, with children snickering all around him. This boy grew quieter and quieter, until a new teacher arrived in the middle of the year and put a stop to the teasing. She came up with all kinds of strategies to help this boy. Mim remembered a book report he read on the last day of school . . . without a single stutter. She would never forget the look on that boy's face when he finished the report—like he had scaled Mt. Everest. Mim tapped her chin with her pencil . . . what were those strategies the teacher gave to that boy? Oh yes! She remembered.

She pulled the typewriter out from under her bed and set it up on her desk. Then she took a fresh sheet of paper and fit it into the roller.

Dear Peter,

I have some tips that might help the next time you are in a situation that makes you feel anxious, like ordering a large coke at the movies or giving a book report in school.

1) Say the words in your mind before you say them out loud.

2) If you have to give a talk in front of your class, avoid looking at any one particular person. Look above the heads of the other students and focus on something in the back of the room.

3) Take up singing. Stutterers normally don't stutter while singing. It will help you build confidence.

4) Try not to put pressure on yourself. One of the things that makes stuttering worse is anxiety.

I hope those ideas might help you, Peter. And I also hope you will not let anyone's teasing cause you to stop talking.

Sincerely,
Mrs. Miracle

Mim pulled the letter from the typewriter and scanned it for typos. She was a stickler for typos. Satisfied, she carefully folded the paper in three sections and placed it in the folder to be returned to the *Stoney Ridge Times*.

Being Mrs. Miracle was a wonderful job.

Mim glanced at the alarm clock on her night table. She had time for one more letter before she needed to go to bed. She was waking up extra early this summer so she could join her mom on pre-dawn walks up in the hills. It was their special time together, just the two of them, and she loved to have those moments with her. She flipped through the pile of new letters and saw one with Stuck's unique scrawl. She ripped it open.

Dear Mrs. Miracle,

It was nice of you to send a letter to me but I am sorry to say you are dead wrong about God. He doesn't exist. If he did, my mother would not have killed my father. She would not be spending her life in jail. If there were a God then someone on this earth would care about me.

Don't bother praying on my account. It's just hot air hitting the ceiling.

Signed,
Stuck

Oh, boy. Being Mrs. Miracle was a difficult job.

◊

When Sammy and Luke galloped past Bethany as she hung laundry on the clothesline, she hollered at them to stop. "Where's Tobe?"

"In the barn!" Sammy said.

"Hunting for something," Luke added. Then they both vanished through the hole in the privet.

Galen King, she thought, was a saint to put up with those boys underfoot.

Bethany finished hanging her dress on the clothesline—a blue one—and she stopped for a moment, watching the dress flutter in the gentle breeze. She was always drawn to the color blue and she couldn't say why. The color gave her a feeling of calm and safety. One of the eagles flew overhead and caught her attention, silhouetted against the sky. Maybe she loved the color blue because it had something to do with the vastness of the sky. Endless, permanent, predictable.

She still had bedsheets to wash and hang on the line to dry, but she wanted to talk to Tobe while no one was around. She walked down to the barn and, once inside, was hit with a blast of pungent moist air: hay and horses and manure. She blinked; it took a moment for her eyes to adjust to the dimness and she heard footsteps above her head. She found Tobe in the hayloft, amidst a sea of opened boxes, dusty old trunks, and broken furniture waiting to be repaired. "Tobe, I've given this a lot of thought. I want the address for Mom."

He looked up at her. "You're not going to get it from me."

Bethany crossed her arms over her chest, furious. "Shootfire! You seem to be keeping a lot of information to yourself these days!"

"My thoughts exactly," Rose said as she emerged up the hayloft ladder. "I have two questions for you, Tobe, and I'd like the answers." She climbed to the top and leaned against a haystack. "Why did you run off last year, and why did you come back?"

Tobe didn't answer her, but his eyes looked a little frightened when Rose asked him those questions, or perhaps only surprised. Like a cottontail caught in a sudden beam of a flashlight.

Rose walked closer to Bethany and Tobe. "Tell me what you're looking for."

He kept his eyes fixed on the ground. His hands were clasped together; Bethany saw them tighten involuntarily. "Just something I left behind. Bethany said that most of the things in the basement got moved up here when you started the inn."

Rose looked around the dusty hayloft. "That's right. The inn has kept me so busy, I haven't had time to organize anything. It's on my to-do list." She brushed some hay off a barrel top. "Tobe, are you looking for something that has to do with Schrock Investments?"

"Maybe I should leave," Bethany said.

"No," Rose said firmly. "Bethany, it's time you understood the bigger picture." She turned to Tobe, who had turned his attention back to the barrel. "I want an answer: are you looking for something that has to do with Schrock Investments?"

Head down, he stilled. "There's nothing more to be done with the business."

"No, that's not true."

He snapped his head up to look at Rose. "The Amish Committee is paying people back. The other investors have already gotten their money from claims. It's going to be okay."

"But that doesn't answer the question of why the business started to fail in such a fast and furious way."

He shrugged and started to go through the contents of the box in front of him. "It was the economy."

"It was more than the economy. You know that . . . don't you?" It wasn't really a question Rose was posing. "Tobe, if you're in trouble, I can help."

He startled. "What makes you think I'm the one who's in trouble?"

"You disappeared for a reason. My guess is that you were frightened. Maybe you thought something was going to be discovered. Something you had done wrong. So you panicked and left."

"Is that true, Tobe?" Bethany asked. She had assumed he had left because he felt like she did, tired of the whole business of failure.

He turned away from Rose and Bethany and opened up another box. "I left because the business was going under and there was no reason to stay."

Rose slapped her hand down on a trunk so hard the dishes inside it rattled. Tobe jumped. Bethany's eyes went wide. "No! That's a lie!" she said. "You need to stop lying to me! You and Jake Hertzler did *something* to Dad's business. This isn't going to go away just because you hope it's all over. It's not. Life doesn't work that way. You're in serious trouble with the law, Tobe." The words echoed and echoed, into the barn rafters.

She surprised Tobe so that his face flushed. He looked at Rose now as if he'd never seen her before. "What makes you say that?"

"There is a lawyer with the Securities Exchange Commission who wants to talk to you."

"There's no reason! I haven't done anything wrong. I haven't." Tobe stared at Rose, silent, then his chest shuddered with a deep sigh. He slid to the ground, his back against a pole, and covered his face with his hands. He started to cry. Rose crouched down on the floor with him and held him in her arms, the way she had held Sammy and Luke when they were little, until he pushed her away. "It wasn't my idea," he protested, his voice breaking on the last word so that he sounded as guilty as he seemed.

"It was Jake's. He falsified bank statements so it looked like we had money when we didn't."

Bethany heard the words but it was her brother's anguished face that broke her heart. A panic gripped her chest so tightly that she thought her heart had stopped beating. She kept discovering new things about Jake that seemed impossible to believe. "How? Why? Why would Jake do such a thing?"

Tobe rubbed his eyes with the palms of his hands. "He said it was to help Dad out. He said that if Dad and I could just keep getting new investors, there wouldn't be any problem. He kept reassuring me that everything was okay."

"How did you find out he falsified bank statements?" Rose said.

Tobe wiped his face with both hands. "Jake usually deposited the checks at the bank. One time, Jake was at the dentist so I deposited for the day. I checked on the balance and saw that it had dwindled down to practically nothing. That was when I first thought that something fishy was going on."

"Then why didn't you tell Dad?" Bethany asked.

Tobe looked up and his hard gaze met hers like a blow. "I was going to! I wanted to. But when I went back to the office, Jake was there, so I showed him the bank balance and asked what he knew about it. He told me that he knew all about it—there was less money in the bank than Dad thought there was, but he knew Dad was having heart problems. He didn't want to worry Dad, so he just changed the statements that he showed him. He said not to tell Dad, not to put him under any more pressure, that things were going to be fine."

"And you believed him," Rose said, but in sadness, not anger.

"I was worried about Dad. Jake said he had enough stress. I wanted to believe him. You remember how tense Dad seemed, and he never slept, and how his heart was beating too fast."

Bethany remembered. She used to hear her father's footsteps downstairs as he paced in the middle of the night.

"Jake wanted Dad to concentrate on getting more investors. He said it could be a very short-term cash flow crunch, if we could only go out and get more investments. Jake had a way of explaining things that made it seem like a good idea. So I went along with him." He picked up a piece of straw and rubbed it between his fingers. "Then the house was foreclosed on and we had to move to Mammi Vera's. Things kept getting worse, not better. So Jake told me he had figured out a way to buy a little more time until the economy improved."

Rose was stunned. "Did you not realize he was setting up a pyramid scheme?"

Tobe shook his head. "Jake kept saying it was a short-term solution. Just to buy some time." He dropped his chin to his chest. "It was the simplest thing. Strangely simple. Jake just whited out the address and account number, using other investors' statements, typed the right address and account number, and then made a copy so you couldn't see that it had been changed."

"And Dad had no idea?" Bethany asked.

Tobe shook his head. "It gets worse." He crumpled the straw and tossed it away. "Checks started bouncing right and left. As word leaked out, shareholders started to try to liquidate, which only made everything spiral out of control. Dad was advised by the bank to declare bankruptcy so they could try to control the implosion and figure out what had happened. That was when Jake showed me that he had been keeping a second set of books. He had given Dad the cooked books. Jake had the real books, the real story—Schrock Investments was running out of money."

Rose rubbed her face. "Then the ones Dad handed over to the SEC were falsified books?"

Slowly, Tobe nodded. "That's right. I was in the office on the day the subpoena was delivered to Dad. He was told that shareholders had organized a lawsuit against Schrock Investments. That was when I started to panic. I took the second set of books and I hid them in the basement. I just needed to get away for a few days, to think. To figure out a plan of how to tell Dad what Jake and I had done." He put his forehead on his knees. "And then Dad died. I couldn't come back. I just couldn't. So I ran. I ran as far away from here as I could get."

"Es is graad so weit hie as her," Rose said. *It's just as far going as coming.*

Tobe squeezed his eyes shut. "I was only trying to protect Dad. He must have known what I had done. He must have figured it out."

"Probably so," Rose said. "He was very upset the night before he died. He left the house and said he was going to go fix everything. I didn't know what he meant by that. The next thing I knew, the bishop and police arrived to let me know Dad had drowned."

At the mention of her father's death, Bethany suddenly

felt aware of how hot and stuffy it was in the hayloft. She felt as if she was having trouble getting a full breath of air. She walked over to the open hayloft window and tried to get some fresh air.

"So," Rose said, all calm and matter-of-fact, "you only came back because you heard that the Amish committee was going to reimburse people for what they lost?"

"Yes." The word had come out of Tobe almost like a gasp. "I thought it would be safe. I thought it was all over."

"Are you looking for ledger books? For the accurate books?"

"I've looked everywhere! I've been combing this hayloft for two days. I can't find them anywhere."

Bethany's head snapped up. "I gave them to Jake."

Tobe stared at her. "You *what*?"

"He was here a few months ago. Jake told me you were in trouble. He said you needed those books. I thought I was doing something to help you."

He let out a short, bitter laugh. "Jake scores again."

"Tobe, we need to talk to the SEC lawyer," Rose said. "Allen Turner is his name. He's been looking for you for the last year."

His head shot up in panic. "You would turn me in?"

"I'm not going to tell Allen Turner anything. You're going to tell him. Everything." Out of Rose's pocket, she pulled Allen Turner's business card and handed it to Tobe.

His face crumpled. "I can't do it. I can't. You don't understand."

"I understand that life doesn't give you many moments like this. You have a very long life ahead of you.

But how you handle this situation will decide the man you're going to be from now on. The man God wants you to be."

He fingered the card. "God has forgotten about me."

Rose shook her head. "He hasn't," she whispered. "You must never think that. His love is always there, Tobe, always there. We're here too. Your family will always support you. That's what families do."

Tobe listened, but said nothing.

"You heard me, didn't you, Tobe?"

Tobe nodded. "I heard you." He wiped his eyes and held up the business card. "I'm going to be different from now on. You'll see. I'm going to be different."

"In what way?"

"In every way. I am going to be a different man."

Bethany looked at her brother. For all his faults—and she had to admit they were manifold—he had a good heart. And as much as he could be frustrating, he could also be amusing and generous and appealing.

"Don't change too much," Rose said gently. "We love you the way you are."

She stood and walked to the hayloft ladder, then swiveled around to face Tobe. "I understand that cash inflow from new investors could be used to pay other investors' dividends. I understand that returns on investments had diminished. But what I don't understand is where all the principal money went. Where is all *that* money?"

Tobe shrugged. "The recession. Plus Dad made some bad investments. Some real estate properties went belly up."

Bethany looked back out the hayloft window. She thought about Jake's new truck with all the bells and whistles he was so proud of. About his new horse trailer. About his cell phone. About the fancy restaurants he took her to. His overly generous tips. It never crossed her mind to ask where that money came from. It never crossed her mind.

And she had trouble getting a full breath of air again.

With all Tobe had revealed in the hayloft, Bethany couldn't shake the feeling that life was spiraling out of control. She had to grab something to hold on to, something to help her feel as if she could find her own way.

Later that day, while Tobe was taking a shower, she sneaked into his room and riffled through his wallet. Tobe kept everything important in his wallet. She noticed exactly how everything was before she took it out so she could be sure to put it back the same way. She went through old receipts, a piece of gum, a few dollars—ah! no wonder he came home when he did—and a folded-up paper from a Schrock Investments' memo pad. She opened it up and squinted, barely able to make out the faded penciled writing:

Mary Miller Schrock, 212 N. Street, Hagensburg, PA

Bingo!

That had to be it. Tobe had said she wasn't too far from here. She heard the shower turn off, so she scribbled down the address on a piece of paper, put the papers and gum back in the wallet, and tiptoed out of Tobe's room.

All day, Bethany kept fingering the paper with her mother's address on it. She wasn't even sure how to get there, or if she even wanted to.

Yes, she did.

No, she didn't.

10

This afternoon, Geena's mind was mainly on dinner. Earlier today she had bought a juicy strip steak at the butcher shop in Stoney Ridge and thought she might ask the Schrocks if she could use their grill. The Amish, she was told, loved to barbecue. And it was still blistering hot, which she didn't really mind because it meant more canceled reservations and her stay could extend at Eagle Hill. The longer she was here, the longer she could put off the inevitable job search.

As she walked out of the guest flat toward the house, she spotted Bethany near the clothesline, a mound of wet bedding in her arms. Of all the Schrocks, she found herself most drawn to Bethany: feisty, opinionated, strong—probably stronger than she knew—yet with an undercurrent of pathos. She wondered what that undercurrent consisted of. Where did it come from?

As she approached Bethany, she could see that something was wrong. Bethany's hands were trembling. "Are you all right?"

Startled, Bethany said, "Of course. Of course I'm all right."

"You're sure?"

Bethany's eyes filled with tears. "I don't know." She looked away. "Maybe not."

"I see." Geena leaned forward. "Would you like to talk? Life gets complicated sometimes. It can help to talk things out."

Bethany shook her head, splattering tears, then ducked her chin in embarrassment. "Shootfire!" she said fiercely. "I'm sorry. I'm never emotional like this. Hardly ever."

Geena patted her back. "Come inside and let's chat."

In the small living room of the guest flat of Eagle Hill, Bethany poured out her life story: her mother's disappearance, her father's untimely passing, her brother's reappearance, and all the pieces in between. "I just want to know why. Why did she leave? Did I do something to make her go? Did my father? I feel as if I can't stop wondering about her—maybe because my father has died. I'll never know anything more if I don't track her down now."

When Bethany had finally finished with her long story, with her tears and deep breaths, Geena encased Bethany's hand like a sandwich between her own and looked deeply into her face. "Maybe you should go find your mother and get some answers to your questions."

"I don't even know how to get to Hagensburg. Buses, I guess."

"I could drive you there. I could go with you."

Bethany's head snapped up. "I didn't mean to ask—"

Geena held up a hand. "You didn't ask. I offered."

"Maybe my brother is right. Maybe it's best to just let sleeping dogs lie."

"Sometimes it is best to leave things alone. But sometimes, a person can't move forward until she faces what's holding her back."

"What if I find out something I don't want to know?"

"I guess that's something you need to decide for yourself."

"I want to know about my mother," Bethany said. "But I don't."

"Sometimes the past can cling to us like cobwebs, getting in the way of the future." Geena patted Bethany's shoulder. "If you want to go, just let me know when and I'll drive you over there."

From the guest flat window, Geena watched Bethany walk back to the clothesline and her heart felt sad. She hoped it had helped for Bethany to talk to her, though the way her shoulders were slumped made her think she had only added to the poor girl's confusion. She would have loved to have dropped everything and driven Bethany right over to Hagensburg, right now, and get answers to those burdensome questions. But going, or not going . . . that had to be Bethany's decision.

Geena wasn't surprised that Bethany had shared personal information with her even though they had only known each other for a short time. People had always told her their stuff, even before she was ordained. Maybe she was easy to talk to. She hoped so. Sometimes people just needed a safe place to unload their troubles. An objective listener. Her counseling classes at seminary had taught her that the best way to draw someone out was just to listen.

But to whom did a minister go to share his or her stuff?

⁂

Early Friday morning, Tobe called Allen Turner of the Securities Exchange Commission. The lawyer told him to sit tight, that he would be there in a few hours.

Bethany had heard the name of Allen Turner for over a year. She had an impression of the kind of man he might be: old, balding, with thick glasses, wearing a detective's overcoat that brushed his ankles, and carrying a fat briefcase with papers sticking out of it. The real Allen Turner turned out to be youngish, sort of. In his mid-forties, she guessed, with a full head of blondish hair and a rather kind-looking face. Not looksome like Jimmy Fisher, sort of a craggy face, but not bad for a middle-aged English man. His smile was kind, lighting up the sadness in his eyes. That was what surprised Bethany the most—his eyes. They weren't the eyes of a ferocious lawyer. They were fatherly eyes.

"This is one case I'm determined to solve," he told Rose and Bethany as they met him at the car and walked to the house.

"Is it still considered to be a case?" Rose said.

"Yes, ma'am, it is."

"It's naïve, I suppose, to hope that there's enough information to clearly show that my husband and son had done nothing wrong with Schrock Investments. Nothing intentionally wrong."

"Yes, ma'am. That would be naïve."

Allen Turner sat at the kitchen table of Eagle Hill, opened his big briefcase—that was one part of him that did fit the image in Bethany's mind—and started to pull out thick files. She had to fight a powerful urge to stand up and fuss with the food or do the dishes, start some coffee. Women, Rose had once said, had to do something with their hands in times of crisis. Boy, was that right. She had to sit on her hands to keep from fidgeting.

Rose sent Mim over to Naomi's to tell Tobe that Mr. Turner was here. And she asked Mim to stay over there, to keep an eye on Luke and Sammy. Bethany was pretty sure Rose wished she could send Mammi Vera away for this conversation too. Her grandmother was hovering in the kitchen, glaring at Allen Turner as if she were a mother lioness and he was threatening one of her cubs. Which, in a way, was true.

When Tobe returned from next door, his face was flushed and not from the heat. Even Bethany was aware this was a significant moment in his life. Tobe shook Allen Turner's hand and sat down at the table.

Bethany caught Rose's eye and nodded her head to the door.

"Would you like us to leave?" Rose said, setting a pitcher of iced tea on the table with two glasses and a plate of cookies. "We can give you some privacy."

"I'm not going anywhere," Mammi Vera announced, seating herself at the table.

Allen Turner took a glass and filled it with iced tea. He took a long sip and set it down, then wiped his forehead with a handkerchief. The room felt like an oven and it was only eleven in the morning. "Please stay, all of you. I have questions for you too. We've got a lot to wade through."

He set a tiny tape recorder on the table and looked up. "I hope you don't mind if I record our conversation." He turned it on without waiting for anyone's permission. "Tobe, start by stating your name and age."

"My name is Tobias Schrock. I'm twenty-two years old . . ."

Tobe answered Allen Turner's questions for over two hours, while Rose and Mammi Vera and Bethany sat at the table, patiently listening. There was nothing new in what Tobe had to say, not to Rose, but something new did occur. Allen Turner pulled out two black ledgers and set them on the table. "Do you recognize these?"

Bethany pressed her backbone against the hard chair. Those were the two books that she had given—searched for and handed over!—to Jake Hertzler, just two months ago. She felt that strange feeling start again in her chest, like she couldn't get a full breath of air.

Comprehension stilled Tobe, but only for a moment. "Those are the actual ledgers for Schrock Investments. Those show the real story. That we were running out of money."

"This case has been pretty unusual for me. Without any computers, there's no paper trail. Everything boils down to these ledgers." Allen Turner opened one of them up. "Maybe you knew that." He lifted his eyes to observe Tobe's response.

"I've never worked with computers. I wouldn't know any difference. That's just the way Schrock Investments kept their records." Tobe bit his lip. "How'd you get those?"

"They arrived at my desk, sent anonymously. A note inside said they belonged to you."

Tobe squeezed his eyes shut. "The entries were made by Jake Hertzler. You can compare handwriting and see that's the truth. But I took the books and hid them on the day the subpoena was delivered and my father was told there was a lawsuit forming against Schrock Investments."

"Why did you hide them?"

Tobe shrugged. "I panicked. It was stupid. I just thought I could protect my father."

"These ledgers only reveal part of the story. Schrock Investments was in trouble but it wasn't only because of poor returns." Allen Turner reached out and took one of Rose's cookies. He took a bite, then a few more. The room had grown quiet, the crunching of the cookie sounded like a cow in dried cornstalks.

"I'm sure there's a perfectly good explanation," Rose said quietly, but she clasped her hands so tightly, the knuckles turned white.

"Quite right, Mrs. Schrock," Allen Turner said, talking around bites of cookie. "Someone was siphoning money from the company."

Tobe jerked his head up. "It wasn't me! I would never have done such a thing."

Allen Turner flattened his palms on the table. "No one's accusing you, son. We think it was Jake Hertzler. He was skimming off the company from the start."

"How did you discover that?" Rose asked.

Allen Turner pulled out another file, with a picture of a man on top. Jake's picture. "It's taken me awhile to piece it all together. Jake Hertzler, aka Jack Hartzler, John Hershberger . . . he's got a number of aliases. He's a con artist. A clever one. He dabbles in all kinds of money-laundering scams."

Quietly, Bethany added, "Horse trading too."

Allen Turner looked over at her as if he just realized she was there. "Wouldn't surprise me. Anything he can get his mitts into, he finds a way to turn a fast one."

Mammi Vera slammed her fists on the tabletop. "That Jake Hertzler always did strike me as slicker than a pan full of cold bacon!"

Allen Turner grinned, a first. "Well, his luck is running out. He got greedy with Schrock Investments and caught the SEC's attention on this one. I'm going to nail this guy." He looked at Tobe. "And if you want to avoid some jail time, you're going to help me."

"Jail?" Tobe asked, color draining from his face. "Why would I have to go to jail?"

"Son, you broke the law," Allen said, his eyes both weary and wary. "You committed felonies."

"How?"

"Concealing records. Withholding information. You're facing jail time. A lot of it . . . unless . . . we can prove Jake Hertzler's involvement as the mastermind behind this pyramid scheme."

"But he was!"

Allen lifted an eyebrow. "Then help me prove it."

"How?"

"You'll need to come back to Philadelphia with me."

Tobe looked at him suspiciously. "So you can throw me in jail?"

"I'm going to do what I can to keep you *out* of jail. But there are people you're going to have to talk to first.

And I need to have your full cooperation to build this case against Jake Hertzler. We need your testimony."

"I'll do anything I can to pin Jake down." A shadow crossed over his eyes. "Anything."

"Tobias Schrock!" Mammi Vera snapped. "Revenge is not an option." She tapped a finger on the tabletop. "Don't forget who you are."

Tobe looked over at her. "Jake should pay for what he did. Is wanting justice so wrong?"

She narrowed her eyes at him. "God decides those matters. Justice belongs to him. You were raised to be a Plain man. You can't toss that away like an old hat."

Allen Turner leaned forward in his chair. "Son, is there something else you know? Something you're not telling me?"

Tobe hesitated. He kept his eyes on the tabletop. "I know he falsified bank statements. I saw him do it."

"Yeah," Allen Turner said. "I figured that out."

"What else, Tobe?" Rose said. "Do you know something else about Jake Hertzler that you're not telling us? Are you frightened about something? Is that why you disappeared?"

Everyone stilled, all eyes on Tobe. He ran his finger along a spot on the oilcloth that covered the table, then finally lifted his head. He didn't back down. If anything, his jaw hardened. "I told you what I know for sure."

Bethany knew her brother well enough to know he was lying. Tobe knew something else he didn't want to say. But what?

Rose must have had the same sense. "I'm going with you to Philadelphia," she said.

Tobe's head jerked up. "No, you're not. I got myself into this and I'm going to get myself out of it."

"I'm coming too," Mammi Vera added. She looked right at Rose. "Don't even try to talk me out of it."

Rose opened her mouth, then clamped it shut with a frown. Both women ignored Tobe, talking over his objections as if he weren't even there.

"I'm due for a three-month checkup with that Dr. Stoltz anyway. I'll just move it up a little. We'll stay at Delia Stoltz's house. She stayed here plenty long." Mammi Vera waved a hand at Rose as if shooing a cat. "You call her today and let her know we're coming."

Rose sighed. It was decided. "Then we'll have to take the boys too. Bethany and Mim have enough to do with the inn and their work at the Sisters' House."

"You can leave them, Rose," Bethany said. "We'll trade off watching them. Tobe needs you right now."

Rose hesitated, nodded, then turned to Allen Turner. "We can't leave for a few days, though. There's a work frolic tomorrow to help build the community garden."

Allen Turner had been watching the family interaction with a stunned look on his face. Bethany thought everything about Schrock Investments probably stunned him. "Mrs. Schrock, this isn't a vacation. Your stepson is under investigation for criminal charges."

Rose lifted her chin. "My *son* is innocent." She didn't like to use the word "step" when referring to her relationship to Bethany and Tobe. As far as she was concerned, they were a family. Period. "And my son is not going to Philadelphia without me. We need Tobe tomorrow for the frolic. And then there's Sunday church. So we can't leave until Monday. You can come back for us then."

"Noooooooo," Allen Turner said, drawing the word out for emphasis. "I am not letting Tobe Schrock out of my sight. I've been trying to catch up with him for a very long time."

"So have we," Rose said firmly.

Bethany nearly grinned, despite the seriousness of the matter. Rose could be surprisingly stubborn.

"Another day or two won't matter in the grand scheme of things," Rose said. "You'll just have to sit tight. You're welcome to help with the frolic. You can stay here, at Eagle Hill."

"Frolic? Under the circumstances, that hardly seems like an appropriate use of time."

Rose's face softened into a faint smile. "It means a work party."

Allen Turner rubbed his forehead. "This is highly unorthodox."

"You have our word, Mr. Turner. We will leave with you on Monday morning."

"Do any of you have an idea where Hertzler might be?" Allen Turner asked. "Favorite places? People tend to do predictable things even when they're in trouble, maybe even more so then."

Tobe shook his head. "Jake won't do anything predictable."

"True, but it's also true that an animal run aground usually finds a way to reproduce the familiar." Allen Turner turned to Bethany. "How did you contact him when he was in Stoney Ridge?"

"I had his cell phone number. I still have it."

Allen Turner's eyebrows shot up. "Well, why didn't

you say so in the first place? We might be able to trace his location."

"His phone isn't on very often," Bethany said. "Usually, I just left messages for him."

Allen Turner turned over his yellow pad of paper to a fresh page. "That's because he knows to keep it off so it can't be located. And if he's smart enough to take the battery out, we can't trace calls at all."

"Jake is freakishly smart," Bethany said.

Tobe scratched his chin. "How can a cell phone be traced?"

"Mobile phones work by hopping from one tower to another. As you drive out of one range, you hook onto another. Each of these towers have a certain range, and the cellular provider can use triangulation and calculate the time it takes for the signal to get from the tower to your phone and back to calculate distance from that point." Allen Turner tapped his pencil on his pad of paper. "So do you have the number?"

"It's up in my room. I'll go get it." As Bethany passed the front door, she saw Geena Spencer come up the steps with her breakfast tray. She hurried to open the door to let her in. "I forgot all about your tray."

"No problem. I'm heading into town so I thought I'd drop it off." Geena handed the tray to Bethany, then looked quickly around the table. Her smile faded at the sight of Allen Turner. She backed up against the pistachio-colored wall, a look of astonishment on her face.

Allen Turner stared at her for a long moment. Then the craggy lines of his face softened in a smile. "Hello, Geena. Long time no see."

Of all the people in all the world over, Geena thought, as she made a hurried return to her guest flat, she would not have expected to find Allen Turner on an Amish farm. She hadn't seen him in years and years, not since the day she had told him she wouldn't marry him.

No—that was only part of it. She wouldn't give up the ministry for him. That was what he wanted from her and it was more than she could give him. She had hoped that Allen would reconsider and discover that he couldn't live without her, but that wasn't the way he was wired. He loved her but wasn't willing to share her with a church. She loved him but wasn't willing to give up the ministry for him. And so they parted ways.

A year or so later, news trickled to Geena that Allen had married. It was for the best, she knew, and she had prayed for Allen and his bride to be blessed. But she'd never gotten over feeling a bit of a sting whenever she thought of Allen.

At that moment the subject of her thoughts knocked on the guest flat door.

"Do you mind if I come in for a moment?" Allen said as she opened the door. He was big, blond, and had the kind of angular face that some might find handsome. She did. The added lines in that virile face had only given him character. His was the kind of presence that filled a room. "I'm going to be staying up in the farmhouse for a few nights. Three, to be exact."

"Did they invite you?"

"Sort of." He wiped the back of his neck with a

handkerchief. “This heat wave is really something. No air-conditioning anywhere.”

“It’s an Amish farm, in case you hadn’t noticed.”

He grinned. “I did, in fact. Geena, I’d like to ask you a few questions.”

She raised a palm toward the sofa. “Well, then, why don’t you sit down.” She sat across from him in a chair. “I take it this is legal business?”

He nodded.

“I don’t know anything, if that’s what you’re wondering. I’ve only been here a week and a half.”

Allen leaned back and raised an arm against the top of the sofa. “What brings you here, of all places?”

“Someone in my church gave me a gift certificate and I finally had time to use it. The inn has been booked up for months, but this heat wave brought some cancellations. So . . . I was in luck. At least until the heat wave breaks, anyway.”

“It is hot. I’ll never take air-conditioning for granted.” He picked up a magazine and started to fan himself. “So, have you been able to get to know the Schrock family? The Amish tend to be utterly private people.”

“They’ve been very welcoming to me. Very pleasant. I’ve gotten to know Bethany, in particular. She’s the oldest daughter.”

“Has anyone mentioned a fellow named Jake Hertzler to you?”

“No. And Allen, even if she did, I would consider it to be a confidence.”

He nodded. “The privileges of the priesthood.”

She bristled. How strange. Twenty years had passed and they were automatically in the roles they had left behind. She stood. "If there's nothing else, I have an errand to run in town."

"Wait, Geena. I'm sorry. I didn't mean that the way it sounded. Really. It was a careless comment. I just meant it as it was—you have the right to hold confidences. Please, sit down. I'd like to catch up with you."

She slowly sat down again. "There's nothing much to say."

"Are you still working at the church in Ardmore?"

How did he know where she was working? "I'm . . . in between jobs right now."

"Is that why you're hiding out here, on a remote Amish farm?"

Okay. That was enough probing. She glanced at her watch. "I really need to head into town to get an errand done." That wasn't entirely an untruth. She had planned to go to the Sweet Tooth Bakery where she could get Wi-Fi and update her résumé on her laptop. And get a cinnamon roll. "If you'll excuse me, Allen." She went to the door to open it.

He rose and walked to the door. "Maybe I'll see you tomorrow."

"I don't think so. I'm going to help the Amish build a community garden tomorrow."

He smiled. "So am I. Wherever Tobe Schrock is, there I will be. See you tomorrow, Geena."

11

On the day of the work frolic, Jimmy Fisher came to Eagle Hill just after breakfast to pick up Bethany. She was waiting on the porch step, shielding her eyes from the bright sunlight that bleached the blue right out of the sky. "Looks like another scorcher."

"Not hardly," he said, drawing out the words teasing and lazy. "Won't be truly hot until the water in the creek gets to boiling." He handed her some drawings. "Last night, I figured out how much lumber we had and drew up some plans for the garden plots. See what you think."

She looked over his detailed sketches. "Why . . . they're excellent. Jimmy, you did a fine job."

He shrugged, as if it was nothing, but she knew it wasn't. He must have spent hours laboring over those plans. And then there was the recruiting he had done to talk dozens of people into volunteering a few hours for the community garden, despite the week's record heat. She handed the sketches back to Jimmy. "Why are you doing all this?"

He looked at her as if she might be sun-touched, then shook his head. "How could anyone in their right mind refuse an opportunity to spend a day slaving like a dog in ninety-five-degree weather with one hundred percent humidity?"

She lifted her chin and tried not to grin. "Excellent point."

By eight o'clock, dozens of Amish had arrived and stood in a large clump, under the shade of the Grange Hall roof, listening to Jimmy Fisher explain how the garden plots would be laid out. By midday they would all be sweltering beneath a blanket of gummy, heavy air. And yet, the heat hadn't stopped anyone from coming.

As Jimmy spoke, Galen stood with his arms folded, until Bethany saw him gesture to someone in the crowd. Then she spied her two brothers, sneaking through the rows of people, tiptoeing with exaggerated silence toward the platter of day-old pastries from the Sweet Tooth Bakery. Galen shook his head. They halted, making gestures of protest. He pulled his brows together and pointed to the edge of the crowd, far from the table of snacks. Deflated, they slunk away.

Jimmy had organized the day quite efficiently. Within minutes he started a group of men measuring and building raised wooden beds. Young boys were given the task of wheeling in barrows of topsoil and dumping them into the beds. Clumps of girls and women planted the vegetable starts that Amos Lapp had donated. Hank Lapp pounded in small wooden placards in front of each one, to identify whose garden plot was whose.

Allen Turner, the SEC lawyer who was investigating Tobe, worked alongside the Schrock family. For a lawyer, he was surprisingly capable with a saw and hammer. But he was never far from Tobe, who was never far from Naomi. Bethany knew Allen Turner didn't want to let Tobe out of his sight—the man was sleeping on the lumpy couch in their living room, which made Mammi Vera furious. But he didn't let Mammi Vera's cold stares bother him. He seemed to Bethany like a man on a mission and that mission was Tobe. Or maybe, in the end, it was Jake Hertzler.

But it was Geena who impressed Bethany the most. She had a pleasant way of getting everyone involved in a task. No one was left out, especially children.

Despite everything that weighed at the back of her mind, Bethany felt it was quite an astonishingly wonderful morning.

After a simple lunch of ham-and-cheese sandwiches had been served by the sisters of the Sisters' House, most of the Amish families went home. The bulk of the work had been done. All who remained were those who wanted to grow and manage a garden plot. Geena had heard about the community of the Amish, but seeing it up close and personal—it was something to behold. They arrived early and slipped seamlessly into a role, as if they all knew where they fit best.

To Geena, it felt like watching Paul's words in action from his letter to the Romans: "We have different gifts, according to the grace given to each of us. If your gift is prophesying, then prophesy in accordance with your faith; if it is serving, then serve; if it is teaching, then teach; if it is to encourage, then give encouragement; if it is giving, then give generously; if it is to lead, do it diligently; if it is to show mercy, do it cheerfully." Watching Bethany, Jimmy Fisher, Galen King, Amos Lapp, Hank Lapp, Rose Schrock, and Naomi King spread out among the newly built plots and teach people how to care for the gardens . . . Geena went suddenly all soft inside with choking that was so close to tears. Every church in the world, she supposed, had a little knot at its solid center. The goodness, the simple honest goodness in some people!

Geena knelt by the Grange Hall garden plot, gloves on her hands, looking at the soft open space with fierce intent. She picked up a handful of dirt, smelling the heady dampness of it. With her spade, she made a row and tucked some pea starts into the dirt every few inches, then patted the earth around each little start. Sammy and his dog Chase appeared at her side.

She held up a handful for him to examine. "This is good earth," she told Sammy. "See how dark it is?"

He nodded seriously, and smelled it when she did, his big eyes always taking everything in. The sun sparkled over the top of his head. "I still don't like peas, though."

"Maybe you'll like them better when they're fresh and you pick them yourself."

Sammy looked unconvinced, then heard Luke call to him, and he ran off, his dog loping at his heels.

"How are you doing?"

Geena had to squint to look up at Allen, and he noticed and moved around to the other side. "Sorry about that."

"Doing fine, thank you. Getting the peas in on this

end. That end will be tomatoes. Maybe pumpkins in the middle, where their vines can sprawl over the edges." She picked up a packet of pumpkin seeds and shook it. The big seeds rattled inside. "Might be a little late to plant these, but we'll give them a try."

"You've done this before, I think." His blue eyes had the gleam of a blue pearly marble she'd had as a child. Such clear eyes seemed as if they could see too much. "Are you going to go back? To the ministry?"

"Of course. I . . . just have to figure some things out." How could he possibly understand how deep her calling to ministry went? To her very marrow.

"It must be hard to be a person of God. When you were trying to eat lunch, I saw that you kept getting interrupted by people who wanted a word with you."

Just one or two. Maybe three. Now that she thought about it, she hadn't had a chance to finish her lunch. No wonder she was still hungry.

"It brought up memories," Allen said. "I remember how mothers always wanted to talk to you, anytime they were worried about something. Doesn't it drive you crazy, people needing you constantly like that?"

Geena thought, with longing, of the way children, teens, even parents from her church would look in her direction when she arrived at their home, or to the waiting room of a hospital, or once at a county jail. When they realized she had come to help them, their upturned faces were expectant, hopeful, grateful. "No." She took a breath. "I love it. I love being needed."

"I guess that's the nature of your job, isn't it?"

Geena didn't know how to answer him.

"You seem happy, Geena. Really happy."

"I am." And she was. Even if, at the moment, she was a youth pastor without a church, she was happy. She knew who she was and what her purpose was.

"You're very lucky." He strolled off before she could say another word.

Geena watched him walk through the middle of the lot, looking at all of the garden plots, smiling at the other gardeners, who smiled back. The sound of happy voices and laughter filled the air. Children chased one another through the pathways between plots, and a few dogs trotted along behind them, the Schrocks' golden retriever Chase among them. He spied Geena and came loping toward her, tongue lolling.

"You look thirsty, ol' boy. C'mon, let's find some water for you, shall we?"

In the kitchen, she found a dented, old stainless steel bowl and carried it outside. She filled the bowl and put it down in the shade and whistled for Chase, who came racing and dove into the water with eager slurping.

Geena went back inside the Grange Hall to wash her hands. A little sunburn gave her cheekbones some color. She took a moment to try to tame her hair and wash the dirt streaks off her face. Even with a big garden hat on, the sun had kissed her. She looked rested and healthy.

Thinking of how lovely Bethany looked even after hours of hard work, she peered into the mirror, wishing she had fuller lips or a bit more chest, or darker eyelashes, or some extraordinary feature, but she was honest with herself. Her eyes were an ordinary brown, her mousy brown hair too frizzy, her cheekbones too broad to ever be considered pretty.

She plucked a few more curls from her ponytail, let them frame her face a little, fall down her neck. Better.

In the mid-afternoon, Bethany sank down at the picnic table under the shade of the Grange Hall roof, took off her gloves, and slapped the dirt from them. Her hands were shaking and she realized she hadn't stopped to eat since breakfast. Geena walked over and brought her a sandwich and a glass of sweet, cool lemonade—just what she needed.

"Look at this," Bethany said, satisfied. "Look what you started, Geena. It was your idea to turn a crummy old vacant lot into a garden." Each plot had small vegetables growing in it: tomatoes, carrots, radishes, lettuce, zucchinis, cucumbers, beans, peas, onions, eggplants, corn shoots. It wouldn't be long at all before those plants started to sprawl, covering up the entire beds with thick green vines and leaves.

"It is beautiful," Geena said, gazing around the garden. "But an idea is one thing. Doing it is something else. This community garden was everyone's doing."

"Mostly Jimmy Fisher, I think. He's spent a lot of time on this." Bethany's eyes had often sought Jimmy out and her chest tightened with a sweet longing. He seemed to be everywhere at once, handing people tools, wheeling in a barrow full of dirt, carrying boxes of Amos's plant starts, scooping up the leftover messes.

Her gaze followed Jimmy as he attached a hose to a spigot at the back of the Grange. Luke and Sammy sneaked up from behind to jump on him, but he must have heard or sensed the imminent attack. He spun around, hosing them down with water. The boys screamed and laughed. They adored Jimmy. He was always surprising people, Jimmy was. Bethany, mostly.

Speaking of surprises, Bethany's little sister seemed to be filled with them. She watched Mim walk slowly along the garden path with Ella, holding the old woman's elbow to keep her from falling. Mim had become Ella's keeper. She shadowed her, helping her along, answering questions, making sure she stayed safe. Ella's safety was a growing concern. But who would have thought Mim would become someone's caregiver? She had to be asked to spend time with Mammi Vera.

There was more to Mim than Bethany had thought—or maybe she just hadn't noticed. Mim didn't know this, but Bethany had started to read the Mrs. Miracle letters that were published in the *Stoney Ridge Times*. Not always, but often, Mrs. Miracle revealed a surprising depth, a startling wisdom. Of course, Bethany wouldn't share that thought with Mim, but she was impressed.

Then Bethany's gaze traveled to a group of wayward girls from the Group Home, clumped together, watching everyone else work. "What do you think those girls are thinking about?"

Geena turned to see. She sighed. "They probably haven't seen people work together like this before. And I think they're watching families work together and feeling great self-pity. Their version of family is nothing like this."

"We're doing this for them, but they won't help." They were invited to pitch in—Bethany had overheard as Geena asked them. And a few seemed willing, until that red-haired girl said no and the rest of them followed her lead. They wouldn't lift a finger to help today, though they did eat lunch when offered.

The red-haired girl was the obvious ringleader. There was something about her that irritated Bethany. She had a permanent look of contempt on her face. Under her breath, Bethany muttered, "That red-haired girl shouldn't be allowed to intimidate the other girls."

"True, but more importantly, why does she feel the need to?" Geena turned around to face Bethany. "Until we walk in someone's shoes, we really can't judge what makes them do the things they do." She patted Bethany's hand. "The garden is the first step toward making a difference in those girls' lives. But the garden needs time to grow and we need to allow God time to work in the girls' hearts."

Time. Bethany had never been one for patience. "Do you know anything about that girl?"

"Her name is Rusty but I don't know anything else about her." Geena slapped her hands on her thighs. "I'm going to find out." She walked over and sat on the ground next to the clump of girls.

Bethany's curiosity about Geena Spencer continued to grow and grow. She was easy to talk to and didn't seem anything like a lady preacher, not that Bethany knew what a lady preacher should be like.

"Anything left that's sweet to eat?"

Bethany turned to see Jimmy Fisher leaning against a support post that held up the Grange Hall roof, one booted foot crossed over the other, his hat dangling from his fingers, gazing at her with an inscrutable look. Flustered, she spied a dish at the end of the row. "One piece of Rose's famous blueberry buckle is left. You want it?"

"Split it with me?"

"I'm already full," she said, leaning over to scoop up the lone square of cake. She put it on his plate. He'd just washed up, for the ends of his hair dripped water and he smelled of Ivory soap. "You've worked hard on this project. Everyone appreciates it."

"Everyone?"

She blushed. "I appreciate it." She looked from his eyes up to the sky, then back to his eyes again, judging which were bluer. His eyes were definitely bluer than the sky.

He leaned toward her, though he was careful not to touch her, cautious about who might be watching them. "So, what do you say about tomorrow night? Will you let me take you home from the singing?"

For one little moment, that vine twined around them again, binding them together as he looked at her. His blue, blue eyes twinkled, but there was also something solid and real there.

"Jimmy! Oh Jimmy Fisher!"

He whirled his head around. And there was Katie Zook, waving to him to come help her carry a tray of seedlings.

Bethany shook her head in disbelief. *That* girl surely needed a copy of *A Young Woman's Guide to Virtue*.

"Be there in a minute." He turned back to Bethany, but it was too late. She'd had enough and was already brushing past him to head into the Grange Hall to help Sylvia with lunch dishes.

Sunday morning was quiet at Eagle Hill. Geena had watched the Schrock family pile into a buggy and head off to church. Last evening, Rose had brought fresh sun-dried towels down to Geena and said that another inn reservation had been canceled due to the heat wave, so she would be able to stay two more nights in the guest flat. She was thrilled. She had no reason to return home. Not yet.

Geena planned to go to church in town later in the morning, after a hike. As she stepped out into the light from the coolness of the guest flat, the sun fell on her skin like a skillet, heavy and hot. She paused for a moment, closing her eyes, letting the early morning heat sink deep into her bones. Unlike most people, she loved warm weather. Maybe she should look for a youth pastor position in Florida or Arizona. Or Texas?

She spotted Allen, leaning against a fence, sipping coffee, and walked over to join him. "You're up early."

"They're early risers, these Amish folk." In the freshness of the morning, the weariness in his face was erased, and she saw only the kindness. He had always been kind.

"I'm a little surprised you let Tobe out of your sight for the morning. I figured you'd accompany him to church."

"Three hours in a sweltering barn, listening to preachers in a foreign tongue—I figured Tobe was pretty safe for the time being."

Geena grinned. "Well, then, want to go hiking? Then we can go to church."

"Hike? Church?" He looked at her as if she'd suggested

bird watching. "I suppose so." He tossed the rest of the coffee on the ground and set the mug on a fence post. He unfolded the stems of his sunglasses, the motion deliberate, and slipped them on. They walked side by side for a few hundred yards until they reached a part of the trail that required single file. He let her take the lead. "I was watching you yesterday. You have a real gift for ministry."

"I miss it," she said honestly.

"So why aren't you . . . ," he paused, searching for the right word, "ministering?"

"It's a long story."

"I have time."

She picked up her pace. "From what I remember, you were always too busy with work to listen."

"From what I remember, you were always talking to other people, not to me."

She spun around, facing him off. "That's not fair. That's what being a good minister is all about. Being available to others."

His face became gentle. "I know that. And you were—you are a good minister."

The fight drained out of her. "And you were—are a good attorney."

"Truce?" He held out his hand to her.

She looked down at it, remembering how big and strong his hands were. Not the kind of hands that belonged to a pencil pusher. It was a hand she had loved once, a hand she had trusted. She reached out and shook it. "Truce."

They started up the hill again, Allen trailing behind Geena. "So you never married."

She shook her head. "I guess I'm married to my work." She glanced back. "I think I heard that you married."

"My wife's name was Alyssa. We were very happy."

Geena felt a strange swirl of jealousy. Where did *that* come from?

"Until she left me."

She stopped and made a sharp about-face. "I'm sorry, Allen." She truly was. Divorce was a terrible thing. "Do you have children?"

"One. A son. He's thirteen now."

"Do you see much of him?"

"I do. We share custody." He was huffing and puffing and his face was turning red. Clearly, the man didn't exercise much. "So why aren't you ministering right now?"

She went ahead of him to reach the top. "I told you. I have a few things to figure out right now," she tossed over her shoulder.

"So you're adrift? That doesn't sound like the Geena I remember."

At the top of the hill now, she ignored him and looked down over Eagle Hill. The pastoral scene took her breath away. She sat down on a rock and he fell beside her, breathing heavily. Slowly, she tipped her head back and let herself be drawn up, up, up into the bright morning sky, the endless and empty sky.

"A body could get lost up there if she isn't careful."

She ducked her head, suddenly shy, aware he was watching her. Down below, the sheep were grazing, milled in a bunch. Just then one of them startled at something, jumping stiff-legged and sideways, and landing with a loud bleat. It spooked the rest of them so they scattered in the pasture.

Geena and Allen laughed at the sight of the silly sheep, and their laughter—his mellow and deep, hers light and airy—wove together. A killdeer trilled sweetly and a chickadee burbled as the wind gently swayed the tops of the trees. "Isn't it lovely?" She turned to face him and caught the look on his face. He stared at her with such intensity that she could almost feel it, like a warm gust of breath on her face.

"You didn't answer my question, Geena. Why are you drifting?"

Hmmm . . . she thought. *Only you would ask that question*. "Allen, are you ever *not* a lawyer?"

He laughed, eyes crinkling at the corners. "Funny you should ask. I'm giving some thought to leaving the SEC. My son needs more of my time. He's a good kid, but when you're thirteen . . ."

"The world revolves around your friends."

"That's true. Exactly right. You always did have a knack for understanding kids."

"You get a lot of experience when you're in youth ministry." She stretched her legs out and put one ankle on top of the other. "So what will you do if you're not an SEC lawyer?"

"Not sure yet. I need to finish up this last case involving Schrock Investments."

"This case seems awfully important to you."

"It is." His gaze shifted down to the quiet farmhouse. "A number of innocent people have been hurt. I'm going to see this through."

She stared at his profile, a face that she had once memorized. "It seems more than that. It seems . . . like there's something personal for you in this case."

He kept his gaze on the sheep, far below them, as if watching them eat was the most fascinating thing in the world. "Anything personal would be a conflict of interest."

Now *that* sounded like the Allen she knew. He loved the law like she loved the church. But something about the determination in his voice seemed a little unusual to her. "Unless the SEC wasn't aware of why it was so personal to you."

He turned abruptly back to her, lifting his eyebrows in surprise. "So, Geena . . . you never answered a question I have tried to ask you several times and still am waiting for the answer. Why are you hiding on an Amish farm?"

Ah, changing the subject. A diversion tactic. "I'm not . . . hiding. I'm just taking a breather."

"Yesterday, you were really in your element."

"What do you mean?"

"You were just tireless, and everybody looked to you for help and advice."

"It's funny how a day like yesterday just"—she made a circle in front of her heart—"pulls me in. Everybody working together for a common good. A day like yesterday makes me feel like I'm a much better version of myself." Before she could stop them, words came pouring out of her mouth. "But I love being a youth pastor. I love working for a church, being part of a whole." Below, the wooly sheep had moved under the canopy of a weeping willow. "I love church, period."

"So why aren't you working?"

She sighed. He wasn't going to let this go. So like the Allen she remembered. "My church fired me. They felt I didn't have the preaching skills, not enough charisma, to match their plans for growth and development. They hired me with expectations to triple the size of the youth group within a year's time." She tossed a pebble against a tree. "Obviously, it didn't."

He wiped his forehead and neck with his handkerchief. "Sounds more like a business plan."

She laughed softly. "Sometimes, it did seem that way."

"So you're 'in between' youth pastoring."

"I miss my work," she said. "I don't know who I am without it."

"Do you have any plans?"

"Not yet." She spoke her own truth. "I have absolutely no idea of where I'll go next. Or what I'll do."

"You say that like it's a bad thing."

"Well, it is. And please don't give me any platitudes. You know it's a difficult question."

"It is that and I don't have the answer for you."

She closed her eyes. "I have to figure this out."

"Yup, you do."

"It's just that . . . I do feel called to be a youth minister."

"Yeah, sure, I understand that. But not called to be perfect."

12

Bethany would never have agreed to go to the singing had Tobe not pleaded with her. He just wanted an excuse to shake off Allen Turner for the evening. She was in no mood to listen to girls' silly chatter and she still was on the fence about going home with Jimmy Fisher. It wasn't that she didn't think he was something special, but that he thought he was something special, and so did most every girl in Stoney Ridge.

Yesterday, she nearly allowed herself to be swept away by Jimmy Fisher's considerable charms. His leadership at the work frolic was impressive—many commented on it. Somehow, in his lighthearted way, he had the whole thing organized like a well-run clock. Yes, she was nearly caught under his spell, but stopped herself just in time. One thing for sure, she wasn't in the market for a boyfriend. Not now, maybe not ever again.

Tobe hitched up the buggy and then hurried next door to get Naomi while Bethany waited in the backseat. As Tobe and Naomi crossed the yard, Bethany was startled by how comfortable they were with each other—heads close together, laughing over something.

Then Naomi remembered Bethany as they reached the buggy, glanced at her, and did a double take. "What's wrong?"

"Why does everybody keep asking me that?" Bethany said, sounding a little more snappish than she intended to.

Naomi looked concerned. "You have dark circles under your eyes."

"Nothing is wrong. I'm just tired."

Tobe and Naomi exchanged a glance. "She's been touchy all day," Tobe said.

Bethany shrugged. "It's the heat. It's getting to me."

"Oh, I can understand that," Naomi said. "This morning I took a stick of butter out of the fridge and it melted on the way to the countertop."

Bethany relaxed. Naomi was a good friend.

It wasn't the heat that was bothering Bethany. She had woken in the night with her heart racing like a drum, gasping for breath. In her dream, she was under water, down, down, down, bubbles coming up all around her. And then there were two hands hauling her up out of the water. She was shivering violently, crying. Crying. Someone held her against her chest. Someone in blue. "I've got you. I've got you. Don't be afraid. You're safe."

She couldn't fall back to sleep for hours. What was happening to her?

She headed to the barn where the singing would take place and where the girls had already gathered, expecting Naomi to follow her. At the barn door, she turned back and saw Naomi and Tobe, still standing by the buggy. Naomi was laughing at something Tobe had said, looking all bright and sparkly as she gazed at him. *Oh Naomi,* Bethany thought, feeling sorry for her gentle friend. *Be careful. I love my brother dearly but he'll just break your heart. That's what men do best.*

In the cool of the barn, Bethany sat at the end of a long table on the girls' side. On the boys' side, she was surprised to see Danny Riehl, Mim's friend, laughing with the other boys and having himself a grand time. She asked the girl sitting next to her why Danny was here and was told he had just turned sixteen. Old enough to attend youth groups.

If Mim knew Danny were here, having so much fun without her, it would make her sad. Mim tried so hard to hide her interest in Danny Riehl. Bethany knew, though. Where had Mim's sudden passion for astronomy come from? It didn't take a genius to put two and two together. But she kept Mim's secret and didn't tell Rose about the stargazing on moonless nights. She might not be the most patient and understanding sister, but who was she to point fingers about boyfriends?

She wondered if she should tell Mim that Danny was here. After giving it some thought, she decided to leave it alone. After all, Danny wasn't doing anything wrong. But he sure was having a good time. He sure was.

Someone announced the first song and everyone started to sing. Now this—*this* was worth coming for. The sounds of harmony were pure heaven to Bethany. In church, they only sang the old hymns, slow and sad, in one voice, no harmony lest any one stand out. But at singings, they could sing different parts and Bethany loved it.

She watched as the girls passed around a glass or two of water, filled from the pitcher that stood in the middle of the long table. On the other side, the boys also had some water glasses to share. A little later they passed a saltshaker around the table. Anyone who was beginning to get hoarse from singing sprinkled a little into the palm of his hand and licked it, like a cow at a salt lick. The first time Bethany had seen that, she thought it was disgusting. Now, it seemed perfectly normal.

Two hours of hymn singing later, one of the boys announced the closing hymn and Bethany realized she had forgotten to tell Tobe they needed to leave right away. Jimmy had glanced at her once or twice and wiggled those dark eyebrows, but she tried to ignore him. She didn't want to give him any reason to think he had her in his pocket. That would have been the worst thing for a boy like Jimmy. He was already far too self-confident.

Where was Tobe, anyway? In fact, where was Naomi?

During the closing hymn, she slipped out of the barn. Tobe and Naomi and the buggy were gone. *Shootfire!*

Bethany knew she could wait for Jimmy to give her a ride home, but she decided against it. She kept her chin tucked to her chest and walked down the driveway quickly, hoping no one would notice she had left.

She almost made it.

"Hey! Hey, Bethany!" Jimmy called to her from the top of the long driveway.

For a moment, Bethany thought about breaking into a run, pretending she hadn't heard him, but then she thought twice. That was a pretty stupid plan. She took a deep breath, let it out, and reminded herself that she was not interested in getting tangled up with another charming fellow. Why was she always falling for the wrong type? Surely something was seriously wrong with her. She would not encourage him, but she could be friendly without being friends. It was just a matter of being polite and keeping her distance.

She pasted a smile on her face and turned around. "Hi, Jimmy."

He was puffing. He'd run down the driveway to catch her. "I thought I was going to give you a ride home. What do you say?"

"Some other time. I just want to be alone tonight." That was sort of true. With everything that was on her mind lately, she wasn't good company. "Jimmy—you and me—I just don't think it would be a good idea."

That part was the absolute truth.

"Look at me, Bethany."

She lifted her head.

"I know you think I'm just playing. But I'm playing for keeps."

And then Jimmy was gone, striding away from her and toward the buggy. The cant of his shoulders made Bethany feel suddenly cold, as if summer had turned to winter in the blink of an eye, though it was a humid and sticky evening. She took in everything as he swung onto the seat: his muscled forearms clutching the reins, his cheeks, clean-shaven in the morning, now shadowed, his gaze, set resolutely ahead. He drove the buggy right up to her. "Hop in."

Shootfire! There he goes, telling me what to do again. Just as she was feeling a little softhearted toward him, he went and ruined it all.

"Bethany, Eagle Hill is over five miles away and your brother left with Naomi hours ago."

"Well, fine," she said as she let him help her up. "But this doesn't mean a thing, Jimmy Fisher."

He slapped the horse's reins to get it moving. The horse snorted and broke into a trot. The buggy creaked and rumbled and clattered over the wooden bridge that spanned a small creek at the bottom of the driveway. Tenderly, Jimmy nudged her shoulder. "You okay?"

She looked up at the brilliant stars in the moonless sky. "I'm fine. Never better."

They weren't far down the road when he pulled up on the reins and turned the buggy to the side of the road. "You want to tell me what's bothering you lately?"

She turned toward him. "What makes you think something's bothering me?"

"Let's see . . . you're jumpier than usual, prickly as a cactus pear, you look like you haven't had a good night's sleep in a while—"

"Enough. I get your point." Why did he have to be so good-looking? She was touched by his concern, despite herself. Bethany hesitated. "Look, Jimmy, there's a lot on my mind right now and I need to get a few things figured out."

"Like what?"

"You wouldn't understand. It's not the kind of thing you're accustomed to."

"There you go again. Thinking that I'm just a one-trick pony. Try me, Bethany. I'd like to help you, even though you're too stubborn to accept it." Jimmy reached out to touch her hand and she nearly jumped out the window.

He turned in the seat. "When are you going to realize how much I care about you?"

"Me and everyone else in Stoney Ridge who wears a dress. Naomi says you go through girls like potato chips."

"She said that? How insulting." Though he didn't seem a bit insulted.

She looked out the window. "The last time I let someone affect me . . . well . . . it was . . . Jake Hertzler."

Jimmy groaned. "I thought he was ancient history."

"He is." She glanced at him. "I'm not the right one for you, Jimmy."

He crossed his arms over his chest defensively. "Wow. That's a pretty smooth brush-off. What comes next? Are you going to tell me you just want to be friends? I'm not playing games with you, Bethany. Maybe you're the one playing games."

She wasn't going to take that from anybody. She stood her ground. "That's not fair, Jimmy. You've done a lot for me, but I never asked you for anything. I've been trying to keep our relationship friendly rather than romantic."

"I see," he said sharply. "Well, you can go on pretending there's no spark between us, but we both know it isn't true. Challenges don't scare me. They just make me more determined." Their gazes met and lingered, then parted. He gathered up the reins and started them on their way again. Finally, in a kinder voice, he said, "Bethany, whatever it is that's troubling you, just remember you're a lot stronger than you think you are. Whenever you figure things out, I'll be here, waiting for you. I'm not going anywhere. Not going after anyone else, either." He grinned in that slow, charming way that made her heart pound. "I don't even like potato chips."

Despite herself, as Naomi watched Tobe drive the buggy away, her heart swelled with hope. Maybe, just maybe, her dream was going to come true.

It was a dream that began years ago, when Naomi was eight and Tobe was twelve. He and Bethany had spent a few weeks of the summer visiting their grandmother and the three of them played together each day, as soon as their chores were done. They rode ponies over to Blue Lake Pond, picnicked on the shore, hiked up in the hills. Those summer visits were happy memories for Naomi.

But it was three summers later that things drastically changed between Naomi and Tobe—at least the way she felt about him. Her mother had died during the winter. Just when school was out for the year, her father had been badly hurt in an accident with a horse. He lingered for over a week, then died suddenly of complications. Everyone had treated Naomi with kid gloves, assuring her that her father would be all right, that he would rally.

All but Tobe.

She had asked him if he thought her father would survive and he had said no, he didn't think so. He said he hoped he was wrong, but to get prepared, just in case. It was the day of her father's funeral that Naomi experienced her first migraine. She couldn't even attend the service for her father. She remained in her darkened bedroom, with curtains drawn because the light hurt her eyes so much.

Tobe shimmied up the rose trellis and onto the roof and knocked on her window to keep her company while the service was going on. He sat on the floor, back against the wall, and read to her, using a small flashlight to see by. The sound of his soothing, calm voice eased the pounding in her head. By the time the worst of the headache had passed, Naomi was thoroughly smitten.

By the age of fourteen, she was crazy about Tobe.

By sixteen, she was head over heels in love. Loving Tobe was as familiar to her as breathing.

But Tobe Schrock had a reputation, even as a teenager, even though he only came to Stoney Ridge in the summers when he visited his grandmother. Naomi wasn't sure how much of his reputation was deserved and how much was inflated, but all her friends warned each other about falling for Tobe Schrock. He was too good-looking, they said. He was unreliable. Lazy as a man could be, her brother Galen often noted. So Naomi kept silent her feelings for Tobe, but she soaked up every mention of his name over at Eagle Hill. His absence hurt her the way it did Rose and Vera and Bethany, so much so that she tried to talk herself out of love with him. She told herself he would never return.

Until this week, when he did return.

Seeing him in the kitchen of Eagle Hill that first night, looking and acting like he'd never left, ruined her resolve to stop loving him. Instead, images rolled in her mind, unsummoned, memories of growing up together. She knew every inch of that beautiful face, the scar across his left cheekbone that he'd received when he and a friend were skipping rocks at Blue Lake Pond and his friend threw a wild pitch that hit Tobe in the face. The heavy dark brows that could signal wrath or disapproval or amusement with the slightest shifts; the prominent eyetooth.

A young Tobe running through the privet, calling for her to come out. Tobe as he grew into a young man, broad shouldered and handsome. Tobe leaning against a wall, watching Naomi struggle to fasten the shafts to the buggy, muscled arms crossed over his chest, wanting to help but holding back because he knew she wanted to do it herself; of Tobe laughing, and frowning, and listening, and telling her the truth no matter what, and the way she felt when he entered a room. She could never stop smiling whenever Tobe was around, though she knew she didn't have the same effect on him.

Until this time, coming home, when Tobe smiled back at Naomi. For the last few days, he courted her carefully, cautious to avoid Galen. She had quietly followed him up to Blue Lake Pond one afternoon, stumbling on him sitting on a log as if she was always at the pond in the afternoon. He invited her to sit down. It was awkward at first, but soon they started to talk and talk and talk. Later that night, long after midnight, he had tossed pebbles at her window until she went to see what was making that noise. She thought it was a bird and was shocked to see Tobe down below, waving to her to join him. "Come on down," he whispered. She had never dressed so quickly in her life.

Each night after that first one, Tobe would toss pebbles at her window and Naomi would hurry down. They walked in the moonlight, up the ridge, to connect to a shortcut to Blue Lake Pond that only he knew about.

Tonight was one of those nights bright with untold numbers of stars. After Bethany left to go to the barn for the singing, Tobe quietly asked Naomi if she would mind skipping the singing and go for a ride. She jumped back in the buggy, quick as a whip, before he could change his mind. They drove to Blue Lake Pond and sat on their favorite log. It was a windless night and the water was so still and calm it looked like a mirror, reflecting the stars.

Naomi stared at it so long that Tobe asked what she was thinking. "The stars are almost like a pattern," she said, pointing to the water. "Can you see it? I'm wondering if I could design a quilt top to match it."

Tobe smiled. "Why do you like to quilt so much?"

It was a question no one had ever asked her before and yet it was such an important one. "To me," she said, "piecing a quilt top seems to be evidence of how God works in this world."

He tilted his head at her in that adorable way he had, his way of encouraging her to keep talking.

"I take all these scraps and leftovers and odds and ends, and turn them into something beautiful. Something useful and purposeful. It just seems like that's what God is always doing, all around us. Taking our jumble of mess and transforming it into something wondrous."

Tobe stared at her for a long, long time. And then he started to confide in her all he knew about Schrock Investments and all he had seen and heard. Every detail.

She listened carefully, trying to understand, careful not to judge, though she felt shocked by what he revealed. His eyes were so weary, so sad. Eyes too old for such a young face. Naomi's heart broke for him.

"I'm leaving in the morning with the SEC lawyer," he said after he finished the long, sad tale. "I don't know what's ahead for me."

The news of Tobe's departure wasn't a surprise for Naomi. Bethany had told her Monday was the day and

Naomi had tried to push it out of her mind. Tried not to think of having to say goodbye to him again.

He took her hands in his. "Naomi . . . I know I'm not much of a catch."

"You're the only catch I want," Naomi said eagerly and Tobe grinned in that boyish way he had. Then he reached out and drew her close to him, and kissed her. Tobe's lips were soft, but his kiss was hard, slow, almost lazy, and so assured. His arms rested at steep angles across the small of her back and the blades of her shoulders.

She melted into the circle of his arms, leaning in, lifting up, softening her mouth. For a few sweet moments, everything felt right to forget and safe to remember.

It was her very first kiss and it was perfect. Absolutely perfect.

◊

On Sunday evening, Geena was finishing up a book an elder from her church had given to her: *Help! I've Been Asked to Preach. Don't Panic: Practical Help to Keep Your Sermon from Sinking* by Maylan Schurch. She took notes as she read, wondering if the elder thought her sermons sank or stank. A knock on the door interrupted her. "Come in."

Rose popped her head in. "Do you have a moment?"

Geena happily put away the book. "I do. Please come in."

"Do you need anything? Towels, fresh sheets, extra shampoo or toothpaste?"

"No. You've provided everything I could possibly use."

Rose held her hands behind her. She seemed ill at ease, as if she had something to say but didn't know how to say it. "It looks as if the heat wave is going to break by Tuesday."

"Oh. Oh!" Now Geena realized what Rose was trying to say. "Your reservations! I'll leave, then."

"Actually, I have a favor to ask. I'm going to Philadelphia tomorrow with Tobe and my mother-in-law. We're not really sure how long we'll be gone."

Geena was well aware that everyone was leaving in the morning. She and Allen had spent all of Sunday together, hiking, church, a brunch afterward, wandering through the small towns and shopping, then dinner together because Tobe went to a church youth gathering. Before Allen said goodbye, he asked her what she might say if he were to call her sometime. Maybe to go out for dinner. "That would depend," she told him, "on how much you can help Tobe Schrock stay out of jail."

"I'll do all I can," Allen had promised. "He's not the one we're after. I want Jake Hertzler."

There it was again. The feeling she got that there was something personal about this case for Allen. "Still," Geena said. "Promise me you'll keep Tobe out of jail."

But Allen wouldn't promise. He did say he would do his best, and if she happened upon any information that might prove useful, please call him. He gave her his business card and kissed her on the cheek. When had she last been kissed on her cheek by a man who wasn't a senior citizen? Years and years and years. It was, she couldn't deny, very nice.

But none of that pertained to Rose Schrock, standing in the middle of the guest flat living room, looking embarrassed. "Geena, I wondered . . . if you're not in a hurry to return . . ."

"I'm not."

Rose glanced up at her, a shy look on her face. "Would you be willing to move into the house and stay with my daughters? Just in case they needed extra help with the boys while they're working and managing the new guests?"

Geena was pleased to be asked. Grateful, too. She wasn't ready to go back to Philadelphia to officially start job hunting. She knew it was waiting for her and she dreaded it. "Consider it done. I'm glad that you feel comfortable asking me."

"Well, I have a confession to make. We're going to be staying at the home of someone who was our first guest at the inn. She has become a good friend. Her name is Delia Stoltz."

"Aha. Now I see." Delia Stoltz attended Geena's church. Her husband, Dr. Charles Stoltz, was new to church attendance but very vocal about his feelings that Geena should be replaced with someone who was a more dynamic preacher. "So, you're probably aware that I was fired."

Rose nodded.

"Don't feel badly. It's not a secret. I told Bethany about it." Geena grinned. "But now you can understand why I have a surfeit of spare time."

"I certainly wouldn't charge you for staying at the house. You'd be doing me a favor."

"I'm happy to be of help, Rose. In fact, I couldn't be more delighted. It's been good for me to be here."

Rose looked at the title of the book on the kitchen table. "Delia mentioned that the problem wasn't with your pastor's heart, it was with your preaching."

"That's about right." Geena rubbed her forehead. "I try so hard to preach well. I try to be just like my father—that's what everyone expects. My father is a wonderful minister. I've been trained by the very best. I prepare detailed notes and put in hours of research . . . and still, something in the delivery goes badly. I bore myself!"

Rose picked up the book and flipped through it. "I don't know much about being a minister, but one thing our preachers don't do is to use notes. They let God's Spirit guide them."

"No notes? None at all? That would have given heart attacks to my seminary professors. Sermon preparation was a major focus. It even has a fancy name: *homiletics*." She pressed her palms together. "They trained us to deliver a nice, tight sermon. Tight. Sixteen minutes long would earn you an A. Studies have found that's the attention span of the congregation."

Rose looked confused. "But how can God's Spirit lead when a minister has it all planned out?"

Geena hadn't thought of it that way. "But don't your ministers ramble and go off on bunny trails?"

"Some do. Some are long winded. But some get right to the point. Those are the ones you can tell have forgotten about themselves—they're just trying to share the word of the Lord because they love it so much. They talk from the heart." She put the book back on the table.

"Maybe . . . you shouldn't try to preach like your father. Maybe you should just try to be yourself." She threw her hands up in the air. "Listen to me! What do I know about preaching?" She shook her head. "Thank you for your help this week. I'm glad you came to Eagle Hill, Geena. You've been a blessing to us."

13

On Monday morning, Bethany made pancakes for Sammy and Luke while Rose finished packing for the trip to Philadelphia. Allen Turner stood patiently by the open trunk of his car, waiting for suitcases to appear. Mammi Vera stood beside the car, frowning at Allen Turner, standing vigil. She didn't like him or trust him, but that was only because she thought he was creating trouble for Tobe. She couldn't understand that he was trying to help him.

Rose was bustling around the kitchen, giving Bethany and Mim last-minute instructions for the inn.

"We'll be fine, Rose," Bethany said. "Besides, as long as this heat wave continues, we're not going to get any new guests."

"The weather is supposed to cool down," Rose said. "I told Geena she could move into the house while I'm away if she'd like to stay longer."

"Mammi Vera did not like hearing that!" Mim said,

grinning. "She said Mom is turning Eagle Hill into a boardinghouse."

"Allen Turner paid us for staying for the weekend," Rose said, scribbling down some instructions on a piece of paper. "He insisted." She glanced at Bethany, then stopped writing and straightened up, looking at Bethany for a long moment. "You look exhausted. Didn't you sleep well?"

"Better not ask her that," Luke said. "I told her she looked terrible and she snapped my head off."

Bethany frowned at her brother. "I'm ready for this heat wave to break."

Rose nodded. "It's supposed to rain Tuesday or Wednesday. Here's the phone number to reach me at Delia Stoltz's. Leave a message and I'll call back." She put down the pencil and looked out the window. Tobe had returned from saying goodbye to Naomi, escorted by Galen, and went to wait by the car.

Galen came into the kitchen to say goodbye. "Better get going, Rose, if you want to beat traffic." He looked at the boys wolfing down pancakes at the kitchen table. "You two, finish up with breakfast. I've got some fence repairing that's waiting on you."

The boys let out a whoop. Luke and Sammy were always glad to have something to do that involved hammering and making noise. Luke rolled up the last pancake, shoved it into his shirt pocket, and shot out the door so fast he made Bethany blink. Sammy followed, a little slower.

Rose smiled as she watched the boys run through the privet to Galen's. She turned back to Bethany and Mim.

"Listen, girls, we'll try to get back to Eagle Hill as soon as we know what's going to happen to Tobe."

"Mom, do you think he'll have to go to jail?" Mim asked.

Bethany saw Rose and Galen's eyes meet over Mim's head. Rose's eyes said, *This is so complicated. How do I answer?*

Galen stepped in. "Tobe says he's telling the truth. He's confessing to any wrong he might have done. The rest is in God's hands. God's good hands."

Rose shot him a grateful look.

It was strange, that wordless communication between a man and a woman who loved each other, the silent signal of caring, the way they checked in with each other. Would Bethany ever have *that* with someone? Or was she destined to make terrible choices? Like her father did. Like Tobe still was. Maybe it was a Schrock family trait. Fixed.

A few minutes later, Bethany and Mim waved to everyone in the car as it drove down the driveway. Galen went back to his farm. Watching the car turn onto the road, Bethany stroked Chase's thick fur, trying to stamp down the worry she felt over Tobe.

"Bethany? Are you listening to me?"

She startled. She hadn't even realized Mim was still beside her. "What?"

"I said I'm going to be up in my room working on my Mrs. Miracle column. It's due for Tuesday's edition and I'm way behind because of the community garden work. You can still drop it by the newspaper office, can't you?"

"Yes, sure, I'll take care of it. By the way, I'll be gone tomorrow."

"Where are you going? I thought you had to work at the Sisters' House."

"They canceled me for tomorrow—they have the Sisters' Bee at Edith Fisher's and it makes them nervous when I'm working in the house and they're not around to supervise."

"I thought Naomi wanted you to join that quilting bee."

"I haven't decided yet. Besides, I'm going on an errand with Geena tomorrow." She hadn't actually asked Geena yet, but she was hoping it would be all right. "I'll be gone most of the day. You'll be okay, won't you?"

Mim looked a little worried. "All day? Watching Luke and Sammy all day long?" She scrunched up her face. "*Luke?* All day long? He doesn't pay me any mind."

"Galen and Jimmy can be in charge of those two." She frowned. "Don't you have a column to write?"

Mim ran up the porch steps and disappeared through the kitchen door.

Chase nudged Bethany's hand, then stood there staring up at her with a worried look in his big round eyes. She bent down to rub his ears, his favorite thing. "Try not to fret, old pal. Tobe will be home soon." But she wasn't sure of that at all. She chewed on her lip, thinking. What if Jake went free and Tobe ended up in jail? Wouldn't that just beat all?

Again the thought of Jake Hertzler filled Bethany with such a huge prickling of red spikes that she almost couldn't catch her breath. She still couldn't get her head around the news that he had stolen money from her father's company. How could he *do* such awful things? Her family had been good to him. Anger added to anger.

It seemed to Bethany that a chain of actions, of people offering trust to Jake without expecting him to earn it, had resulted in the trouble they were facing. She should never have introduced Jake to her father . . . her father should not have given Jake access to so much of Schrock Investments before he knew him well—he had left the cat to guard the cream. Tobe shouldn't have accepted Jake's rationale about the diminishing money at the bank when he sensed something wasn't adding up. Jimmy Fisher should never have trusted Jake so easily when buying a horse from him . . . and of course she was at fault for falling prey to Jake's charms. The start of it all was Jake Hertzler.

All her life, Bethany was taught to love her enemies. Jake had become her first true enemy. How could she forgive him? It wasn't over—Jake kept on hurting the people she loved. She hated him, even though she knew she wasn't supposed to hate, that it was a sin. And she hated herself for harboring such darkness.

Standing there with the morning sun pouring down hard on her head, Bethany had half a mind to stomp to the phone shanty and call him. Why not? Why shouldn't she? She would! She would call him and tell him just what she thought of him.

Hands shaking, she dialed the number for Jake's cell.

As she waited to see if the number still worked, if it would connect, the first wave of doubt floated along. Maybe it wasn't smart to call Jake and tell him off. Maybe she should hang up. *Tell him off. Don't tell him off.* Back and forth she went, a battle between anger and good sense.

But the call connected and clicked right over to voice

mail. She took a deep breath and banished those niggling doubts. "Jake, this is Bethany. Bethany Schrock. My brother Tobe came home. He told us what you did to my father. To all of us. He said you were trying to frame him by giving those books I found for you to that SEC lawyer."

She felt a surge of fresh anger, invigorating anger. "How *could* you? How could you be so cruel to people who trusted you? My father, my brother, all the investors—and then Jimmy Fisher and that horse." She was on a roll. It felt good to tell Jake just how she felt. She never had before. It felt so good! "You're not going to get away with this, Jake. It's catching up with you, but fast. People like you think they can do anything to Plain people because we won't defend ourselves. Well, you're wrong. Tobe's going now to tell that SEC lawyer everything you've done."

She stopped and sighed, the fight slipping away from her. "Shootfire! What's the point? I'm just wasting my time. You don't care about anybody but yourself." She slammed the phone down and marched out of the shanty. She was officially *done* with Jake Hertzler.

If Mim had more time, she would ponder what was going on with her sister lately. One minute Bethany was fine, the next minute she was distant and preoccupied, the next—she was stomping mad. But there was no sense in stewing over Bethany's mental state. At least not at this moment. Mim had to get her Mrs. Miracle column prepared for today's deadline. Just saying the word filled her with a secret delight. She had a deadline!

Under her bed, she kept a box of the Mrs. Miracle

columns that she cut from the *Stoney Ridge Times* newspaper. It wasn't easy to collect them because her family didn't subscribe to the newspaper. But . . . the sisters at the Sisters' House did. They loved to read, anything and everything. Whenever Mim was over at their house, she would tiptoe around the house, hunting for the latest edition of the newspaper—which was never in the same place twice—tear out Mrs. Miracle's column, fold it carefully, and tuck it into her dress pocket.

A few days ago, Ella came up behind her and caught her in the act. "Do you need scissors, dear?"

"Uh, no," Mim said, cheeks burning. "Just something I wanted from the paper. I didn't think you'd mind."

Ella was looking right at the Mrs. Miracle column in Mim's hand, *right* at it! Then she gazed at her for a long, long moment with an inscrutable look on her face. "Well," she said at last, "we are a reading household. Papa always wants us to have good reading material. But I don't suppose he'll miss one column."

How strange, Mim noticed, for Ella to talk as if her papa was nearby. He must have passed decades ago. Then the wave of guilt hit—Mim hadn't realized the sisters ever actually read the paper, only collected them, and she certainly never meant to lie to anyone, especially Ella. That, she decided right then and there, was the last time she would take the column from the sisters. She'd find another way to collect those columns. Maybe she could ask Bethany to get them from the receptionist at the newspaper.

In her bedroom, Mim pulled the manila envelope out from under her mattress and set the typewriter up on her desk. She dumped the letters on her bed.

Dear Mrs. Miracle,

I have been happily married to "Phillip" for ten years. We have a nice-sized farm where we grow beets.

Last spring, a neighbor lady, recently divorced, asked if Phillip would teach her how to use a tractor. At the end of each day, Phillip goes over to give her tractor lessons. It has been three months and he is still teaching her to drive a tractor. Each time I mention that the neighbor lady has had enough time to learn how to drive the tractor without help, he says she is a slow learner. He comes home late and is very tired. I am starting to feel suspicious that more is going on than driving lessons.

Gratefully,
Beet Farmer's Wife

Dear Beet Farmer's Wife,

If your neighbor lady hasn't learned how to drive a tractor by now, she should consider getting a horse. It would be much easier for her.

Sincerely,
Mrs. Miracle

Dear Mrs. Miracle,

Nancy and I have been best friends since we were girls. We've never kept secrets from each other. Recently, I found out that Nancy's husband, who is a dentist, is having an affair with his dental hygienist. Should I tell Nancy? Is it ever wrong to keep a secret?

Signed,
Wringing My Hands

Dear Wringing,

Would you want Nancy to tell you if she knew your husband were having an affair?

Sincerely,
Mrs. Miracle

Mim was particularly proud of that answer. It was inspired! She had no experience with marriage or affairs and didn't want to mislead anyone. This answer put responsibility for the decision back on Wringing. Yes, that was an ideal answer, and she felt it would prove beneficial to her many readers. She always tried to choose letters for the newspaper column that many readers could relate to.

She opened another letter to read:

Dear Mrs. Miracle,

I thought I had something special with my girlfriend, but then she broke up with me.

I stayed in bed. I fought with friends who meant well. Once, I got into a fist fight that I knew I would lose just so I could feel a different type of pain, but nothing hurt more than my broken heart. It's been seven months and I still have not moved on. I think I'm ready. I finally shaved. But my heart still races with anxiety when I think of losing my girlfriend. I mean, I was really in love.

Just Wondering What to Do Next

Mim felt stupefied by the letters about broken hearts. She thought she understood love—after all, she loved Danny Riehl and planned to marry him one day—but she did not understand what brokenheartedness felt like and she hoped she never would. It sounded awful. It sounded like a person's heart had been ripped open, without anesthesia, and was bleeding inside his chest. Mim couldn't imagine how dreadful it would be to have a truly broken heart. She set Just Wondering's letter aside, unsure of how to answer.

She read through the stack of letters from last week's pouch and placed them into piles on her bed: Answer, Don't Answer, and I Have No Idea How to Answer.

She almost missed a small envelope at the bottom of the pile. It was from Stuck.

Dear Mrs. Miracle,

Sometimes I feel like leaky dynamite—just waiting for the spark to make it explode.

Yours truly,
Stuck

Mim leaned back against her bedframe, holding the letter in her hand. How in the world should Mrs. Miracle handle *that*?

14

Early Tuesday morning, Bethany wiped her feet on the mat before stepping into the guest flat's bright living room. It was hard to believe this was the same dreary space, filled with old junk, that it was a few months ago. Rose had transformed it and she'd done it on a shoestring budget. Now it was a cheerful space with buttery yellow painted walls, white woodwork, a large window that let in bright light. The window overlooked Rose's flower garden near the barn. The transformation was amazing. The guest flat was much cooler, too, than the house above it. "Geena?"

"In here!" Geena was in the bedroom, packing up. "You're just in time to give me a hand. I thought I'd move my things up to the house so I can clean the guest flat when we get back later today."

"You don't have to clean anything," Bethany said. "You're our guest. Mim and I have it down to a routine." She plumped a pillow. "Besides, if the heat wave doesn't break, I'm sure those folks will cancel."

"Supposed to rain tomorrow." Geena looked around the room and grabbed her purse. "Well? Ready to go meet your mother?"

Bethany took a deep breath. "As ready as I'll ever be."

An hour or so later, they were driving into Hagensburg. "At the next street make a right onto the bridge," droned the GPS in Geena's car.

"Almost there," Geena said.

This might be a huge mistake, Bethany realized. Over the years she had learned to live with her mother's abandonment. Why did it need to change now?

Bethany felt her stomach lurch. Coming here had been a bad idea. A really bad idea. And she found herself simply wishing she could talk to . . . not to Geena, not to Rose, but to Jimmy Fisher.

Where had that idea come from? Why would she feel a longing for the counsel of Jimmy Fisher, of all people? What might he say to a complicated situation like this, anyway? What could he possibly know?

A ridiculous notion! But she could almost hear his voice: *You've gone this far, Bethany. Don't lose courage now. You need to get your answers if you're ever going to get through this gray stretch in your life.*

The car stopped in front of an old but cared-for house with wooden ramps leading up to the front door. Bethany took in a deep breath. This was it. This was where her mother was. An eerie sense of something lost moved through her chest, cold and hollow.

Geena turned off the ignition. "Let's go get your answers."

They pressed a doorbell button and waited until someone came to the door. An older woman, skin like chocolate and hair like a salt-and-pepper Brillo pad, looked Bethany up and down as if she recognized her.

"We're here to see Mary Schrock," Geena said at last. "She might go by the name of Mary Miller."

The woman was still eyeing Bethany. "Didn't expect you folks till the end of July."

Bethany was confused. "I've never been here before."

Now the woman looked confused. "Who are you?"

"I'm Mary's daughter. I'd like to meet her."

The woman rolled her eyes and sighed. "Oh Lawd—jez like that boy that come 'round here awhile back."

"My brother, Tobe."

"Child, whatever you're looking for, you ain't gonna find it in your mama."

Shootfire! Everywhere Bethany went, she hit the same brick wall. Everybody thought they knew what was best for her. "I'd like to decide that for myself."

Geena put a calming hand on her shoulder. "Ma'am, this is Bethany Schrock. She'd just like the chance to meet her mother. That's all. Seems like a daughter should be able to meet her mother."

The woman fixed her gaze at Geena, as if she'd just noticed her. "And who are you?"

"I'm the Reverend Spencer. A friend of the family's."

Something changed instantly in the woman as soon as she learned Geena was a minister. It was like a free pass. She opened the door wide. "Mary's in her room."

Bethany and Geena followed behind the woman. They went through a room where a few elderly women sat on the couch, watching television. Only one noticed Geena and Bethany and stared at them.

"Mind if I ask," Geena said, "what kind of home is this?"

The woman stopped and turned toward Geena. "It's a home for ladies with mental health issues."

"What kind of mental health issues?"

"Bipolar, manic depressive, clinical depression, psychotic, schizophrenia, paranoia—"

"So my mother runs this home?"

The woman looked at Bethany as if she had a loose bolt. "Say what?"

"I thought you were taking us to her office."

The woman's face softened in understanding. "Oh, baby. No, no, no, no, no. She ain't running the place. She's a patient. She's been here for a long, long time. Longer than I've been here."

Everything went upside down. A funny tingling feeling traveled through Bethany, starting with her toes. By the time it reached her head, she felt she might faint. The room started to spin and she dipped lower, as if her knees might give way, but Geena grasped her around the shoulders.

"Are you okay?" she whispered.

Bethany nodded. She had to be strong. She just had to. She took a deep breath. In, out.

Geena turned to the woman, still holding Bethany's shoulders. "Why is Mary here?"

The woman's back went up. " 'Cuz it's better than an institution. We try to make it homelike. Most of the staffers have been here for years and years. They know all these patients. They treat them like family."

"I meant . . . what's the diagnosis?"

"I can't tell you that."

Geena held her gaze.

"It's them stupid HIPAA laws." The woman pressed her lips together. "I could lose my job."

"Please," Bethany whispered.

The woman looked at Geena. "You really a preacher? You ain't wearing a collar. You don't look much like a holy roller."

"I can assure you . . . I am an ordained minister."

The woman hesitated, wavering. She turned to Bethany. "Your mother is a chronic schizophrenic."

"What is that?" Bethany asked, confused. "I don't know what that means."

"Her brain is sick, baby."

"It's a mental disorder that makes it hard for the patient to tell the difference between what's real and what isn't," Geena said.

"I don't understand," Bethany said, her voice gravelly and dry. "How does someone get schiz . . . schizo . . ."

"Schizophrenia," Geena finished.

"Was my mother born that way? Had she always been sick?"

The caregiver glanced up and down the hall, then lowered her voice. "From what I heard about your mama, it started with acute schizophrenia when she was in her late teens, then it went on to chronic schizophrenia. She's on some heavy antipsychotic meds. They help her with her hallucinations, long as she stays on it—and she can be tricky that way—but even on her best days, she can't take care of herself and she can't live on her own." She started walking down the hall again and stopped in front of a door. "Baby, you look awful pale. Why do you want to do this?"

Bethany followed behind her. "I need to."

"You sure you're up for this?"

Bethany closed her eyes. Was she? She heard Jimmy's voice: *You've come this far. And you're stronger than you think.* "Yes."

The woman opened the door. "Mary, honey, you got some company."

Bethany hesitated before she stepped toward the open door. It was a small room with a single bed, a nightstand, and a chair in the corner next to the window. Curled up in the chair was a small woman, staring out the window, her long dark hair pulled back severely into a ponytail.

As Bethany crossed the room and stood beside the chair, she could feel her heart pounding. There was a salty, bitter taste in her mouth that she recognized as fear. Her gaze searched the woman's face, then went slowly over the rest of her. She was small boned and fine featured and her skin was so pale that Bethany could see the blue veins on the insides of her wrists. Eyes shaped like Tobe's—half moons with those thick lashes that Bethany had always envied—but these eyes seemed flat and empty.

Bethany groped for a thought, something she could say. How did a person introduce herself to the woman who gave her life? "My name is Bethany. Bethany Schrock." She enunciated each word slowly and carefully.

The woman—this was her mother!—blinked her eyes rapidly but looked at Bethany without recognition.

She tried to clear the gritty feeling out of her throat. "Do you remember me? I'm your girl. I'm Bethany. Your daughter." She reached out to touch her arm, but the woman flinched. "Tobe is my brother. Dean Schrock was my father. Your husband."

The woman clutched and unclutched her hands. The lines at the corners of her mouth pulled deeper.

Bethany crouched down so she was face-to-face with the woman. "I came because I wanted to see you." She tried to sound calm but couldn't quite keep the quiver out of her voice. "I've missed you. My whole life, I've missed you. I've never stopped missing you."

"No," her mother whimpered. She drew her legs up tight against her chest and started to rock back and forth, her arms tightly around her knees, her eyes squeezed shut.

Bethany noticed her hands. She held her hand up next to the woman's. "Look. Look how similar our hands are. Even the nails. Tobe always teases me that my hands are small. They're just like yours."

The woman responded by balling her hands into a fist and ducking her chin to her chest. "He said not to give it to anyone."

"Give what?" Bethany asked. "Who said such a thing to you?"

"No, no, no, no, no." Her whole body was so rigid it shook.

The caregiver stepped in and put a hand on Bethany's shoulder. "She's getting agitated. Maybe you need to come back another time, baby. This isn't a good day for her. Don't feel bad. Even before you came, I knew it wasn't a good day for her."

Bethany reached out a hand toward the woman's shoulder, then dropped it so it hung limply at her side. Slowly, she rose and walked toward Geena, waiting by the door, then turned back for a final look. The woman was sucking in great gasps of air, breathing, breathing, breathing frantically, as if she dared not stop even for an instant.

This was her mother. This was her *mother*!

Tobe was right. She should have left it alone. Once you know something, you can't unknow it.

Bethany turned and stumbled toward the door, fumbling for the tissue she had put in her dress pocket. She squeezed her eyes shut against the burn of tears, but they came anyway.

The caregiver told them to wait for her in the hallway while she tended to Mary. "Any doubt if she's actually your mother?" Geena asked. "There could be a mistake."

Bethany shook her head, splattering tears. "No doubt." Those eyes, that hair, even the shape of her fingernails. There was no mistaking the family resemblance. She dabbed at her eyes with the tissue, then lifted her head slowly and glanced upward. "All my life, I assumed my mother was living a grand life somewhere, happy to be rid of us, never giving us another thought. I never ever imagined her life to be . . . to be like . . . *that*."

The caregiver came out of the room and walked them to the front entrance.

"Can you tell me anything more?" Bethany asked. "How long has my mother been here?"

"Don't know. I started here about six years ago. All I know is that she's been here a long, long time, and her bills are paid for every month, right on time. That's all I know."

Geena tilted her head. "When we first arrived, you

said something about not expecting anyone until the last day of the month. What did you mean by that?"

"That's when the ladies come to visit her. Three or four of them, like clockwork. They pretty her hair and fuss over her. The last day of every month, rain or shine, unless it's a Sunday. Then they come on Monday."

"What made you think Bethany was part of that group?"

The caregiver looked Bethany up and down. "Well, because she's dressed the same—with them little bonnets."

"They're Amish?"

The caregiver nodded. "They sit and quilt with Mary. It's her best day. She's always real calm after they visit."

Bethany leaned forward. "Did you say they quilt?"

"Yes. They're a quilting group, they say. Call themselves the Sisters' Bee."

15

Jimmy," Naomi said, resting her forehead in her hand as she talked, "for the tenth time, I don't think you did anything wrong."

"But I told Bethany I'd take her home from the singing. She didn't say anything about having to leave early. I did end up giving her a ride, but she was mostly quiet. She's never quiet. Usually, she's complaining about my bad character. She even wore that lavender dress that I like so much. She looked beautiful. A little tired, though. Did you notice?"

"I did." Naomi sighed. Jimmy was her friend. So was Bethany.

"I just don't understand what's happened," Jimmy said. "At times, I think she's genuinely interested in me, you know? And other times, she acts like I'm invisible."

"I don't think you should be worried. She went to the singing, didn't she? If she wanted to avoid you, she wouldn't have even gone."

"That girl flashes hot and cold faster than I can keep

up." He worried his hat in his hands. "Doesn't it seem like something's bothering her lately? More than her usual fiery temper?"

It did seem so to Naomi too, but she had no idea what exactly was troubling Bethany. "Maybe there's just a lot on her mind with her brother's coming, then going." Tobe was certainly on the top of Naomi's mind.

Jimmy wiggled his eyebrows up and down. "By the way, you and Tobe sure did make a fast getaway at the singing."

Naomi froze. "Did anyone else notice?"

He grinned. "Your secret is safe with me." Then his smile faded. "So do you think you could talk to Bethany?"

"If there's a chance to talk, then I'll try. No promises. I'm your friend, not your matchmaker." That wasn't entirely true, Naomi did enjoy matchmaking and thought she had a talent for it. But she hadn't had any time alone with Bethany for quite some time now. She didn't even know where she'd gone today.

Naomi looked out the window at Sammy and Luke, racing behind her brother Galen as he led a horse into the ring for training exercises. Those two boys never seemed to walk in a straight line. Instead, they ran in zigzags. What would it be like to have that much energy?

"I'd better get out there before Galen wonders where I've gone," Jimmy said. At the kitchen door, he stopped. "Hank Lapp told me the other day that there were only two women in Stoney Ridge who could ever manage me on a full-time basis—Mary Kate Lapp, who spurned me for Chris Yoder, and Bethany Schrock. Think he's right?"

Naomi grinned. "Let's just say I think you and Bethany are perfectly suited."

"Me, too. I just need to convince her of that." He fit his hat on his head. "Thanks, Naomi. You're a good pal."

The ride home from Hagensburg was a silent one. As they drew closer to Stoney Ridge, Geena glanced at Bethany and wasn't surprised to see tears pouring like hot, silent rain over her face. She fished a small package of tissues out of her purse and handed it to Bethany. "Do you want to talk?"

Bethany pulled a tissue out of the package and wiped her eyes and cheeks. "All these years, as long as I could remember, I was so angry with my mother, so angry that she'd torn our family apart. How could I even have thought such a thing? If I could, I'd take them all back. Every resentful thought, every hateful word. I feel riddled with as many holes as a wormy apple." She blew her nose.

"You didn't know," Geena said kindly. "You had no idea what had happened to your mother. Is that typical of the Amish? For your father to not tell you the truth about your mother?"

"I don't know if he knew the truth. Knowing Dad, he might have sugarcoated my mother's illness, but he wouldn't have lied." Then the tears started again. "How can God ever forgive me for being so hardhearted? At times, I hated her," she whispered.

"But he does forgive, Bethany. He does." Geena turned off the highway onto the back roads that wound toward Stoney Ridge. "Sometimes," she said softly, "we have to make decided efforts to let go of the past. Not so that we pretend hard things didn't happen, but so that the power of hard things is lessened. In the Bible, Isaiah talks about forgetting the former things and not dwelling on the past."

"It's not that easy."

"No, it's not. 'The past is not a package one can lay away.' Emily Dickinson said that."

"Who's that?"

"She's an American poet. Lived in the 1800s."

"Well, no wonder I've never heard of her if she's passed on."

Geena swallowed a grin. At times, Bethany seemed wise beyond her years. Other times, she seemed so young, so naïve. "Are you going to tell the sisters from the Sisters' Bee that you know they're visiting your mother?"

Bethany turned toward the window. "I don't know. I just don't know what to do about that piece of news. I'm still stunned. I've been working for them for months now and they've never said a word about my mother. Though, not long ago, I discovered they were feeding lunch once a week to thirty people. They are a puzzle, those old sisters."

"Mind if I give you some advice?"

"Please."

"Don't do anything about it for a while. Just give yourself some time to wrap your head around what you found out about your mother today. After all, the only thing you know for sure about the sisters is that they visit your mother once a month. That's not such a bad thing."

Bethany glanced at her from the corner of her eyes. "Keeping it a secret is."

"Bethany, just pray long and hard before you talk to

the sisters. Make sure God is the one leading you to talk to them, if you do it at all."

Bethany nodded. "Now *that* is some advice I could've used recently. Any time I get all puffed up and self-righteous, I make a mess even bigger." Laughter broke through her self-pity. "I need a nap. It's been an emotional day."

Geena patted Bethany's arm. "In a good way."

Bethany closed her eyes and Geena drove past rolling fields, farmhouses with clotheslines flapping, horses hanging their heads over fences. The weather was changing—gray clouds were moving in from the north and the wind was picking up. Geena rolled down her window. The air was at least ten degrees cooler now than it was when they headed to Hagensburg this morning.

She was glad she had gone with Bethany today. She wasn't sure if the caregiver would have been as forthcoming with information had Geena not slipped into the conversation that she was in the ministry. Finding the truth today was much harder than she expected, but she couldn't help but feel it was necessary for Bethany to come to peace about her mother.

For the first time in months, perhaps in years, Geena had a sense that she was right where she was supposed to be.

A headache came over Naomi in the afternoon that was so painful she had to come inside the house to rest her eyes from the bright sunshine. She brewed a cup of tea from the spearmint leaves that Sadie Smucker, the local herbalist, had given to her. Sadie had recommended that she distract herself from the pain, rather than lie in bed and dwell on it. So Naomi sat in the living room and tried to put a binding around a quilt, a Basket Garden pattern she had just finished.

Sitting quietly and sewing the bright green binding inch by inch to the border, covering all the uneven edges and raveled threads with a smooth band of green, seeing all those different bits and scraps of fabric come together, stitch by stitch, into a neatly finished whole, did help lessen the pounding in her head, just a little.

She had made this quilt with all kinds of scraps from her piece bag, and the scraps brought up happy memories of her siblings when they still lived at home. There were five brothers and sisters in between Galen and Naomi—they were the bookends, their mother had called them. They were the most alike too. Quiet, thoughtful, introspective, and frequently underestimated by others. Her sisters, now married with families of their own, had invited Naomi to come live with them, but she didn't want to leave Galen. She understood him. She wondered when he would get around to asking Rose to marry him and what that might mean for her. Knowing Rose, she would want Naomi to remain with all of them. One big happy family.

And that was tempting, especially when Naomi considered Tobe, which she did quite a lot.

She wondered how the week was going for Tobe and hoped he was being completely candid with that lawyer. She had encouraged him to tell everything, to not hold back anything. Tobe seemed skeptical, but then she reminded him that he had spent most of the last year hiding from the truth and where had that gotten him? Honesty, she said, was always the best way.

Even if being honest might open up a Pandora's box of troubles? he had asked her.

Even then, she said.

Naomi had been stitching around a corner, which took careful attention to set the tucks just right, when the headache took a severe turn. She put down the fabric pieces and rubbed her temples.

Outside, the sun disappeared as if someone had popped a lid over it. She went to the window and saw the weather was changing—no wonder she had such a headache. Whenever the barometric pressure in the air changed suddenly, she felt the pressure in her head. She watched streaks of lightning light the sky, muted and hidden by low-lying clouds. Not rain clouds, just those empties. "Always threatening, never delivering," Galen called them. She saw Galen and Jimmy lead some horses from the paddock into the barn. No more training would happen today if lightning flashed in the sky.

Finally, she went down to the darkest part of the basement to curl up and rest on a cot. The basement was usually her last resort, but the quiet and the darkness often helped to alleviate the headaches. Sometimes she felt as if tiny men were inside her forehead, pounding on it with little hammers. She closed her eyes and tried to sleep. The lightning was closer now, with large cracks of thunder quickly following. The sound filled her with such tension that she didn't think she could endure it. If it went on much longer, she felt it would twist her like a wire.

A gust of wind rattled the basement window and she

shivered. For no reason she could have named, Naomi felt a ripple of foreboding. In her mind flashed images—bright lights, like a spinning police siren. She smelled freshly turned earth, then saw a shovel and . . .

Naomi's eyes popped open and she was on her feet. Something terrible was about to happen.

Jimmy listened to Naomi's vision and didn't know what to make of it. Sometimes, when Naomi had a fierce headache, she would have these . . . visions or dreams or second sights . . . and while they often turned out to mean something, just as often they didn't. He wished Galen were here, but he had gone into town to pick up some liniment for a horse's lame leg. Jimmy appeased Naomi by saying he would check every horse on the entire King farm.

"It's not here," Naomi said, trembling. "The trouble isn't here."

"Then, where?"

That . . . she didn't know. Jimmy saw Hank Lapp saunter up the driveway with a fishing pole in his hand and waved him into the kitchen. Maybe he could make sense of Naomi's vision. At this point, Jimmy wasn't sure what else to do. Hank listened carefully to Naomi, asking details as if she were a witness to a crime and not just dreaming the whole thing up. He suggested they check over Galen's livestock first, so he walked with Jimmy through the barn, then out to the pastures, but the horses were all accounted for and nothing seemed awry. "I'm not sure what to do to appease Naomi, Hank," Jimmy said, walking back to the house. "Those headaches can make her a little . . ." He whirled his finger around his ear.

"Her vision might not be real," Hank said, "but it's real to her."

And then Mim came flying through the hole in the privet hedge. "Jimmy—we have to get to the community garden! I just got a call from Bethany. Something's going on down there."

Jimmy fetched a buggy horse from the barn and Hank hitched it to the shafts in record time. Mim jumped in the buggy and Naomi came out of the house to join them, but Jimmy discouraged her from coming along by promising to stop by later with news. He could almost see the headache pain radiating from her eyes. He climbed into the buggy, slapped the reins on the horse, and started to take off, when Sammy and Luke ran through the privet. "We're coming too!"

"HOP IN, BOYS!" Hank bellowed.

Jimmy stopped the buggy and let them climb into the backseat. He glanced at Mim. "What exactly did Bethany say?"

Mim's hands were gripping the sides of the buggy. "She and Geena were driving past the community garden on their way home and saw that the garden had been trashed."

"What?" Jimmy glanced at her. "By who?"

"She didn't say. It was a quick call."

"Where were Geena and Bethany coming from?" He hadn't seen Bethany all day, and he'd been looking.

"I don't know."

No one said a word for the rest of the ride. Jimmy detoured down a road for a shortcut, across a fire path in a field, and pulled the horse to a stop at the back of the garden, behind a fence. He jumped out of the buggy, tied the reins to a tree, and helped Mim down. The boys raced around the fence corner. Then they stopped abruptly, stunned. Jimmy, Hank, and Mim joined the boys; the five of them stared at the gardens with blank expressions.

Here was Naomi's warning.

It looked like cattle had stampeded through, trampling the new and carefully tended plots. Plants were smashed, dirt was scattered, leaves and blossoms lay in clumps, gravel from the pathways was churned up. Some of the wooden boards that held the plots were smashed into splinters.

They were ruined.

Rage rose in Jimmy as he strode through the gardens. Nearly every plot had been damaged, but it was capricious, like a tornado. Some gardens had been trampled and yanked up badly. Others had only sustained wounds. A handful of others had taken a hit, with broken plants, footsteps in the middle. He started counting. Two very badly damaged plots. One of them was the Grange Hall's kitchen plot. That was better, he felt, than if it had belonged to a needy family or the Group Home. He picked up a stake, shoved the support in the ground, tenderly knelt and propped up a listing tomato cage. Within, the tomato plant had a few broken arms that Jimmy pinched off, but its main stem was intact. It would survive.

The wanton destruction trailed off toward the far end of the gardens, as if the vandals had been chased away. Or interrupted.

He heard a slight moan and turned around to see

Bethany, standing with her fist clenched against her mouth. He walked up to her. "This is unbelievable," she said.

"Mim said you and Geena were driving by when you saw that the gardens had been wrecked. Did you see anyone?"

She pointed to the back of the garden. "In the shadows back there, I saw some figures moving. Two, maybe three people. When Geena pulled over, they ran off." Something fierce crossed her face. "How could anyone do such a thing? Why? This is food! They're gardens. They're only meant to help people."

He looked around the plots, teeth clenched together. "I don't know. I just don't know." Then he turned to face Bethany. "But we're not going to let them think they've taken something away." He peered at the sky. "It might rain soon, but until it does, we're going to start fixing things."

"Now?"

"Now."

Mim had been standing nearby, listening to their conversation. "I'll go to the Sisters' House and let them know." She took off running.

"WAIT FOR ME, MIM!" Hank called. "I'll use their phone to start the Amish telegraph." Mim waited for him to catch up and the two hurried off together to the Sisters' House.

"Jimmy," Bethany said, "who is capable of this kind of violence?"

"It doesn't matter," he called, walking backward toward the Grange Hall to get tools from the shed. "What matters is that the garden keeps growing."

Soon the word spread and church members started to arrive. Everyone surveyed the damage, faces masked with shock and sadness. "Why would anyone do such a thing?" Amos Lapp asked, lifting a smashed zucchini plant. He tried to brace the broken boards of a raised bed, but they kept falling over again.

"I have no idea," Bethany said. She must have said it over and over. She still couldn't believe what had transpired here today.

A few girls from the Group Home drifted over and Geena set them to cleanup tasks. Bethany admired how easily Geena related to those girls. Bethany avoided them, was intimidated by them, but Geena always went right up and drew them into conversation.

Sammy stood by the garden plot Bethany had planted for the sisters' soup kitchen. He was peering at his pea shoots, which had been twining up a trellis he had made out of stakes, and made a roaring noise. "Someone wrecked my peas!" he cried, hurt crumpling his face, and Bethany wrapped her arm around his shoulder.

"No, Sammy, look," she said, bending down to examine the plants. "Some of the pea vines are broken, but not all. They'll keep growing. Peas are hardy things." She spied some stakes and reached out to grab them and put them back in the ground. "I think if you leave those peas alone, they'll survive."

Luke ran over to see the plot, a scowl pulling at his face. He jammed his fists on his hips and jutted out his chin. He whipped his head around to Bethany, his eyes flaring brightly. "Until they do it again." He stomped off down the garden path.

Sammy's mouth trembled. "What if it happens again?"

Gently she brushed the hair out of Sammy's eyes. She hardly had to reach down to do so anymore, he was getting that big. He would be nine years old come fall. Before long, he'd be growing past her, like Luke already was. "There's no point in worrying about what-ifs. Let's see what can be salvaged."

Kneeling, she plucked leaves from an eggplant and removed a crumpled stem of a sunflower. The carrots and potatoes and onions and garlic would be fine, tucked deep under the earth. A swath of corn shoots was crushed. She tried to appear calm, for Sammy's sake, but as she tossed the ruined plants aside, she saw that her hands were shaking.

Jimmy walked over to where she and Sammy were working. "Sammy, Amos Lapp brought some flats of mixed bedding plants from his greenhouse to help replace those that had been lost. Run over and see if there are some plants he'll let you have." As Sammy ran over to Amos's wagon, Jimmy examined the two boards of the raised bed. He pulled out some nails from his pocket and hammered the corners together. "That'll hold for now. I'll get corner latches on it tomorrow."

Bethany still couldn't imagine who would have done this. She glanced over at the Group Home and saw Rusty and her friends on the porch, watching others clean up the gardens. Maybe she *could* imagine whom. But why? What could cause those girls—Rusty, if she were honest—to commit such a reckless act? "What would make her do something like this?"

Jimmy raised an eyebrow. "Why'd you say that? Why'd you say 'her'?"

Bethany didn't know for sure that Rusty had done it. If so, she certainly would have needed help from her friends, but that wouldn't have been too difficult. Rusty said jump and they asked how high. "Just a hunch."

"Well, you might be on to something." He glanced over at Rusty. "The only plot that wasn't damaged was the Group Home's."

"We were just trying to do something for the community, to make things a little bit nicer." She wiped at some dirt on her cheeks. "People think they can do anything to us because we won't fight back."

"I know," Jimmy said quietly, not looking away. "But we shouldn't stop trying to do good. Things are damaged, but most of it is fixable."

Geena walked up to them. "Whoever did all this has been damaged too, or they wouldn't choose to do this kind of destruction."

"Well, we probably can't fix them, but let's see what we can do about this garden." Jimmy reached down and picked up his hammer and extra nails. "Where've you been all day, anyhow?"

Bethany stilled and her eyes pricked with tears. She glanced at Geena for help.

"Taking care of some old business," Geena volunteered. "Jimmy, you're absolutely right. Let's see what we can do about this garden."

16

In less than a week, Bethany's missing brother had returned and was being investigated by a big city lawyer, her church had built a community garden, she had discovered that her mother was mentally ill, and to top it all off, the brand-new community garden had been trashed . . . and rebuilt.

Still, the sun rose on Wednesday morning and Harold the Rooster crowed and new guests were due at the inn this afternoon. It was strange how time moved along, like a river rushing to meet the ocean. Nothing could stop it.

Right after breakfast, Mim and Bethany scrubbed and cleaned the guest flat, washed the windows, changed the sheets and towels, and prepared the rooms for new arrivals. Now the sisters were expecting Bethany to help serve lunch at the Grange Hall. As she put on her bonnet to walk to the Sisters' House, Chase greeted her at the door, barking his big, deep bark, wagging the whole back half of his body. "You want to come with me, don't you?" Chase tilted his head toward her for a nuzzle. She scratched his back, rubbed his ears. "You're the best." She didn't know how anybody could get along without a good old dog.

The rain from last night had stopped, but the air was thick with it, dense to breathe, smelling of damp soil. Now and then a slight whiff of horses wafted through. Geena invited herself along and they walked to the Sisters' House, Chase trailing behind, sniffing and baptizing every bush along the way.

On the way, Geena asked how she was processing through all of yesterday's events. "As I thought about it last night, I realized you probably have more questions than answers. And most likely, the sisters have the answers. Some of them, anyway."

"I've thought of little else." Bethany blew out a puff of air. "I had to bite my tongue last night when I saw the sisters at the garden—I wanted to ask them what they knew about my mother. Wanted to but didn't. I'm not sure I can handle knowing anything more. I doubt it's good."

"Wait for God's timing on this, Bethany."

Bethany glanced at her, a little annoyed. "I told you—I didn't say anything."

"Waiting on God doesn't mean forgetting or ignoring. It means you pray for God's timing. Ask him to let you know when the time is right. Don't act until you sense God's leading. Waiting on God isn't passive. It's very active."

"Then what happens? Should I be on the lookout for a burning bush or something?"

Geena laughed. "I don't think you'll need something quite that dramatic. For me, it's more like a knowing, deep inside. The more I pray, the more familiar I've become with getting direction from God. I try not to act until I get his prompting."

It never crossed Bethany's mind to pray the way Geena prayed—asking and expecting and asking some more. She had no idea a person could talk to God like that. No idea at all. She'd been in church all her life—different churches too. Amish and Mennonite. Never had she heard that prayer was a two-way conversation. Was it that her churches didn't encourage that kind of praying? Or had she just not paid attention?

As they turned onto the road that led to the Sisters' House, Geena brought up Naomi's warning. "Does she get those . . . presentiments . . . often?"

"She thinks of them as intuition. Gut feelings. And she thinks everyone has intuition but people don't listen to it enough. But I've noticed they seem to be related to her migraine headaches." Bethany kicked a stone off the sidewalk. "Naomi is an interesting person."

"Her voice reminds me of a librarian, hushed and refined. She seems like a gentle soul."

"That she is. She does generous and loving things without even a second thought. But she's stronger inside than she might seem on the outside."

Geena grinned. "That's the opposite of the girls from the Group Home. They look tough on the outside, but inside, they're still little girls."

"Why do you like those girls so much?"

"I've always been partial to teens," Geena said. "That's why I love being a youth pastor. If I were running that Group Home, I'd start a weekly Bible study for the girls. And I'd try to organize a mentoring program for them, so they could be matched with people—" she held her palm out to Bethany "—people like you, who have so much to teach these girls."

Oh no. No thank you.

"I guess the thing I like about teens is that they're less jaded than adults, more vulnerable, more willing to believe."

"But you're going to look for another youth pastor job?"

"Oh yes. I like supporting teens during their impressionable years—to make them feel part of the church, to listen without lecturing them, all while pointing them toward God's highest and best."

"But what if a church wasn't in a building?"

Geena opened her mouth to say something, closed it, opened it again, closed it. She seemed flustered by the question, yet it seemed so obvious to Bethany.

Sylvia was in front of her house and called out to them when she saw them coming up the road. "Turkey Rice Soup on the menu today." She was filling a little red wagon with jars of homemade turkey stock.

"It's the first time all summer that serving a hot meal sounds good," Bethany said. She and Geena took the wagons on ahead to the Grange Hall while Sylvia gathered her sisters.

Chase wasn't allowed in the Grange Hall kitchen, so he moseyed over to the community garden to visit with a few gardeners working on their plots. Geena unlocked the kitchen and started to unload the wagon. Bethany stopped for a moment to gaze at the gardens. It was amazing to see that the garden didn't look all that different today from how it looked on Saturday afternoon—neat and tidy and full of promise.

"REMARKABLE SIGHT, AIN'T IT?"

Bethany flinched at the loud sound and spun around to find Hank Lapp standing a few feet away from her. "Morning, Hank. What are you doing here?"

"Thought I'd give some help to the gardeners."

"That's nice of you."

"Well, some of them are new at this. That family there—" he pointed to a mother with two little girls—"they're planting onions next to beans. That'll stunt the growth of the beans." He shrugged his shoulders. "If you haven't been raised Plain, you don't know about gardens."

Well, that might be stretching things a little, but it was true that the Amish passed their know-how from generation to generation. Bethany picked up a sack of flour, glad to see it. She'd ask Sylvia to see if she could get some flour so she could start making biscuits for lunches. That store-bought white bread had no taste at all. She glanced at the Group Home. She wondered if those girls ever had a homemade biscuit before, hot from the oven, topped with a pat of cold butter. Maybe today, if she could get started soon.

Hank shielded his eyes, looking over the garden plots. "You'd never know this place had been such a mess."

In her other hand, Bethany picked up a big jar of broth. "When I think of what happened last night to the gardens—yes, it is remarkable."

"I wasn't talking about last night. I was thinking about how it looked just a week ago. The whole lot was a mess."

She smiled and handed Hank the jar of broth, then

another. If he had time on his hands, she had things for him to do. "I suppose you're right."

"Takes a pretty determined woman to have seen all that through."

She looked at him in surprise. "You mean me? Oh no. I was just a small part of it. These gardens were a community effort."

"Look at this," he said, spreading his free hand to encompass the garden. "Do you remember what a wreck this was? A less determined woman . . . a less stubborn woman would have given up before she even started. Not Bethany Schrock."

She grinned. "Stubborn—now that label most of my family would agree with."

"There are worse things than being stubborn."

Chase noticed a few girls from the Group Home in the garden before Bethany did. He went flying over to greet them. To her surprise, Rusty bent down and rubbed his head all over.

Hank was watching the interaction too. "I think we should call it 'The Second Chance Gardens.'" He handed the jars of broth back to Bethany and sauntered off to help the mother and her children in their garden plot.

She watched him walk down the garden path. When she first became acquainted with Hank Lapp, she thought of him just like everybody else did: an odd fellow who made church a little more interesting. She remembered countless Sundays when Hank would fall asleep during the sermons, snore loudly, then jerk awake. He would look around the room, startled, blinking rapidly like a newborn owl, oblivious to the disruption he had caused. Another time, his stomach growled so loud that the minister stopped preaching and looked right at him. "Die Bauern haben gern kurze Predigten und lange Bratwürste," Hank told him in his usual loud voice. *The belly hates a long sermon.*

Hank Lapp had always been amusing to Bethany, but that was all.

After Jimmy started to work for Galen, Hank dropped by Eagle Hill and the King farm often and she discovered other sides to him: his kindness, his good intentions, and his love for the Plain life despite his stubborn streak. He had a good heart, Hank Lapp did. She held the kitchen door open with her foot and motioned to Geena to start the assembly line to unload the little red wagons.

By the time the sisters arrived, the wagons were unloaded, the biscuit dough was resting, and Bethany was chopping vegetables for the soup. Geena stood next to her, staring at the cutting board as Bethany took the last onion, made six quick, deep cuts into the flesh, another six crossways, then chopped through the onion.

"The speed that you cut an onion is amazing," Geena said.

"No man is his craft's master the first day. That's a saying my grandmother likes to quote. In other words: do enough of anything and you'll get good at it."

"Except for preaching," Geena said with a grin.

Just then the girls from the Group Home slipped in early—something Sylvia didn't normally allow. She thought Sylvia or Fannie might shoo them out but they were preoccupied with taking turkey meat off the carcass and chopping it up for the soup. Lena, Ada, and Ella, setting the tables, were too softhearted to ask them to wait outside.

Bethany would have liked to give those girls jobs to do to help get lunch ready—set places, sweep the floor, fill glasses with that sugary Dr Pepper and juice drink—but when she brought it up once, Sylvia disagreed. She said it wasn't time yet. Bethany didn't know what she meant by that—as far as she was concerned, there was work to be done and those girls needed to work.

Geena left the kitchen and went over to talk to the girls from the Group Home. She pulled out a chair and sat next to Rusty. They talked awhile—sadly out of Bethany's earshot. Geena patted her on the shoulder. Why? Rusty didn't seem like the type to pat much.

Bethany had been watching Rusty since she came in. Inside her battled a war: her basic nature was to be confrontational and she knew, she just *knew*, Rusty had something to do with the trashing of the community garden. But she also knew it was wrong to accuse others. Hadn't it been drilled into her for as long as she could remember? What right did she have to accuse another of a sin when she was a sinner herself? And she was.

Still, wasn't it important to be held accountable for one's actions? To face consequences. Isn't that what Rose was trying to get Tobe to understand? But then . . . Rose wanted Tobe to take responsibility for himself. That was the rub, right there. Bethany wanted someone else to hold Rusty accountable. She could feel the pointed finger of judgment brew within her, and that was where pride gained hold.

"It's good of you to show interest in those girls," Bethany said when Geena returned to the kitchen.

"It's always illuminating to me," Geena said. "It really boils down to the fact that the girls want to feel understood, accepted, and heard even while they struggle to understand, accept, and hear others. I guess it's not that surprising when I stop to think about it. That's what everybody wants and what everybody finds so hard to do."

Bethany took a pan of biscuits out of the oven. "I guess that's the difference between the Amish and the English. Being English means you struggle to find your place. Being Amish means you belong."

Geena found a spatula in a drawer and scooped the hot biscuits into a basket. "Don't forget these girls are on the extreme side of your definition of being 'English.' Most of them have never been wanted by their families; they've never belonged anywhere. I remember something one of my seminary professors had said: 'Most people are in way more pain than anybody knows.' That is so true." Geena carried the dirty spatula to the sink and rinsed it off. She put the spatula away in a drawer.

Bethany started to ladle out the soup into empty bowls set on the countertop. "I guess I haven't thought about why the girls were the way they were. I've only noticed how they act. Like they're always pushing people away from them."

Geena set the soup bowls on a tray. "What I've come to learn is that hurt people push others away because they want someone to come and get them, to say they haven't forgotten about them, to show how much they're wanted and needed."

Bethany fit three more bowls on Geena's tray. "Maybe if those girls made a little effort in the right direction, it might be easier for people to want and need them." There it was again: judgment. It was gaining a foothold. "Don't listen to me. I'm still frazzled from yesterday."

"It's been a big week for you, Bethany. It's a lot to process. Give yourself time." Geena squeezed her arm before she took the tray to the dining room.

Process. Geena had used that term before. She made it sound like thoughts and feelings were in motion, and maybe they were. Bethany felt like she was trying to sort things through and put them where they belonged. It was as if her cluttered mind was a version of the Sisters' House and she was trying to get it organized.

Bethany ladled out more bowls of turkey rice soup and put them on a tray to take to the table of Group Home girls. They always sat in the same place—the farthest table. One clump on one side, one clump on the other, as if they didn't like each other and, probably, they didn't. She tried to focus on what Geena had mentioned—that these girls, including Rusty, were hurt souls, longing to be loved and valued. Noticed.

With a sigh and a prayer, she took the tray over and set it on the table. One by one, she served a bowl of soup to each girl. She forced herself to smile and make eye contact. Then she came to Rusty. The two of them locked eyes almost like clockwork.

As Bethany reached across the table to serve the bowl to Rusty, she slipped Bethany a note. She put it in her dress pocket. When she went back into the kitchen, she pulled it from her pocket and read it. A chill moved through her, tickling down her spine.

Yesterday was just a warning. Tell Tobe to leave it alone.

It was in Jake Hertzler's handwriting.

17

Shootfire! When it came to Jake Hertzler, Bethany made mistake after mistake after mistake. She was the one who had introduced him to her father, years ago, on a Sunday morning at church. She mentioned to her father that Jake had accounting skills and was looking for a job. She had done it intentionally—she thought Jake was charming and handsome, and he was. But he was also crafty and cunning and shrewd . . . and now she had discovered that he could be threatening.

Her anger evaporated as she realized, *It's all my fault*.

Why had she called Jake and left that message, tipping him off to Tobe's whereabouts? She was ashamed of her action, embarrassed by it, unsure of what to do about the note from him. What had she done? What did Jake mean—warning Tobe to "leave it alone"? Leave *what* alone?

Why did she always seem to underestimate Jake?

She knew why. She was raised to believe the best in others—it was ingrained into her. How many times had she been told that if you search for the best in people you're bound to find it?

But what about people in whom there was no best?

Chase had been following her from room to room as she paced through the farmhouse, never leaving her side for longer than he absolutely had to. She sat at the kitchen table and he slumped under her chair and gazed at her, a worried expression on his furry face. Then his tail began to wag. She bent down and stroked his ears. She knew she needed to start dinner soon, but her thoughts couldn't leave that note.

She looked at it again. It was definitely Jake's distinctive handwriting. Rusty must have some involvement with Jake—which made it all the more likely that she had played a role in trashing the garden. Bethany thought back to those three figures she had seen at the back of the garden. She didn't think any was a man, but Jake had a slight build. Maybe one of those had been Jake, along with Rusty and one of her friends.

She wished she could talk to Rose. Or Galen. Geena? Should she call Allen Turner? Rose had left his business card on the kitchen countertop. But if Tobe heard about this, he would clam up and stop talking to Allen Turner. And then, without realizing the ramifications of clamming up, he would end up taking responsibility for the illegal things Jake had done to the business. She knew her brother's nature. He would avoid conflict at all costs. Why else had he disappeared for nearly a year?

She folded up the note. She just didn't know who to talk to or even how they could help. She tried to think straight and gather facts.

One fact in particular stared back at her: Jake was nearby.

Each afternoon, around five-ish, Mim waited at the phone shanty, hoping for a call from Danny Riehl to go stargazing. If he did happen to call, which wasn't often, it would be around that time of day. He would have finished his evening chores and be checking phone messages for his father before he'd be expected back at the house. She didn't really think he would call because there was a full moon tonight, round and creamy. Beautiful for the soft light it shed on the fields but too bright for stargazing. Those were the thoughts that were running through Mim's mind as the phone rang. She took a startled step backward, then lunged for it, sure it was Danny.

Instead, it was Rose, Mim's mother. "How's everything going, Mim?"

"Everything's fine. Well, at Eagle Hill, anyway. Bethany moved into my room so Geena Spencer could stay in her room. There's a new couple staying in the guest flat. They seem nice, but they're not around much. Turns out the lady is allergic to horses so she runs from the guest flat to her car with a pink handkerchief over her mouth."

"I wonder why she came to an Amish farm if she's allergic to horses."

Mim had the same thought. "And she needs her food to be gluten free. We've been giving her scrambled eggs and applesauce for breakfast and told her they're gluten free."

"Mim—those things have always been gluten free."

"We know. But the lady seemed impressed so we decided not to say anything more."

"Do you think Geena will stay on for the rest of the week?"

"I hope so. She helped clean up the mess at the community garden."

"Wait. What? Why was there a mess?"

"Someone trashed the gardens on Tuesday afternoon."

"What? Why? What happened?"

"Nobody knows."

Silence. "I'm sorry about that. You've all worked so hard on those gardens."

"No kidding. But everybody has. And the same people helped clean it all up. It almost looks as good as it did on Saturday afternoon. Almost."

"What else have you been doing?"

"Me? Um . . . I . . ." She'd been sifting through letters for Mrs. Miracle and hoping to go stargazing with Danny Riehl, but she couldn't tell her mom any of that. "The usual. Chickens, horses, goat."

"Are the boys behaving?"

"Same as usual. Galen keeps them so busy that they fall asleep early."

Her mom laughed. "Good for him. That's pretty smart."

"How's Mammi Vera holding up?"

"She's sticking close to Tobe whenever we're at Allen Turner's office."

"Mom, is everything going to turn out all right for Tobe?"

"I . . . don't know yet. I hope so. He's spending a lot of time in depositions."

Mim knew all about those. She'd read up on depositions after a letter to Mrs. Miracle mentioned them. "But he'll be coming home soon, won't he? Won't all of you be home soon?"

There was a long pause. "I'll know more in a day or two. Are you managing by yourselves? Do you think Geena might stay until we return?"

"I can ask her. She doesn't seem to be in a hurry to get home."

"You can ask Galen for help too."

"I know. He stops by each day."

"Is Bethany doing all right?"

"She's been awful quiet." Mim wasn't sure where Bethany had gone on Tuesday, but she had come home a different person. Quiet, defeated. Another reason she was glad Geena was staying.

"I guess we're all shaken up by Tobe's return. Give her time, Mim." Mammi Vera's voice was calling in the background. "Your grandmother needs some help. I'll call again when there's news. And feel free to call Delia's house. The number is on the kitchen countertop. Bye, Mim."

Mim hung up the receiver and walked to the house, up to her bedroom, and back to her secret role as Mrs. Miracle. She wished she could talk to her mom about a problem that was brewing for Mrs. Miracle. Bethany had brought over the mail from the *Stoney Ridge Times* office and the envelope was bursting at the seams. Nearly every letter was about Mrs. Miracle's advice to Wringing My Hands. Readers had all kinds of opinions about whether it was right to meddle in marriages. Four to one ran against Wringing My Hands telling the truth to her friend, Nancy. But what distressed Mim was the actual response from Wringing My Hands. She had absolutely no idea how to respond back to her:

Dear Mrs. Miracle,

I took your advice and thought about whether I would want Nancy to tell me if my husband were having an affair. I would be grateful to my friend for the courage to tell me the truth and not let me remain a fool. So I told Nancy that her dentist husband was having an affair with his hygienist.

Nancy didn't believe me and said she will never speak to me again.

Really *Wringing*
My Hands

Mrs. Miracle's sterling advice might not have been quite as wonderful as Mim had thought. Then another letter completely baffled Mim:

Dear Mrs. Miracle,

Have you ever noticed that you often answer a question with a question? Why is that? Are you trying to avoid giving an answer?

Cordially,
Wants an Answer

Oh, boy. What could she say to that? Then she realized

she had just done the very thing Wants an Answer accused her of doing.

She pulled out the next letter.

Dear Mrs. Miracle,

I messed things up. And now I don't know how to fix them.

Sincerely,
Stuck

Mim chewed on the inside of her cheek. Now *this*, she thought she knew how to answer. For years, her mom had disciplined her two little brothers in just this way and it always worked:

Dear Stuck,

You can do two things:

1) Apologize (sincerely).

2) Do something that helps someone else.

Sincerely,
Mrs. Miracle

◊

On Thursday, after Bethany and Mim had spent a few hours tackling another corner of the Sisters' House, they walked into town to take care of a few errands. Chase had tagged along with them to the Sisters' House, where the sisters kept slipping him snacks, and then trotted behind the girls as they walked to town. When they reached Main Street, Mim handed Bethany the envelope that contained next week's Mrs. Miracle column. She was proud of herself for being ahead of her deadline.

"Be sure to ask for my paycheck," Mim said.

"You mean, *my* paycheck," Bethany said. "Don't forget that it's made out to me."

Mim frowned. "I'm going to get something at Pearl's Gift Store. Come on, Chase. We'll meet you back at this end of Main Street in ten minutes." Chase's ears pricked up at the mention of his name. Tongue lolling, tail wagging, he trotted behind Mim.

Bethany went into the *Stoney Ridge Times* office and asked the woman at the receptionist's desk for the envelopes for Mrs. Miracle. She wasn't the usual receptionist and peered curiously at Bethany as she handed her the manila envelope. "I'm Penny Williams. I'm a new hire. Just started today. You can't be . . . you aren't . . . Mrs. Miracle?" Her voice was hushed in awe.

"No," Bethany answered truthfully. "Her true identity is top secret."

"Of course you couldn't be Mrs. Miracle. She's got to be an old woman! Please tell her I love the column. It's getting a lot of buzz—everyone thinks Mrs. Miracle gives such comforting wisdom."

Bethany had to bite hard on her lower lip to keep from bursting into laughter. What would Penny Williams say if she knew Mrs. Miracle was a fourteen-year-old!

As the receptionist went to get Mrs. Miracle's paycheck, Bethany heard the sound of tires screeching, then a blood-chilling scream that sounded like Mim. Bethany dropped the column on the receptionist's desk and bolted to the door. She ran all the way down Main Street. Her bonnet blew off and a car had to stop short to let her cross the street.

There, lying in the middle of the street, was Chase. Mim was beside herself, shrieking that he'd been hit by a car, tears running down her face as she hovered over the poor dog. Bethany lifted Chase's head, and his eyes opened but he didn't even whimper. Between Mim's sobs she could hear him breathing hard. He was still alive. A crowd of people started to gather and suddenly beside her was Jimmy Fisher. He knelt down and put a hand on Chase's chest. He looked up at Bethany. "Go get my buggy. It's in front of the Hay & Grain." She hesitated, not wanting to leave Chase. "Go now."

She ran to it and drove the buggy over to where Chase lay. "Hurry, Jimmy. We can get him to the vet."

But Jimmy didn't hurry. His hand was still on Chase's chest. A soft look passed over his face. "I'm sorry. He's gone."

Bethany looked at Chase, feeling utterly helpless. Sweet old Chase lay dead. She would not let herself cry, not now. She needed to be strong for her sister. Mim held her hands in tight fists against her mouth.

Jimmy took over and lifted Chase in his arms. "I'll take him to Eagle Hill and bury him." Bethany spread a buggy blanket on the floor of the buggy and gently laid Chase on top. As Jimmy guided a stricken Mim into the buggy, Bethany remembered her bonnet and walked down the block to look for it. She found it in the gutter and bent down to pick it up. When she looked up, she noticed Rusty from the Group Home, about one hundred yards away, standing against a tree, watching the whole thing with an unreadable look on her face.

Bethany locked eyes with her, until Rusty did a sharp about-face and walked away.

Back at the buggy, Bethany asked Mim if she had seen who had hit Chase. "No. It happened so fast. I was crossing the street and Chase was behind me. The next thing I knew, I heard the sound of a big thump, then a car rushed off."

"Did you recognize it?" Jimmy asked. "Or the driver?"

Mim shook her head, tears spilling. "I can't remember the car at all. It happened too fast. All I could think about was Chase, lying there on the ground." She put her face in her hands. "I should have been watching him more carefully."

"It's not your fault, Mim," Jimmy said. "These things happen."

"But Mim—"

"Bethany, not now," Jimmy said sharply. "Hop in." He helped Mim and Bethany into the buggy, then climbed in and drove them back to the house. He took the dog out, and Chase drooped in his arms, which started Mim sobbing all over again. "Bethany, where's a shovel?"

"I'll get it." Bethany went to the barn and brought back a shovel. She would not cry. She would not.

Sammy and Luke bolted out of the house, Geena following behind. When they saw Chase in Jimmy's arms, they stopped abruptly on the porch stairs. It was Luke who pierced Bethany's heart. Understanding settled over him first, she saw his face go utterly stoic—a strange look on an eleven-year-old boy. His head was up and slightly tilted, his gaze focused on Jimmy, and something about him seemed like their father in every way.

"What's wrong?" Sammy said, his forehead puckered

with worry, his eyes too wide and bright. "What's wrong with Chase?"

"He's dead," Luke said coldly. Sammy burst into sobs. His whole heart shone on his face.

Tears prickled Bethany's eyes and she bit her lower lip to hold them back. *Not now. Not now.*

Geena joined them as they walked to the hill beside the house. Mim said Chase loved to sit on that hill and watch the sheep in their pen, so Jimmy chose a beautiful tree with a large canopy and started to dig. He laid Chase gently, ever so gently, in the hole, then put a big handful of dirt in the boys' hands. Geena said a few reassuring words about what a good dog Chase was and sang a hymn that no one else recognized, but they liked it. Then they dropped their dirt on the little grave, and made a great ceremony of filling it and piling rocks. By the time the funeral was over, the afternoon was nearly past.

Geena and Mim walked down the hill with Jimmy and Bethany and the boys trailing behind. "I don't know how I'll tell Rose," Bethany said, about halfway down the hill. "She adored Chase."

Luke spun around and glared at Bethany. "It's your fault!"

She stared at him, trying to understand him. "That's not true, Luke. It's not true and it's not fair."

"With Mom gone, you were supposed to take care of us!"

"Wait a minute!"

Luke's eyes flashed, and he started to protest, but Bethany wouldn't let him interrupt. He shook his head as she came up to him.

"Listen to me," she said. "This was just a terrible accident. It was no one's fault."

"It's your fault!" Luke shouted as he lifted his face. Angry tears filled his eyes. "You should have been watching out for him. You should have stopped this!"

"Luke, I—"

He didn't wait for her answer. He lurched around and ran back up the hill, disappearing over the ridge.

Bethany worried so about Luke. She knew he was edging up to manhood, his heart sore and lonely with grieving for their father. He'd taken to doing and saying things he'd never have dared to try to get away with when their father was alive. She started to follow, but Jimmy grabbed her arm.

"Let him go. It wasn't your fault."

A wave of guilt crashed over Bethany. She was sinking beneath it. "Luke's right. If I'd been paying attention . . ."

"Don't think like that. It wasn't your fault, understand?" He turned her so she had to look at him. "Bethany, did you happen to see that pickup truck that hit Chase?"

"No. I was in the newsp—I was in a store." She looked up. "You must have, though, if you knew it was a pickup truck."

"I can't be sure . . . and I only saw it once before, at twilight. Months ago. It was at Windmill Farm, at Hank Lapp's birthday party."

Bethany stilled. *Oh please, no.*

"It looked like the same black pickup that Jake Hertzler drove."

Another warning from Jake.

Later that night, Bethany tiptoed into Luke's room and sat on his bed. She rubbed his shoulders to soften the ache she knew was there, and to comfort him. "I'm sorry about Chase, Luke. So very sorry."

Luke wiped his eyes with his pajama sleeve. "There'll never be another dog like Chase."

"No. Chase will always be special. But there will be another dog to love. Chase wouldn't want you to stop loving another dog just because you loved him so much. He'd want you to honor his memory by loving again. We'll find you a special dog."

"Chase came to us. We didn't go to him. That's the way it is with the best dogs. They find you."

"Then we'll be waiting."

They stayed like that a long time, just listening to Pennsylvania night sounds through the open window—the soft hoot of a great horned owl and the harsh squawk of a Northern Mockingbird and, now and then, the steady clip-clop of a horse pulling a buggy—each of which had their own way of giving comfort.

18

After the long sick worry of a week, Bethany helped Naomi sew a binding on a quilt top on Friday evening and found it strangely calming. As soon as they finished, Naomi wanted to drop it off at the Sisters' House so it could be wrapped and taken to a fundraising auction in the morning. A full moon cast eerie shadows all around Bethany and Naomi as they drove home from the Sisters' House in the buggy.

The more time Bethany spent around the sisters, the more amazed she was at their quiet and purposeful lives. Now she understood why their house was a mess—they had better things to do with their time than clean and tidy and iron and dust. And they didn't just talk about doing things—they did them. They even cared for Bethany's own mother.

She still didn't know the story behind that, but she was taking Geena's advice to sit on it and pray about it. Geena said she would know when the time was right, but so far, nothing. She hoped Geena was right. This praying and expecting and waiting for an answer to come was new to her. She would prefer a burning bush.

"I'm glad for the chill in the air," Naomi said as Bethany turned the horse down the road. Bethany stopped and looked both ways when they reached the intersection, although she knew there wasn't a car in sight. She tugged the horse's reins and murmured, "Tch, tch," to urge him forward.

All of a sudden, Naomi grabbed her arm. "Look out, Bethany!"

She pulled back on the horse and slammed on the buggy brake, stopping no more than a yard in front of something lying across the road. If Naomi hadn't spotted it in time, the horse would have tried to jump it and the buggy could have been wrecked. "Shootfire! That was close. What's in the road?"

"I don't know."

They got out of the buggy together and walked to a large tree limb that was lying crossways in the road. "How in the world did that get there?" Bethany looked up. "There aren't any big trees hanging overhead."

"Maybe it fell off a truck," Naomi said. Bethany leaned down to pick up one end of the tree limb and was about to ask Naomi if she would pick up the other when Naomi said, "Something's not right here. Quick, Bethany. Get back in the buggy. We can go back down the way we came."

"Why? That'll take a lot longer to get home."

"I can't explain it. I'm just getting a funny feeling."

"I thought you only got those when you had a headache."

"Hurry! We need to get out of here!"

She straightened up to see what Naomi was so anxious about, and just as she did, a man emerged out of the cornfield. She opened her mouth to ask for his help, but before she could utter a word, it dawned on her that tree limb wasn't there by accident. The man came toward her, slow and deliberate, and stopped just as he reached the buggy headlight. He took a step closer, moving across the beam of the headlight off the buggy, and she saw who it was.

Jake Hertzler.

He walked right up to her and smiled, but his eyes showed no warmth, only a cold, hard gaze. "Hello, Bethany."

She stood like a statue, frozen to the spot.

"Bethany, who is he?" Naomi asked in a trembling voice.

"I'm Bethany's boyfriend, Jake Hertzler. Bethany, honey, I've come for you." Jake's voice was soft and charming, like always, and there was the faint scent of Old Spice aftershave lotion, like always, but he didn't look the same and he didn't act the same. He had a strange look on his face that scared her. Something had changed, something essential, deep down. Even then, Bethany thought it was odd that she'd noticed such a thing.

"What is it you want, Jake?" Bethany practically spit the words. "You killed Chase. You ruined the gardens. What more can you take from my family?"

Jake sneered and his eyes narrowed slightly in the way of a man studying a mildly perturbing question. "I need to talk to Tobe and I think it's best if you're with me."

"She doesn't want anything to do with you," Naomi said boldly. "Nobody does."

Jake waved his hand at Naomi, as if he were brushing away a pesky fly. He kept his eyes on Bethany.

"I'm not going anywhere with you," Bethany snapped. "You keep away from me!"

He gave her a slow look over, up and down, in a way that made her feel filthy.

"Don't you touch me," she said, teeth chattering. She didn't want him to see how cold she was. She was shaking with it, she was feeling so cold. She took a step back.

Jake lunged toward her and grabbed her wrist. "You know you don't mean that. You know you belong to me."

She tried to yank her hand away, but he slapped her across the face with the back of his hand, then hit her again with his palm. She tried to get away, but he held on to her wrist tight as a trap.

By now Jake's cool exterior had vanished; he was seething. She looked into that face, into eyes that were relentless, ruthless.

"What's the matter, Bethany? Aren't I good enough for you anymore?" Jake put his hand on her throat and moved it down over her body. She began to shake all over even while she was trying so hard to be brave.

"Leave her be, Hertzler." A voice spoke out calm and clear in the dark.

Jake stilled.

"Hertzler, I told you to leave her alone," the voice said a little louder. In the beam of the buggy headlight stood Rusty.

Jake dropped Bethany's wrist as if it were a hot potato

and spun around. Bethany's legs gave out and she fell into the dirt. Naomi ran to her side.

"Run along, kid," Jake said. "You've been paid for your work."

"You can keep your money," Rusty replied in the same calm voice and pulled out a handful of crumpled bills from the pocket of her jeans. She threw them at Jake's feet. "Leave the women alone." Bethany realized she had never heard Rusty's voice before. She spoke as quietly as a person in a library. "They won't fight you, being Amish, but I will."

Jake laughed at Rusty, sizing her up and dismissing her. He turned back to Bethany and grabbed her arm. "Get up. You and me are going for a ride."

Rusty pulled the buggy whip from its socket and whipped it, like a flash, against the back of Jake's hand so that he released Bethany. "I told you to leave her alone."

Jake gripped his stung hand. Then he swung at Rusty, but before he could land a single punch, she kicked him in his privates. He bellowed out with pain and she kicked him again so that he dropped his hands to the front of his pants and doubled over. Rusty pulled something out of her back pocket and held it up high, in front of her, so Jake would see it in the beam of the buggy headlight. In her hand was a six-inch knife. It looked familiar, like the knives that belonged to the Grange Hall kitchen.

"Now, why don't you just get along back to that rock you live under," she said, still in that calm, quiet voice.

Strangely authoritative, Bethany realized, and wondered why her mind was working though her body wouldn't budge.

Jake turned to run and Rusty kicked him in the small

of this back. He made a *whoomp* sound and limped off into the dark.

Rusty watched, making sure he was gone for good, before she turned to Bethany, her breath coming as easy as if she'd been out for a walk. "You all right?"

"Where did you come from?" Bethany's voice was high and shaky, and she cleared her throat.

"Just heading back to the Group Home."

"Thank you," she whispered.

Rusty nodded, shifting from one foot to the other. "I'll move that tree limb out of the road. Then I'll be getting on."

"No!" Naomi cried. "What if he comes back?" She was as pale as a ghost.

Rusty hoisted the tree limb and shoved it to the side of the road like it was a feather pillow. "I don't think so. Not tonight, anyway. He'll be hurting for a while."

"I can't drive the buggy," Bethany said. "My hands are shaking too much." Naomi was trembling even more.

"I'll drive you," Rusty said. She hopped right into the driver's side of the buggy. Naomi helped Bethany in, then got in and sat in the backseat. Bethany wanted to know more about Rusty, to ask how she happened to be right there when they needed her, how she knew Jake, why she was willing to fight him off. And how did she know how to drive a buggy? But Bethany's cheek was smarting where Jake had hit her and her teeth kept chattering and she wasn't sure she could get the words out in any order that made any sense. Rusty didn't volunteer any information—she just drove the buggy down the road like she'd been doing it most of her life.

When Rusty pulled up to Naomi's house, Jimmy came

out of the front door. "Galen was just wondering where you were, Naomi." He stopped short as he realized there were three in the buggy. "What's happened?"

From the backseat, Naomi poked her head out the buggy window. "Bethany needs help."

Jimmy jumped the porch rail, landing near the buggy.

"We just had a scare, that's all," Bethany said.

"The scare of our life," Naomi added.

Jimmy yanked open the buggy door, and Bethany slid out and fell into his arms.

"Let's get her inside," Naomi said, hurrying to climb down from the buggy.

Jimmy wrapped his arm around Bethany and helped her up to the house. Her legs still felt shaky—she couldn't have walked to the house without his help. They reached the porch steps before she remembered Rusty and turned back to the buggy.

"Rusty!" she called, but there was no answer in the darkness.

Galen opened the door. "I'll put the horse and buggy away . . . ," he started to say, then stopped when he saw the bruise on Bethany's face. "Do you want me to get a doctor?" he asked.

"No," Bethany said.

Jimmy set her in a chair as Galen grabbed a sweater hanging on the wall and wrapped it around her.

"I'll get a cold rag for your face," Galen said.

"I'll start some tea," Naomi said, her voice sounding stronger. "Tea always helps everyone calm down." She filled the teakettle with water and put it on the stove to boil.

Jimmy knelt down in front of Bethany. "Are you all right?"

Bethany nodded, her eyes on her lap, where her hands twitched.

"Look at me, Bethany," Jimmy said.

She raised her head as slowly as she could, glancing at him, then turning to the stove where the teakettle was starting to sputter.

He covered her hands with his. They were so warm and she was so cold. "Are you sure you're all right?"

"Yes," she said in a squeaky voice. "He didn't . . . he tried to make me go with him . . ."

"Who?"

Bethany kept her eyes on her hands that were tucked under Jimmy's. She took too long to answer, so Naomi spoke up. "Jake. Jake Hertzler."

"Oh no . . ." Jimmy grabbed Bethany out of her chair and hugged her so hard she could hardly breathe.

"I'm all right, Jimmy. Truly I am."

The teakettle started to whistle, so Naomi filled a teapot with hot water, then dipped four teabags into it. The cinnamon scent of the tea filled the air, calming Bethany's racing heart. Galen brought a cold rag and she held it up against her cheek to keep the swelling down. Every few minutes, without saying anything, he took the rag and refolded it so it would be cool, then put it back against her face.

Naomi set the teapot and four mugs on the kitchen table, then sat at the kitchen table and poured tea for everyone. Bethany looked up and saw Naomi gazing at her with concern, handing her a mug of hot tea, and she felt so lucky to have such good friends that tears came to her eyes.

As Naomi's nerves settled, she was able to start at the beginning. Bethany filled in parts she missed, so that soon Galen and Jimmy heard every detail, including the rescue by Rusty.

When the girls had finished, Jimmy hit the table with his fist. "I'm going after him!"

"No!" Naomi said. "No. You can't catch him. You shouldn't even try."

"Naomi's right," Galen said, "but we should call that SEC lawyer. He needs to hear—"

"No," Naomi said firmly. "We should let God alone deal with this."

Bethany looked at Naomi. "What else did you see tonight?"

Hesitating, Naomi kept her eyes fixed on her tea mug. "Jake Hertzler cast two shadows. I saw it in the moonlight, plain as day."

A chill traveled down Bethany's spine. Jimmy and Galen exchanged a look.

Naomi's hands were wrapped tightly around the mug. "That man is possessed."

Early Saturday morning, Jimmy arrived at Galen's to start work. Galen was in front of the barn, waiting for him, a tight, serious look on his face.

"I thought I'd stop over at Eagle Hill before the day begins and see if Bethany's doing all right after last night's scare."

"Hold on a minute, Jimmy."

"What is it, partner? You look like someone has died. Naomi's all right, isn't she?"

"She's fine. Jimmy, when I got up early this morning, I noticed that the barn door was wide open. Someone had been in there during the night. But I never heard a thing."

Jimmy snapped to attention. "What's happened?"

Galen rubbed his chin. "It's Lodestar. He's gone missing."

Bethany sent Luke and Sammy outside with a basket to gather eggs in the henhouse because Jimmy said he wanted to talk to her privately. He pulled out a kitchen chair. "Bethany, sit down. There's something I need to tell you before your brothers find out."

At the kitchen sink washing breakfast dishes, Bethany wiped her soapy hands on a dishrag and sat at the table. She could hear the drip of water in the sink as she waited for Jimmy to say what was on his mind: *plink, plink, plink.*

He cleared his throat. "Lodestar was stolen."

Bethany's shoulders shivered faintly. She squeezed her hands together into tight fists. "Jake," she said in a deadly quiet voice.

"Probably. Can't prove it but probably so."

Bethany sat there fuming for a few seconds, then she slammed her palms on the tabletop. "It isn't fair. It isn't right! He takes everything we love." She shook her head as if trying to shake off an image of Jake. As quickly as it came, the fury drained out of her and a ripple of hope crossed her face. "Do you think you can find Lodestar?"

"I don't know." He lifted his hands, showed his palms. "Maybe . . . it's for the best."

"How so?"

He leaned back in the chair so the front two legs lifted. "My mother has been after me to manage the chicken and egg business, full-time."

"But you hate chickens."

"I do indeed. But she's my mother and I do love her. And maybe I've been making too much of being a horse trainer. It's created nothing but tension with my mother. I left Paul alone to handle the chicken business and that wasn't fair, either. Sometimes, the things we love can turn into our glory. My sense of purpose, my significance—I put it into something finite. Maybe horse training has become too important to me."

Bethany pressed the heels of her palms into her eyes. "Jimmy," she whispered, wiping guilty tears with the back of her hand. "I'm just so sorry . . ."

He crossed his arms over his chest. "Why? You didn't do anything."

"If I hadn't introduced Jake to my father in the first place, he wouldn't have swindled all those people, and you wouldn't have lost Lodestar."

Jimmy's mouth split into a grin and he shook his head. "Boy, you sure think a lot of yourself, Bethany. I'm perfectly capable of making my own mistakes, thank you."

"But . . ."

"I'm the one who was dazzled by Lodestar and bought him from Jake without getting a bill of sale. I did that all by myself. Maybe I've lit too many firecrackers in my day," he said, rapping his head with his fist. "Or maybe I'm just stubborn. Probably that. But whatever I am, whatever I've done, I've done myself. So quit trying to hog all the credit, will you? Besides, I'm glad things happened the way they did."

Seeing her open mouth, he laughed. "Don't look at me like that. I mean it. I'd been thinking about all this even before Lodestar went missing. I've ignored my mother's need for help with the chicken farm. I think maybe God had to shake me to get my attention."

"You think God arranged for Lodestar to get stolen?"

"Well, I don't think God opened the stall door or anything like that, but I do think he used the situation to shake some sense into me. Galen said once that the hardest choices in life aren't between what's right and what's wrong but between what's right and what's best."

He leaned forward to brush tears from her cheeks. "And who knows? With that horse's penchant for running, maybe I won't have to find him at all. Maybe he'll come back to me."

She tried to smile, but it came out all wrong: sad and pitiful.

"So, think you don't mind being courted by a chicken farmer?"

Bethany's back went straight up. "And who said anything about courting, Jimmy Fisher?"

He wiggled his eyebrows up and down. "When are you going to admit you're crazy about me?"

She gave him a sly look. "You want me to turn into a quiet, timid little Amish girl."

Jimmy grinned. "Not hardly."

"Let me tell you something, Jimmy Fisher. I am not the kind of girl who cares about silly things, like whose cobbler tastes best at Sunday potlucks or what anyone might be saying about an early winter or an early thaw or if the wheat might blight this year due to heavy rains."

"I want you just the way you are. Spitfire and all." He scooted his chair closer to her. "You know you're sweet on me, Bethany."

"Maybe I am, but that's beside the point."

"What is the point?" He scooted his chair even closer to her, his gaze fixed on her lips. "The only thing on my mind is kissing you."

"You need more on your mind, Jimmy Fisher." She turned her chin away, trying not to think about being kissed by him, so of course all she could do was think about it. His fingers were brushing her hair from her neck and then his lips fell there, on her nape, which made her shudder. He noticed. "Look at me," he said quietly.

And as if her body belonged to someone else, that's what she did. She turned to face him and he kissed her. Sweetly at first, full of tenderness. Gentleness. She felt safe here, in his arms.

Luke and Sammy ran past the kitchen windows, holding a basket between them full of freshly gathered eggs.

"Bethany!" Luke shouted. "Open the kitchen door. The basket's heavy and we're hungry!"

Jimmy released her. "What happens if we give it a try, Bethany? This relationship thing?"

She only looked at him.

Jimmy smiled his slow, wonderful smile and plopped his hat back on his head. "I'll talk to you soon."

19

Geena had been right to encourage Bethany to wait before asking the sisters about her mother. She felt better prepared to hear the truth than she had last week, when it was fresh. Painful. She had needed time to "process," as Geena would say.

But the time had come to find out more. Bethany had woken up on Monday morning with a strange inner knowing that it was time. Could it be she was finally sensing the intuition that Naomi said belonged to everyone? Or maybe it was the prompting from God that Geena had said would come, in good time. And here it was.

Over the weekend, Bethany had confided in Naomi, telling her everything she knew about her mother, and Naomi had repeated her standing invitation to the quilting bee. "Come to the quilting bee on Monday," Naomi said. "Come and ask."

Bethany hadn't given Naomi a definite answer, but all morning long, she kept getting a tug she couldn't ignore.

More like a push. At noon, she appeared at Naomi's front door. "I'm going to go."

Naomi smiled, as if she knew all along.

The Sisters' Bee was meeting at Edith Fisher's house. A Log Cabin quilt top, pieced from purple and blue fabrics, was stretched onto a large frame in the living room, with chairs positioned around the frame. The women were just finding their places as Jimmy Fisher darted in and handed his mother a bag of lemons. His eyes locked on Bethany's and he made his eyebrows do that crazy up-down dance, which always made her grin as hard as she tried to squelch it. Edith Fisher caught their look and glared suspiciously at Bethany, who ducked her head in embarrassment.

Edith held up the bag of lemons. "I'll put the teakettle on. I'm serving my shortbread," she announced as if it were a surprise.

"I'd hoped you would," Naomi said kindly.

Bethany had hoped she would not, but fat chance. She was amazed that Naomi—who was a fine baker—could be so charitable about Edith Fisher's rock-hard shortbread. A person could chip a tooth on it.

The ladies chatted to each other in a mingling of Penn Dutch and English. For a moment Bethany closed her eyes, letting the harmonious sound of the two mingled languages fill her. The best sound, she thought. Like music.

"Has anyone seen my favorite thimble?" Ella asked Bethany and Naomi. "I've misplaced it."

More and more, Bethany felt a spike of concern about Ella's with-it-ness. She was always looking for that one lost thimble, the one with the band of roses around its base, though she had plenty of other thimbles.

When the women had settled in their seats and pulled out their needles and thread, Bethany took a deep breath and blurted out, "I have a question to ask and I would like an answer."

Heads bobbed up. The sisters looked curiously at Bethany.

"I want to know the truth about my mother."

Hands stilled. Chins dropped to chests and eyes riveted to needle and thread. All but Naomi. She kept her head high. Bethany was so glad she was beside her. "I went to Hagensburg. I saw my mother. I know she's schizophrenic. I also know that some of you visit her once a month." She hoped someone in the room would speak, but it was as quiet as death.

The ladies peeked around the circle at one another, avoiding Bethany's eyes; then each turned to Edith Fisher, just as they always did when there was a difficult decision to make. It was remarkable how much authority Edith possessed. She would have made a fine deacon, Bethany thought, and wondered why in the world she was thinking such a stray thought when she was waiting to hear the truth about her mother.

"What's that you were saying?" Edith Fisher said stonily.

"I said I wanted to know the truth about my mother."

Sylvia let out a deep sigh and set down her needle. "I always thought we should have told her, right from the beginning. Do I have your permission, sisters?" She looked around the circle for approval. "Edith, is it all right for Bethany to know our secret about Mary?" Everyone waited.

Bethany looked at Edith Fisher. She shrugged her big shoulders up and down, but at last, she muttered, "I suppose we knew this day would come, sooner or later."

Sylvia picked up her needle and thread and set to work. "Bethany, your mother started this quilting bee," she said. "When she married your father, she moved here to Stoney Ridge and asked Ella to teach her to quilt. Ella has always been known for her fine quilting and for her bottomless well of patience." She nodded at her sister.

Ella seemed pleased with the compliment. "Patience is a virtue."

"That it is, dear," Ada said. "And in short supply today."

Oh no. Once the sisters veered off topic, it was never a short trip back.

"She called us the Sisters' Bee, your mother did. And soon a few others joined in who weren't good quilters. Edith, for example."

Edith's sparse eyebrows lifted.

"It's the truth, Edith," Fannie said. "Your stitches were long as inchworms."

"They never were!"

"Knots the size of flies," Lena added.

Edith's lips flattened into a thin line of disgust.

Lena waved that away. "It wasn't your fault, Edith. You just hadn't learned right. You've made a lot of progress over the years."

Bethany cleared her throat to remind them of the topic of her mother.

Sylvia picked up on Bethany's cue. "Your mother was

a pretty girl, just as pretty as you. She and your daddy made a fine pair. But your mama was awful young when they married. And she started showing signs of the sickness before Tobe was born."

"What kind of signs?" Bethany asked.

"She grew fearful," Ada said.

"Oh yes, yes," Fannie said, nodding her head. "I remember that now. She thought someone was after her. She wasn't always sure what was real and what wasn't. But she had good days, when she seemed right as rain. We all thought the sickness would go away after the baby came."

The sisters nodded. "We did think that," Sylvia said. "But after Tobe was born, the sickness came on her and didn't leave. It hit her hard. We all tried helping out—sometimes new mothers get the baby blues."

Fannie shook her head. "This wasn't the baby blues."

"No, it wasn't," Sylvia said. "It was something we didn't know how to handle. Our church was different back then. We had a different bishop—it was after Caleb Zook's time—"

Ella spoke up. "Caleb Zook would have known how to help her. He was a fine, fine bishop."

All five sisters nodded. Even Edith gave a curt bob of her head. Just one.

"Our bishop at that time was hard on Mary," Ada said. "He convinced her that she was being punished for her sins."

Sylvia poised her needle in the quilt, then looked up. "Poor Mary got sicker and sicker—strange, strange behavior. That doctor gave her some medicine, but she didn't like the way it made her feel. She slept almost around the clock."

"All day and all night," Ella echoed.

"And they didn't know as much about mental illness twenty-some years ago," Sylvia said. "Mary couldn't tolerate those drugs, sleeping all the time, not with a little toddler running around. Your daddy took her to more doctors and tried more medicines. One doctor said she would need to be locked up before she hurt herself. Then your daddy heard about a *Braucher* in Ohio and they paid him a visit. When they came back from the faith healer, they threw away her medication. They both thought she was healed. Your daddy—" she sighed, "well, the need to believe things were going to be all right was a powerful one. And for a little while, she did seem better." She looked around the room at her sisters. "Remember that?"

Capstrings bounced in agreement.

"Then she became in the family way with you," Sylvia continued. "And the sickness came back to her and wouldn't leave. One of us took turns staying with her, all the time."

A hot, crushing sensation sharpened in Bethany's chest. "What happened then?"

The sisters exchanged a glance, then their eyes settled on Edith Fisher.

"It was a hot summer day and I was on duty with her," Edith said. "Tobe had fallen outside, so I ran out to see if he was hurt. Your mother was resting, and you were in your cradle, sound asleep. But when I came back in, I found her . . ." She stumbled on the words, then stopped. She puffed air out of her cheeks and looked away.

Whatever Edith was trying to say, it was hard for her.

She turned back to look straight at Bethany. "I found her trying to drown you in the bathtub. She said you had a demon in you."

What did that mean? The heat of the afternoon made Bethany feel like she might faint. She opened her mouth to speak, then stopped. The hot spot on her chest grew hotter and larger, spreading up her neck to her cheeks. This truth . . . as it settled in, it was searing her heart.

"So we packed Mary up and took her to that little house for sick ladies," Sylvia said. "And we never told your daddy or anybody else where she'd gone."

Bethany's breaths came in rapid pants and her throat was so dry. "You did that? You let my father, all of us, think she had run off? Just abandoned us?"

"We did," Sylvia said gently, firmly, "and we'd do it again."

"But . . . why? How could you do such a thing?"

"We were afraid your father would go get her and bring her back and then we didn't know what she might do. To herself, to you, to Tobe. We couldn't risk that."

Bethany dropped her hands in her lap and looked hard at Sylvia. "But that wasn't fair! It wasn't right. Not to my father, not to the rest of us. To not know where she'd gone or why."

"It might not have been fair," Sylvia said, "but it was better than the alternatives."

"How could you put someone away without their will?"

"It wasn't against her will," Edith interrupted impatiently. She'd let Sylvia be in charge long enough. "This was all Mary's idea. She had asked us to help her, begged us, if there came a point when she couldn't take care of you or Tobe. We loved her. We did what she wanted. We even helped with the divorce papers even though it went against our beliefs."

"Against everything we believed in," Fannie said.

"We didn't think it was the right thing to do. If the bishop knew, we would've been in hot water ourselves."

"Terrible hot water," Ella echoed.

"Kneeling on the front bench," Ada added.

"We tried talking Mary out of it," Edith said, "but she was adamant."

"But . . . you helped her get a divorce? My father would never have divorced my mother, no matter how sick she became."

"That's true," Sylvia said, "but he also wasn't willing to protect her. His need to believe everything was all right was stronger than the facts."

Bethany felt a chill run down her spine. Hadn't she heard Rose say the same thing to her father as Schrock Investments imploded?

"I know this is hard for you to understand," Fannie said, "but your mother was desperate. She had moments of clarity that horrified her and she knew the sickness was getting worse. Your mother needed help and your father wouldn't get it for her. He could never accept what her sickness was doing to her. He refused to believe that she was as sick as she was. We felt desperate too, Bethany. That was when the Sisters' Bee had a talk and we agreed to do what Mary asked us to do. We didn't know how else to help her. I suppose we thought this was her only chance to keep herself safe—for her own sake, for others, to give her some peace of mind."

Edith rose. "We never abandoned Mary. We still take

care of her. We rotate a schedule and visit her every month."

Sylvia gave Bethany a sad smile. "This is why we keep quilting. We raffle off our quilts at local auctions and pay Mary's monthly bills."

Bethany tried to steady herself, tried to breathe, as she absorbed this news. "I need to think about it all. I want—I just—" She stood, hoping her knees wouldn't buckle. "I can't take it in." She headed for the door, then stopped and turned around. "How did you know she would never get well? How could anybody predict that?"

The question hung in the air as they all grew quiet again, eyes on Edith. There was something more, a final part of the secret.

"I knew your mother as a girl," Edith said. "We were childhood friends. I introduced her to your father." There was a tremor of sadness in her voice. She looked down at her hands, then lifted her head and looked straight at Bethany. "Mary's mother had the sickness too. She knew what her future looked like."

Bethany grasped the top of a chair. She felt a blow, as real as if someone had kicked her in the stomach. And that was when it hit her. It was genetic. Her mother's sickness was hereditary.

"So *that's* why you don't want Jimmy to court Bethany," Naomi said in a quiet voice.

Edith spoke right to Bethany. "Die Dochder aart der Mudder noh." *The daughter takes after the mother.*

"Edith! That's an awful, awful thing to say," Sylvia scolded.

"It's the truth," Edith huffed.

Sylvia crossed the room and reached for Bethany's

hands, covering them with her own hands, wrinkled and speckled with brown spots. "We kept this secret because we didn't want you to grow up with such a burden hanging over your head. Not you or your brother Tobe." She squeezed Bethany's hands and held them close to her heart. "Just remember one thing, Bethany. Your mother loved you. Don't you see? She loved you and your brother and your daddy enough to give you up."

Bethany had to get out of that house, that stuffy room, away from the looks of pity on the sisters' faces, and she was relieved Naomi didn't follow her. She spotted Jimmy in the cornfield and skirted quickly around the chicken hatchery to reach the road, hoping he hadn't seen her. She desperately needed to be alone.

As soon as she reached the shady, tree-lined road, she slowed. She gulped in air and tried to find words to pray, but she couldn't find them. Her thoughts were on her mother as a young woman—about how she must have walked down this very road when she was Bethany's age—when she felt her heart start to race and she had trouble taking a full breath of air. Her stomach cramped. A tingling sensation ran down her arms to the ends of her fingers. She stopped on the side of the road and sat on the grass under a tree, hoping it would pass. What was happening to her?

After a few long moments, her heart stopped racing, she could breathe again, and she was left with a wave of exhaustion. A sort of oppression settled over her—weighing her down, stealing her energy. This wasn't the first time she felt like something might be wrong with her. Each time, it felt different. A few days ago, her hands couldn't stop trembling. Another time she woke in the night in a cold sweat, convinced she was suffocating. She hadn't slept more than two hours at a stretch in the last week. Was she too young to have a heart attack? Her father had heart trouble.

Or . . . was she going crazy? Like her mother? It wasn't the first time she had thought such a thing. After meeting her mother last week, the worry had been lurking at the back of her mind. All summer long, she had been turning into all moodiness and distraction. She tried not to think she was losing her mind, but that was like trying not to think about a cricket that was chirping. The more you don't think about it, the louder it gets.

Schizophrenia could be inherited. Hadn't Edith Fisher just admitted as much?

She had to go talk to Jimmy Fisher.

◊

"You're breaking up with me?" Jimmy's mouth opened wide and his eyes quit twinkling. "And we haven't even started courting yet?"

"I've given it a lot of thought since we talked, Jimmy," Bethany said, trying to sound clear and strong and brave. No wavering. "It's for the best. It's good that nothing's gotten started yet. It'll be easier. We were friends before and this way we'll remain friends." It hurt too much to look in his eyes so she didn't.

He grabbed her shoulders and made her face him. "What have I done wrong?"

Tell him. Don't tell him. "Nothing. It's nothing like that. It's just . . . I'm just not right for you." To her horror, tears sprang to her eyes and she bit her lip, trying to make them stop. It had been such a long afternoon and she was dangerously emotional, teetering on a breakdown.

"Whatever I did, I'm sorry. If you'll just tell me, I promise I won't do it again."

That pulled her up short. Sympathy was the last thing she expected, or deserved. *Tell him. Don't tell him.* She turned her head away and looked at the chicken hatchery in the distance. "You wouldn't understand."

He gave her shoulders a gentle shake. "Then help me to understand. Why are you suddenly going cold on me? Usually, you're only mad if I've done something stupid."

His face looked so sad, she wanted to hug him, but of course she didn't dare. "I'm not mad at you. I'm not."

His shoulders slumped. Just as he was about to say something, she stopped him. "Please. I just need to be left alone. Can't you understand that?"

He shrugged, but not in a good way, as if he accepted what was coming and was bracing himself for it. "Yeah, sure. Absolutely." He let her go and took a step back, then his eyes turned to a snapping fire for a second and his mouth broke into one of those reckless smiles that made her feel as if her heartbeat missed a hitch. "Don't you worry none about me, Bethany," he said, the words clipped, hard. "I'll get along just fine."

But then she never doubted that and it was hardly to be wondered. Him with his mighty faith, so strong and solid. It was herself she doubted. "I know. I know you will."

He gave her a probing look, one she couldn't read. "Just answer me this . . . what are you so afraid of?"

She turned her head from his hard gaze and felt burning tears flood into her eyes, causing her to sniff like a baby. He just wouldn't leave well enough alone and made her look at him square in the face. "Tell me."

She hesitated for a moment before giving him the only possible answer. "Of making a terrible mistake."

20

Early Tuesday morning, Mim found some sheets of used, slightly wrinkled wrapping paper and tape in her mom's desk and sat at the kitchen table to wrap the present. She had never been so excited to give someone a gift before.

"What have you got there?" Bethany asked as she came into the kitchen with an apronful of gathered eggs.

Mim spread out the wrapping paper and ran her hand along it, trying to smooth out the wrinkles. "I found a thimble for Ella. She's always looking for her thimble so I thought I'd get her one."

One by one, Bethany put the eggs into a bowl and set them in the refrigerator. She came over to the table and picked up the thimble. "Mim, it's sterling silver."

"I know," Mim said, pleased. "Look at the band of wild roses around the base. Just like the one Ella keeps looking for. The one her mother gave to her."

Bethany held it up to the light. "It's dated from the 1890s."

"I know."

"Where did you find it?"

"At Pearl's Gift Shop on Main Street. I saw it in the shop window and knew I had to get it for Ella. That's what I was looking at the day . . . when Chase got . . . hurt."

"But Mim . . . this must have been expensive."

Mim smoothed out a few pieces of tissue paper and tried to figure out how to wrap up such a tiny thimble. If she wrapped it too tightly, Ella's arthritic, knobby fingers couldn't open it. "That's why I wanted you to get my paycheck from the newspaper. I wanted to use my Mrs. Miracle money."

Bethany handed her the thimble and sat down in a chair. "You realize that Ella will probably lose this thimble."

Carefully, Mim cut out a piece of wrapping paper. "No she won't."

"Oh Mim, don't you see? Haven't you noticed how forgetful Ella is? She's always losing things."

"Everybody loses things. Luke can't keep track of a hat for longer than a week."

Bethany blew a puff of air out of her cheeks. "This is a different kind of forgetfulness, Mim."

"No, it's not." She set the thimble in the center of the square and folded the paper up around it. "Ella lost her thimble and she needs a new one. That's all. Stop being mean about her."

"I'm not being mean. I'm just trying to help prepare you—" She stopped and gave Mim a look that she couldn't understand—sweetness and sadness, all mixed together. "Hold on. I might have a box you could fit the thimble in. That would make the wrapping go easier." Before she left the room, she gave Mim a kiss on the top of her prayer covering.

◊

No girl had ever broken up with Jimmy Fisher before—he'd always been the one to cut ties. Was this how it felt? Was this the pain he had inflicted on so many girls? Most recently, Katie Zook? It felt like he had been sucker punched. Left for buzzard pickings under a hot sun. Like someone tore his heart out of his chest with a dull kitchen knife.

Jimmy had hooked the team of horses to a cultivator and was working the soil between the rows of corn, taking out most of the weeds, but not all. Some of them were particularly stubborn and had to be hand pulled.

The horses had done this many times and knew what to do. They walked evenly without stepping on the corn. The rain last week had loosened the soil so the chisel teeth of the cultivator turned the spaces easily: new upturned earth, thick and black against the green stalks of corn. Jimmy kept at it steadily all afternoon, up and down the field, as his mind spun in circles.

For the umpteenth time, he reviewed everything Bethany had said to him as she crushed his heart. Then how, to his shock, she had walked over and put her head against his chest. She put her arms around him and held him tightly. It was so surprising that he almost lost his balance. He put his arms around her to steady himself. She didn't raise her head for what seemed like minutes. He could feel her body trembling and could smell her hair—a scent of vanilla. Then she stepped back from him as abruptly as she had come to him, though she caught one of his hands and held it a moment. Her cheeks were wet with tears.

Bethany's expression had been so full of pain. Why was that? A flare of hope burned through his mind. Maybe it wasn't that she had stopped caring about him. Maybe there was something else that was causing her to be so hot and cold with him.

Naomi. She would know.

He looked at the sun and the corn in the field and decided he had done a good day's work. Fair, anyway. If he hurried, he might be able to talk to Naomi while she was making dinner.

He found Naomi in the kitchen, just like he thought he would, a warm smile on her face. The scent of supper enveloped him, onions and pork and something sweet. She had become, he realized, the sister he never had. "I need some advice."

He sat at the kitchen table as Naomi brought him a cup of coffee, and spilled the sad tale of the breakup. He looked for answers in Naomi's patient gaze.

Letting his head droop, he heaved a melodramatic sigh and pretended to beat his head against the table. "This is pathetic." With his head still on the table, he mumbled, "I hate this."

Naomi rose and set three places of silverware at the table, working around Jimmy. "I'm sorry."

He jerked his head up. "You should be. This is all your fault. You're the one who thought we were meant for each other. You're the one who encouraged me to pursue her. I should never have listened to you. Now I can't get her off my mind." He peered glumly into the bottom of his coffee cup, annoyed that she wasn't giving him anything but sympathy. He was sure she knew more. He was putting her in a hard position, he knew that, but he was desperate.

She set a platter of steaming pork tenderloin, smothered in onions, in the middle of the table. "Bethany has so much on her mind right now. Be patient with her. She just needs some time."

Jimmy kept his eyes on the platter of food. He loved pork and onions more than a cat loved sweet milk. "Or maybe she's just not that interested in me. Not like I thought she was." He forced himself to stop looking at that steaming pork. "Can't you do something? Talk to her or something?"

"No, I can't. You're twenty-three years old. You're acting like a moonsick fifteen-year-old." She rolled her eyes.

"I am moonsick. And that girl makes me feel like I'm fifteen." He dropped his head into his hands. "Pathetic. I'm just a pathetic case."

She caught sight of something out the window and said, "Galen's on his way in. Would you like to stay for dinner?"

Jimmy lifted his head and smiled. "That, I could do."

Bethany felt as if she were living underwater. People said things to her but the words were muffled in her mind. She was going through the motions, doing what she must, stupidly and slowly, as if trying to wake from a deep sleep, to shake off a bad dream that refused to end.

She hadn't called Rose to tell her about Jake's attack or about Chase's death. Or that Lodestar had gone missing. She thought about it, quite a lot, but Naomi's vision of two shadows stopped her short. She hoped Rusty was right—that Jake was gone for now.

She didn't want to give any credence to Jake's "warnings." If Tobe knew of them, she was pretty sure he would stop talking to Allen Turner. That was the way it was with Tobe—if he could avoid difficulty, swerve from facing bad things, he'd find a way. And then Jake would win again.

Whatever Tobe was telling Allen Turner, whatever was taking so long, needed to be said. She had a strange feeling that Tobe's time in Philadelphia was pivotal, though she didn't know why or how.

Late Tuesday evening, she couldn't sleep. The wind was blowing hard through the treetops, rattling the leaves and branches against the windows. Bethany shivered. It was a warm night, but the wind made it sound cold. She went downstairs to make some chamomile tea and found Geena at the kitchen table, scribbling away at her yellow pad.

Geena looked up when she saw Bethany. "Do you know anything about résumés?"

"Not a thing," Bethany said. She filled the teapot with water and set it on the stovetop. "Would you like some tea?"

"No thanks." Geena took her glasses off and rubbed her eyes. "I'm trying to update my résumé and jazz it up. Give it a little punch. It's hard, though, to figure out how to word the fact that I've been fired from my last job. I have to make it sound like a positive thing."

Bethany was half listening, but her gaze fell to her hands. As she waited for the teapot to boil, she was gripping and releasing, gripping and releasing, small handfuls of her nightgown. She made herself stop. "Getting any idea about what to do next?"

Geena shook her head. "I've asked God, but haven't gotten any word back yet. Not a single word." She grinned. "But I'll keep asking till I get my marching orders. 'Ask and ye shall receive.'" She stretched her arms over her head and rolled her neck from side to side to get out the kinks. "Does your neighbor Galen ever talk much?"

"He's not particularly chatty. Why?"

"He brought the boys over, pointed to the hose, shook his head, and walked away."

"By any chance were Sammy and Luke covered in mud?"

"They were! Head to toe."

"That explains the trail of mud up to the bathroom." The teapot whistled, so Bethany turned off the burner. "I'm sure they're sorely trying Galen's patience while Rose is away. Luke, especially. He's the ringleader for mischief."

Geena rose and walked over to the stove. "How are you doing?"

"Fine." Bethany got a teabag out of the cupboard and put it in her mug, then filled it with hot water. She put her hands around the mug.

"How are you doing, really and truly? You hardly said a word at dinner tonight."

Bethany paused for a moment, lifting her eyes to the ceiling and blinking. Her throat had been getting tighter and tighter, as if a hand had wrapped around her neck. She was desperate to talk—she felt she might explode if she didn't get this out—and Geena might just be the right person. Everyone else was too connected to the problem. She needed someone neutral. Geena had an objectivity that no one else did—not Rose, not Jimmy, not Naomi. But she wanted to get through this without losing her composure. She hated tears, they made her feel weak and frightened, and she wanted to be strong. She always wanted to be strong.

Bethany took a deep breath. "I think . . . I'm going crazy . . . just like my mother." Out spilled yesterday's revelation by the sisters, all she knew about her mother as a young woman. The coming of the sickness, her father's refusal to accept the illness, the near drowning, the Sisters' Bee intervention. "I'm about the same age—maybe even a little older. I found out my grandmother had the sickness too. I've been waking up in the night frightened, scared to death . . . and I don't know why."

She swirled the teabag in the water, watching the dark color seep out of the bag and infuse the water. She would not, would not, would not look at Geena's eyes. If she saw eyes filled with pity, she thought she might scream. She needed help, not pity.

"Do these episodes only happen in the night?"

Bethany's head snapped up, surprised at the matter-of-fact tone in Geena's voice after hearing such a sordid tale. "No. Sometimes it happens when I'm just walking down the road. It must be the beginning of schizophrenia."

"Any other symptoms?"

"My heart races so fast it feels like it's going to explode. I have trouble getting a full breath. My palms get sweaty."

"How long has this been going on?"

Bethany kept slanting looks at Geena, expecting to see more than mild concern on her face. Didn't she realize all she was confiding in her? Didn't she care? But Geena was only considering her with a detached professionalism. This, Bethany realized, must be the ministerly side of Geena. Up until this moment, Bethany had viewed her as first a guest in the inn, then as an interesting woman, then as a friend. "Two weeks. At first it happened every few days. Then last week, every day. I had the worst one of all this afternoon."

"Are you having bad dreams?"

"Terrible."

"So when it happens in the daytime, have you ever noticed what you were thinking about?"

Bethany tilted her head. "Today, it happened right after I'd been at the Sisters' Bee and heard what they had to say about my mother. I was thinking about how my mother might have walked down that same road when she was my age. That's when I started to feel dizzy. Confused."

Geena nodded. "There could be all kinds of reasons you're having those episodes. It would be a good idea to have a physical exam—just to rule out anything like—"

"You think I'm going crazy, don't you?"

Geena smiled. "I was going to say, like low thyroid. Anemia. There could be a lot of physical reasons you're having those episodes."

"But you think I'm getting schizophrenia, don't you?"

"I'm not a doctor. I've had a few counseling classes in seminary, but I really can't make a diagnosis—"

Bethany squeezed her eyes shut. "You do. You think I have the sickness." She thought she might start to cry and she swallowed hard a few times. Only a few tears trickled out of the corners of her eyes, and she surreptitiously wiped those away with her sleeve.

Geena sighed. "I don't think you're describing mental illness. I think you're describing panic attacks. Frankly, that makes a lot of sense, given all that's been going on in your life lately."

Bethany's eyes popped open. "Panic attacks?"

"Yes. Just like it sounds. They're very real. And very frightening. But they can be managed too. Panic attacks typically begin suddenly, without warning. They can strike at almost any time—just the way you've described. Waking up in the night or walking down the road. Symptoms usually peak within about ten minutes, and you can be left feeling worn out. Exhausted." She put her hands on Bethany's shoulders. "Look, I shouldn't be diagnosing you. But I will help you find a good counselor, if that's what you need. A counselor can give you coping tools. First, we need to get you to a doctor. That's the best place to start. You may just be run-down or needing vitamins or something simple like that."

"What if it's not simple? What if I'm going to get the sickness?"

"Then we'll deal with that. There's lots of treatments now, Bethany, much better ones than when your mother was diagnosed. If you were showing signs of schizophrenia, and I truly don't believe you are, but if you were, you would be at the earliest stages of the illness and at the most treatable point."

A breath eased out of Bethany in an odd sigh.

"Can I give you one piece of advice?"

She nodded, but she couldn't quite meet Geena's eyes.

"I know it's been a hard week, a hard summer . . . well, just a hard year for your family. But you need to hold on to what is in front of you, not spend your life looking for what's been lost or what might never come."

She gripped Bethany's shoulders firmly to make her look at her. "You do not have to live the life your mother lived. Or your grandmother." She softened her grip, then dropped her hands. "Don't start going down that worst-case path. Just put it out of your mind for now."

If only it were that easy to put things aside. To send it to the back of Bethany's mind like she sent Sammy to bed when he was tired. If only life were that simple. "So . . . what should I do?"

"Pray," Geena said, then immediately closed her eyes and lowered her head.

Geena was going to pray here? Now? Out loud? Prayers were said in private silence, as was the Plain way, unless it was the Lord's Prayer. Feeling awkward, she followed Geena's lead, closed her eyes, and ducked her head down.

Quietly, in everyday language, as if Geena were speaking to someone she knew well and respected enormously, she thanked God for Bethany, for bringing things to light so that Bethany could deal with them and not be frightened by them. She asked for guidance and direction to help her get answers for why she was having these episodes and the support she needed so that she could keep doing the good work she was doing—helping her family, the community garden, and the soup kitchen.

"Amen," Geena said, then looked up at her and smiled. "There. That wasn't so hard, was it?"

Bethany shook her head. "No. Not hard. But a little casual, considering you're addressing the Holy Maker of the Universe."

"Yes! Isn't it amazing?" Geena clapped her hands together in delight, like a child. "That a wondrous and majestic God would want us to talk to him like we're talking to our own father! And he does. Says so in Galatians 4:6."

Bethany didn't know how to respond. She had lived her life attending church—observing traditions, obeying rules, following guidelines—and yet there was so much she didn't know about God. She wanted to know more. Geena made faith sound easy, enjoyable, fortifying. Exciting. Geena's faith gave color to the way she viewed the world and those around her, like strong coffee. Bethany's faith . . . well, if it colored anything, it would be a mild tint, like weak tea.

"God will answer. Trust me. 'I call out to the Lord, and he answers me from his holy mountain.' Psalm 3:4. It's a promise."

"Okay," Bethany said, but doubtfully. If talking to God and getting answers back were really as easy as Geena made it sound, she would have liked sky writing or a booming voice, or maybe a parting of the Red Sea. Some dramatic, no-questions-about-it sign. Some kind of guarantee from God that she wasn't going crazy.

The air was soft and warm after the morning rain shower. Naomi walked over to Eagle Hill as soon as she saw Geena's car drive into the driveway. She'd been watching for it all afternoon after Bethany told her she was seeing a doctor today, sure she was going certifiably crazy.

By the time Naomi slipped through the privet bush, Bethany was out of the car, beaming ear to ear.

Naomi felt a wave of relief. "What did the doctor say?"

"Geena was right! I'm having panic attacks. I'm not getting the sickness!"

Naomi beamed. "I knew it! I was sure you weren't getting it. But I'm so glad that you know it for certain."

"The doctor sent me right over to talk to a counselor in his practice. She gave me some strategies to cope, next time I get a panic attack." Bethany sighed happily. "But at least I don't have the fear attached to it that I'm coming down with schizophrenia like a bad cold."

Geena laughed and reached into the backseat for a bag of groceries. "You two talk. I'm going inside to start dinner."

The girls went up to the porch. Naomi sat in the swing that Galen had built for Rose. She kicked off the swing with her two feet so that it gently swayed. "What was it like to talk to a counselor?" More and more, she heard of church members who were getting counseling and it seemed like a good change. Everybody needed help now and then.

Bethany leaned against the porch pole. "She was so easy to talk to. She told me all about panic attacks and how to discern between true fear and anxiety, and gave me some books to read."

"What *is* the difference?"

"True fear is a constructive emotion. Like . . . do you remember last winter when Sammy and Luke were wrestling up in the hayloft? And I saw Sammy start to fall and ran to catch him before he fell onto the concrete down below."

Naomi nodded. She and Bethany had just walked into the barn and heard the boys overhead. Suddenly, Bethany was at the hayloft ladder, arms cast wide, as Sammy tumbled down the opening, headfirst. She caught him before he hit the concrete floor.

"I moved so quickly—yet it felt like it was all happening in slow motion. I've never moved that fast in all my life and doubt I could again. But fear made me move like that—constructive fear. It was helpful. Anxiety is nameless and vague, and doesn't provide anything constructive. That's what I seem to be experiencing in those panic attacks."

Naomi stopped the swing from swinging so Bethany could sit on it.

"The counselor also agreed with what the doctor said—that there was nothing in my symptoms to indicate a presentation of schizophrenia."

Naomi let out a breath. "What a relief to hear that."

"It doesn't mean I'm immune to it, but the doctor didn't think it was likely." She pushed off so the porch swing started swaying again. "He said that one in five are affected by mental illness. One in five! It shouldn't make me feel better to know that, but somehow, I don't feel quite so alone."

"Speaking of alone, Jimmy Fisher came to talk to me," Naomi said. "He's terribly upset that you broke things off with him." She glanced at Bethany. "Maybe you'll reconsider, now that you have a better idea of what's been troubling you."

"It was hardly a breakup. We'd only talked of courting for about five minutes."

"So, you'll reconsider?"

Bethany looked at Naomi, eyebrows lifted. "Since when did you become such a matchmaker?"

Naomi just smiled. "Only when I get a certain feeling. Like with Galen and Rose. Or you and Jimmy."

"What about you and Tobe? Do you have a certain feeling about that?"

Naomi looked away, feeling a blush warm her cheeks. "Don't be silly. Your brother would never be serious about someone like me."

"Don't sell yourself short, Naomi. Any fellow would be lucky to have you. I mean that. But as much as I love my brother, he's a ways off from being serious about someone."

Naomi grew somber as the smile swept away from her eyes. "What makes you say that?"

"Tobe spent a long time trying to be what my father wanted him to be. And then he spent a long time running from that. I think he needs time to figure out who he wants to be. He still has a ways to go." She grinned. "But I won't deny that he noticed you. Even better was the look on your face when he was around."

"I don't know what you're talking about . . . yes . . . I do." Naomi covered her face. "How embarrassing."

Bethany reached out and covered Naomi's hand with hers. "I just don't want you to get hurt."

"Duly warned. Enough about me. Maybe you should try noticing how Jimmy Fisher looks at you."

"How does he look at me?"

"Well, I wouldn't want to spoil it for you." She smiled her old-soul smile. "He's the one, you know."

"The one?"

"Yes. The One. The one you've been waiting for. The reason you didn't run off with Jake. Deep down, you knew God had someone better in mind. He's the One."

"We'll see."

She nodded. "You'll see. I know."

21

Mim waited on the porch for the taxi to arrive. Her mom had left a brief message that they were heading home this afternoon. She wished for her brother Tobe, with his easy laugh. She even wished for her grandmother, all pinch-mouthed. Most of all, she wished for her mom. She searched the road, straining to hear for an approaching car, needing to see her mom's face. She thought if her mother hadn't left, most of the bad things from the week might not have happened. There was something about her mom that felt like a shield.

Close to five o'clock, the taxi drove up to Eagle Hill. Her mother opened the car and helped Mammi Vera out. Mim ran over to meet them. "Where's Tobe?"

"Geduh is Geduh." *What is done and past cannot be called again.* Mammi Vera walked up to the house, slower and older and a little hunched over, different than she seemed nine days prior. Luke and Sammy barreled out of the house, Bethany behind them.

While the taxi driver got the suitcases out of the trunk, Mim's mom dipped her head into the back of the taxi and came out with a six-month-old golden retriever puppy, wiggling and squirming in her arms. Luke and Sammy lunged for the puppy. "Wait, slow down, boys. Let him get used to you."

Holding on to the blue nylon leash, she set him carefully on the ground and let the puppy sniff. "Mim, this is the puppy that you gave to Delia Stoltz on the day she left Eagle Hill. Turns out her husband is not fond of having a dog in the house, so when Delia heard about Chase, she thought it would be best to return him to us."

Mim bent down to pat the puppy. "She called him Micky, right?"

Mim's mom laughed. "That's right. Short for *Miracula fieri hic*."

Tears sprang to Mim's eyes and she blinked them away, keeping her head bowed. "Remember, Luke? This pup's father was Chase. His mother is Daisy, from the Lapps over at Windmill Farm."

Sammy bent down immediately, nose to nose with the round-eyed pup. Luke didn't utter a word. He just watched the puppy, almost reverently, as he made his way sniffing around the suitcases. Then Luke hugged his mother, hard, and took the leash from her. "Let's go show him around, Sammy."

Bethany, Mim, and their mother watched the two boys and the puppy in a footrace down to the barn.

"How did you know about Chase?" Bethany asked.

Uh oh. Mim had called Delia Stoltz's house each afternoon, around five or so, after she was sure Danny wasn't going to call to go stargazing—which he hadn't, not in a while—and left long phone messages for her mom. She had told her mother everything, but she accidentally-on-purpose neglected to tell Bethany that she had called. Bethany had said she didn't want to worry her mom or Mammi Vera, but Mim couldn't help it. She couldn't hold all that worry inside her. Besides, Galen had called and talked to her mom each day too. Bethany didn't know that, either.

Before her mother could answer, the taxi driver wanted to be paid and Galen and Naomi came over to welcome them home. Mim saw Galen exchange a look with her mom that seemed like married people who sent messages without talking. Their eyes met. His asked: *You okay?* Hers answered: *I'm okay. Not great, but okay.*

"Where's Tobe?" Mim repeated.

"Tobe isn't coming back for a while," her mom explained. "He ended up pleading guilty to withholding evidence and was given a light sentence. He'll be transferred soon to a federal prison camp in central Pennsylvania to serve out the sentence."

"He did the right thing," Naomi said firmly.

Galen gave her a look that was a mixture of surprise and confusion.

"Well, he did," Naomi said, her chin lifting a notch. "He showed courage."

Mim looked at Naomi and realized she had changed from a young girl to a woman this summer. Naomi seemed whole and strong and complete inside herself in a way she never had before. How did people change so quickly?

"Rose," Bethany started, "Jake Hertzler—"

"There's a warrant out for Jake Hertzler's arrest."

Rose looked at Bethany. "Tobe got a light sentence because he agreed to provide evidence about Jake Hertzler."

"Rose, Jake is far more sinister than we ever realized."

"I know, honey." Her mother's eyes filled with tears. Mim had never seen her mom cry before. Not ever. Her voice choked on the words. "Mim told me all about it."

"You what?" Bethany glared at Mim.

"Don't blame your sister. She was worried about you. But after I told Tobe what Jake had done to you—what he had tried to do—he pled guilty and self-surrendered that very day."

"But why?" Bethany asked, her eyes filling with tears. "Why would he do that?"

"I don't know. I just . . . don't know." She held out her arms and Bethany sank into them.

Bethany arrived at the Grange Hall early on Wednesday morning, though the sun was already searing the morning sky with a blinding light. The sisters weren't expected for hours, but Bethany thought if she could get the bread rising early enough, it would be baked in time for lunch. Just as she pulled the flour bag out of the cupboard and up on the countertop, she heard a knock on the door. When she opened it, no one was there but a note was taped to the door.

On it were scrawled only two words: *I'm sorry.*

Bethany saw Rusty kneeling next to the garden plot of the Group Home, thinning radish starts. She was wearing jeans that were too short and a ratty-looking brown sweater that was much too big. Sunlight streamed on her tangled bird's nest of long red hair, making it seem as if it had caught fire.

Bethany stood a few yards away for a while before letting Rusty know she was there, and looked at her, truly looked at her, as if she were seeing her for the first time. She looked beyond the angry eyes and tough-girl attitude, and saw a young, mixed-up teenager.

A purple martin darted between them, flapping its wings in sudden terror. Bethany spotted a cat slinking toward them on a garden path. She smiled. Jimmy's purple martin houses were attracting all kinds of creatures. She sat on the edge of the wooden garden bed. "How'd you like to learn how to bake bread?"

The funniest expression crossed Rusty's face—wariness and calm and hope, all mingled together. Then she dropped her eyes and tugged on her cutoff jeans. She shrugged. "Beats weeding, I guess."

"Good. Put your tools away and meet me in the kitchen in the Grange."

A few minutes later, Rusty joined Bethany in the kitchen. Bethany pointed to the sink. "Wash your hands. Then wash them again. Get the garden grit out from under your fingernails. Scrub them like a surgeon heading to the operating room."

Rusty scowled at her—which didn't surprise Bethany because she knew Rusty didn't tolerate anyone telling her what to do—but she went to the sink and started to scrub.

Bethany stirred a packet of yeast into a jar of warm water and set it aside. She measured flour into a big bowl, created a well, and added a tablespoon or two of oil.

Then she picked up the yeast, now stirred to life—thick and bubbly—and dumped it into the well.

Rusty peered over her shoulder. "That gray stuff is alive."

Bethany laughed. "It is. It's a living organism. When water is added to yeast, it wakes it up." She picked up a sturdy wooden spoon and stirred it together, stirred and stirred, until it was a thick, lumpy blob of dough. She scattered a layer of fine white flour across the surface of the countertop, divided the dough into two pieces, one for each of them, and gave half to Rusty. "It's going to be sticky to start with, but just keep kneading and it will get better. If it's too sticky, dust it with a little more flour."

Rusty pounded it with her hands.

"Whoa! Keep it steady. Watch me. Do what I do." She pushed the heel of her palm into the dough and it squeezed upward, cool and clammy. "You knead dough by folding it, and then pressing the heel of your hand into the fold, like this." She folded, pressed, folded, pressed. Bethany loved the way it felt, spongy and cold, and how it started to change under her palm as she kneaded it.

"Why do you have to knead it so much?"

"You're releasing the yeast into the flour and water and salt. It's a miracle, in a way, to think of delicious bread coming out of such simple ingredients." She glanced over at the sticky lump in Rusty's hands. "Add a little bit of flour as you go so it doesn't stick to your hands."

"How do you know when it's done?"

"The more you bake bread, the more you'll just know, but until then, there are a couple of ways to know for sure: If it holds its shape when you lift the ball in the air. If you poke it and the hole fills in." She grinned. "Or if your arms get tired." She stretched her ball of dough and pounded it down on the countertop. "It's not ready until it's not sticky. It should seem like a smooth, firm ball. Good thing is, you can't knead it too much. Not like pastry dough."

Rusty crinkled up her face in confusion and Bethany realized this girl knew absolutely nothing about cooking. She probably had never tasted a homemade piecrust before, buttery and flaky. "When the ball is elastic and doesn't stick to you at all, it's time to let it rise for a few hours. Then we pound the air out of it, knead it some more, let it rise again, and bake it."

"That's a ton of work for a slice of bread. Why don't you just buy a loaf of Wonder Bread from the store?"

Bethany gave her a look as if a cat had spoken. "Later today, after you eat a piece of this bread right out of the oven, with butter melting on it, then I'll ask you the same question." She watched Rusty push and pull the dough, a serious intent on her face, and thought she might just be enjoying herself. "But if what you're really asking is why anyone would bother to go to all this work—I love to bake bread. I love to cook from scratch."

"Why? It's simpler to just buy stuff."

Bethany was surprised. Rusty was easier to engage in conversation than she would've expected. Almost as if she was just waiting for someone to show genuine interest in her. Geena, no doubt, had probably discovered that right away. "I get a lot of pleasure out of nourishing and feeding people. It makes me happy."

Rusty mimicked Bethany's movement: pressing the dough with her palm, then rolling and pressing it again.

Drumming in Bethany's head was Geena's prophecy

about being a mentor to these young girls. It gave her a shivery feeling down her spine, like how she felt after one of Naomi's visions came true.

As they pushed and pulled at the dough, Bethany said, almost whispering, "Rusty, do you have any idea where Jake Hertzler is now?" She had told herself not to ask Rusty about Jake. Told herself, yet out it blurted. She didn't want to talk about him, to think about him, but in the back of her mind, she had a hope that Rusty might be able to help the police find him.

Cornered and knowing it, Rusty pressed her lips together and stilled. "No," she said at last. "I haven't heard from him since . . . that night."

"I'm not judging you. I know Jake can be a smooth talker. But I wondered how he found you in the first place."

A tiny shade of relief passed over Rusty and she started to push and pull the dough again. When she had her words lined up, her voice dropped to that calm tone she'd used on the night of the attack. "I've known him for a while. He used to get drugs and stuff for me and my friends. He drove by the Group Home and recognized me. Paid me a bundle to destroy the gardens." A combative light came into her eyes as she looked squarely at Bethany. "But I didn't hurt your dog. I wouldn't do that. That was all Jake. I didn't know it was you he was after."

"I'm grateful for your help that night." Back and forth with the dough, back and forth, pushing and pulling.

"He'll be back. Your brother's got something he wants."

Bethany froze. "What? What could it be?"

"I don't know. I don't know if it's a thing or if it's information. I just know he's determined to get something.

I'd tell you if I knew anything more." Rusty jammed her fist at the dough. "He's a bad one, that Hertzler. Bad through and through."

That he is. Bethany hated the man, hated the man with such force she shuddered with it and felt no shame for it. She should, though. It shamed her that she felt no shame.

Rusty didn't offer up another word about Jake and Bethany was fine with that. She didn't think she could stand one more fearful thought about Jake Hertzler. "So what's new at the Group Home?"

"Old Biddy Green is leaving."

Bethany looked up. "The housemother? She's leaving?"

"Yup. Her mother is about to kick the bucket so she's gonna go take care of her."

"When is she leaving?"

"As soon as they find some sucker to take her place."

Bethany grinned. "Mrs. Green wasn't so bad."

Rusty rolled her eyes. "She spends most of the day on the couch watching soap operas."

Bethany shaped the bread into balls and put them in a large wooden bowl, then covered it with a damp dishcloth and set it near the oven. *Someone to take her place.* She glanced over at Rusty, an idea starting to surface. With a sense of sudden purpose, she said, "You might be surprised. Mrs. Green's replacement could be an ideal match."

◊

Geena woke in the middle of the night and somehow knew, without a doubt, the time had come to leave Eagle

Hill. Rose and Vera had returned, the Schrock family didn't need her help any longer, and she sensed that inner prompting she was always listening for. It was time. "I get the message, Lord, but what am I going home to?" She waited for an answer, eyes on the ceiling.

Nothing.

"I'd really prefer to get the full picture, Lord, if you don't mind. I've never been good at that step-by-step thing."

Nothing.

"Well. Fine, then. I'll head back to my apartment in the city and wait for further orders."

Nothing.

In the morning, Geena stripped the sheets off the bed in Bethany's room and packed her suitcase. She looked around to make sure she had left the small room the way she found it. She would leave, but not until after breakfast. She wasn't about to miss her last Amish breakfast. She thought she smelled the sweet scent of freshly baked blueberry cornbread all the way up in her room. It was the Inn's specialty and always served at the first breakfast for new guests.

When Geena went downstairs, she found Bethany alone in the kitchen. The kitchen clock chimed softly while she helped herself to a cup of coffee. "You're up earlier than usual."

"The new guests in the guest flat are bird-watchers. They wanted breakfast at 4:30 a.m. so they could go birding at dawn."

"And you accommodated them?"

Bethany smiled. "Not me. Rose did. She likes birds herself."

Geena sat at the kitchen table and set her mug down. "It's time I head back to Philadelphia."

Bethany glanced up, disappointment on her face. "So soon? Do you have a job? Do you know what you're going to do?"

"No. God hasn't told me that part yet." Not yet. Soon. She felt confident of that. Each day, she went to the Sweet Tooth Bakery for coffee and a cinnamon roll, then spent a few hours in the corner of the bakery using the Wi-Fi. She had emailed dozens of résumés and sent emails to colleagues. She had received one answer back from a church that showed mild interest. They were looking for a youth pastor, though she would have to move to a remote section of South Dakota. She was willing. She would go anywhere God called her. Even South Dakota.

Bethany turned off the burner at the stove and set down the spatula. "Geena, would you consider applying for the job as housemother at the Group Home? Mrs. Green can't leave until she finds a replacement, and Sylvia told me just yesterday that there haven't been any qualified applicants. Being housemother probably doesn't pay much money and you'd be doing more counseling than preaching. I know it's not quite what you had in mind, but you're so good with the girls. Would you consider it?"

The suggestion caught Geena by surprise, so much so that she hesitated a moment before answering. "Thanks, Bethany, but I'm committed to serving in churches."

"But who's to say what kind of church? Isn't serving God what you want to do? You're wonderful with those girls. And being a housemother is a position that plays to your strengths. You've said that was important."

Geena managed a kind smile and hoped it didn't look

as patronizing as she felt. It was sweet of Bethany to worry about her, but how could an Amish girl possibly understand what it was like to be a trained seminarian? Just as Bethany opened her mouth to say something more, Geena cut her off. "Breakfast sure smells delicious."

Bethany clamped her lips shut. A loud clunk hit the ceiling and her eyes rolled upward. "I hear those boys stirring upstairs. I'd better finish up."

An hour later, Geena had said her goodbyes to the Schrock family with promises to return, and drove away from Eagle Hill. She passed by the Sisters' House, the Grange Hall, the community garden, the Group Home. As she turned the corner onto Main Street, she heard the voice of God. It said gently, *Stop. Go back. Feed my sheep.*

Instead, she headed down Main Street and noticed the Sweet Tooth Bakery. She loved that little shop.

She heard the voice again: *Geena, make a U-turn. Watch over my flock.*

She checked her GPS for the road that would lead her east on I-76. To Philadelphia. She clicked on her blinker.

Again, she heard the voice: *Go to the Group Home and care for those girls.*

As soon as the words formed in her head, she understood. She had been asking the wrong question: *Which church should I serve in?* Surely the answer was to look around and see the church was everywhere. She hesitated. And she almost went back. Instead, she stopped at the Sweet Tooth Bakery and bought a cinnamon roll. She loved those cinnamon rolls.

Then she went back.

22

School started on a gray mid-August morning with a rainstorm due at any moment. The wind had picked up, the sky had darkened. As a few drops started to fall, then more and more, Teacher M.K. rang the bell to call everyone into the schoolhouse a little early. For a moment, everything felt normal to Mim. She had been worried Teacher M.K. wouldn't be here this term, but there she was!

Teacher M.K. had an odd look on her face as she welcomed the class back for another term. Happy and sad, all mixed up together. "I have some news," she said at last, and Mim's hands started to feel cold and clammy, even though the air in the schoolhouse was heavy and humid from the warm summer rain. Mim never did like change and she sensed change was coming.

"Since I'm going to be getting married and moving to Ohio, I won't be able to teach this term."

Mim hung her head. She had been holding out a tiny glimmer of hope that maybe Teacher M.K. would keep teaching or postpone her wedding. Just one more term—then Mim would graduate and it wouldn't be a problem if the new teacher were awful.

"The school board has been looking for a replacement for the last few weeks and, so far, hasn't found anyone. In the meantime, they have decided on a substitute teacher. This is someone I recommended to the school board. This person is the smartest student I ever taught. And even though he's a little bit younger than most teachers, he was born to teach. I am counting on each one of you to support him." She was staring right at Luke when she said that.

The door opened and all heads turned to see who was coming in. First, all they could see was a big black umbrella, dripping with rain. Then it dropped to the floor and there stood Danny Riehl.

Mim's heart soared.

Danny shadowed Teacher M.K. all day. Mim stuck around after school let out, hoping they might walk home together. Hoping he might ask her to meet him on the hill behind the schoolhouse and stargaze. After the rainstorm that swept through Stoney Ridge this morning, the skies were clear, the moon just a sliver of a thumbnail, and it would be a perfect night to observe Orion. But Danny didn't look at her, not once, and he stayed close to Teacher M.K.'s desk, peppering her with questions about teaching.

It was getting late so Mim quietly slipped out the door to head to Eagle Hill. As she reached the road, she heard Danny call to her. Her heart soared again as she waited for him to catch up with her.

"I need to go back in and work with Teacher M.K."

She nodded. She understood.

He pushed his glasses up against the bridge of his nose. "I just found out about substituting a few weeks ago. The school board has been looking for teachers all summer and couldn't find anyone. No one wanted it. That's why they finally came to me. I wasn't supposed to tell anyone."

"That's all right."

He looked down at the tops of his shoes. "The thing is, Mim, I want to do well in this job."

"Of course," she said. She twirled her apron corner around one finger. "Of course you do."

"So . . . I . . . won't be asking you to go stargazing anymore. In that . . . I'm your teacher now."

Oh. *Oh!*

"And I need you to do me a favor."

"What?"

He kept his eyes on the waving cornstalks that rustled in a gentle breeze. "You should call me Teacher Danny." For a brief moment he met her gaze. "You called me Danny a couple of times today. I think it would set a good example to the younger students."

She tried to look casual and nonchalant, but she knew it probably looked weird and tight and forced. Her disappointment was massive and she had never been good at hiding her feelings. If she didn't leave soon, she would start to cry and that would be mortifying. She had to swallow twice before she could speak. "I understand perfectly. I'd better get home. Mom will be wondering where I am." She turned and hurried down the road.

"Mim," Danny called.

She stopped but didn't turn back.

He walked up to her. "I'm sorry."

Mim started for home, feeling halfway sad and blue, halfway stupid. As tears slipped down her cheeks, she thought now she could finally answer questions for Mrs. Miracle about love and broken hearts.

Summer was slipping away. The air had gone quiet, falling into the purple hush of dusk as the sun slipped suddenly behind the ridge that framed Eagle Hill.

A hummingbird buzzed through the air, paused to stare at Bethany as she turned on the garden hose, and then settled on the edge of the watering can. It dipped its little bill into the water three or four times and watched her again. A glistening drop of water perched on the tip of its beak. She stopped moving to see what the tiny bird would do, but it flew away. When she turned around, there was Jimmy Fisher.

She walked up to him. "Hello, Jimmy. I haven't seen you around." Now that he wasn't working at Galen's any longer, she hadn't seen him in quite some time.

"You said you needed some space. I've been trying to give it to you."

The expression on his face was so full of pain. She couldn't bear him being hurt. She simply could not bear it. She had to look away. "I guess I owe you an explanation."

He stilled.

She raised her head. He was looking down at her with those spectacular blue eyes of his. A muscle ticked in his cheek and she could see the pulse beating in his neck, fast and hard. "My mother has a mental illness. That's why she left Stoney Ridge the way she did—she disappeared when Tobe and I were little and we grew up thinking she had abandoned us. I didn't know the truth until just recently. I tracked her down and visited her, and I met her." She had a hard time talking around the knot in her throat and her voice cracked a little. "But she didn't seem to know me at all. She's . . . in bad shape. Though she's in a good place. I mean, she's well cared for."

A sadness welled up inside Bethany, choking off the words. She shut her eyes and pressed her fingers to her lips. She hadn't wanted to cry and didn't think she would, but in the next instant scalding tears pushed against her eyes. She buried her face in her hands, but just for a moment. Then she let them fall to her sides, curled into balls.

She swallowed and drew in a deep breath. "Turns out, my grandmother had the same sickness. I thought . . . well, lately, I've felt so confused and upset and moody—I might be getting the sickness too. That's why I ended things with you, before they got started."

"You didn't even give me a chance." He said the words simply, his voice low and flat.

His comment surprised her. She wasn't sure what she expected him to say, but not that. "I know." She looked down at her hands, which were now twisted up into a knot with her apron. With a deliberate effort she unclenched her fingers, smoothing out the bunched material. She lifted her head. "I'm not sure you can understand this, but I felt so scared, Jimmy. I was sure I was getting the sickness. I broke things off with you because I couldn't bear the thought of tangling you in this sickness. I even went to a doctor, and now I'm seeing a counselor. I've been having panic attacks and she's helping me." She bowed her head.

"You didn't think you could tell me any of this?"

"I'm sorry. My mother's situation . . . well, it's complicated. And messy." She shook her head, splattering tears. "Shootfire! If I told you, it would scare you to kingdom come."

His expression grew quite sober. "Think you're the only one with skeletons in your closet? We Fishers have plenty of our own. Let's see, there's old Rufus, who had six toes on each foot. My father passed on at an early age because of high blood pressure . . ."

"Jimmy, those are physical things. Mental illness . . . that's another beast."

"Okay, then. Okay." He bit his lip, as if he was weighing whether or not to say something. "My mother's father lost his mind. I don't know what kind of sickness he had—he died before I was born—but I know it was pretty bad."

"Your mother's father? He was mentally ill?"

"She won't talk about it. Not with anyone."

Edith Fisher, she was discovering, was very good at keeping secrets.

"Bethany, life comes at you like a hurricane, and you do what you can with whatever it blows into your hands, good and bad. I don't think we have any idea about what we're going to be faced with in life."

"Do you really believe that? You think that fate is lying

there like a snake and it'll take you no matter what you do to try to stop it?"

"No, no. That's not what I meant at all. What I'm trying to say is that we don't know what the future holds, only God does, and there's no point in trying to avoid trouble. Like . . . genes. They're a mystery. Who knows what makes us the way we are? Or what triggers an illness? Nobody knows, Bethany. It's amazing how fast life can turn its course—"

"On a nickel and give you some change."

He nodded. He bent over and took her face in his hands, his thumbs lightly tracing the bones in her cheeks. "The only thing I'm sure of," he said, in a voice so loving that it brought fresh tears to Bethany's eyes, "is that I'd rather have you, just the way you are, than never have you at all."

Then, just as suddenly, he turned away abruptly to head down the driveway.

If she'd been holding on to any illusions about how much she cared about Jimmy Fisher, that last speech would have clinched it. And suddenly she was completely aware of this exact moment—the sweet smell of fresh-cut grass, the sound of horses neighing to each other in the pasture, the bleating of the four little sheep, the clatter through the open kitchen window of Rose putting dishes away—because as she watched Jimmy head through the privet hole, she realized that she loved him. Whatever happened, as much as she had tried, she couldn't un-fall in love with him.

On the way home from school one afternoon, Mim stopped to pick up the mail in the mailbox before she walked to the house. There was a thick envelope addressed to her in Ella's spidery handwriting. She dropped her lunch box and sat down under a tree to read it.

Dear Mim,

The silver thimble you gave me is very special. I will treasure it. Sylvia is holding on to it and only letting me use it during our bee time, so it doesn't get lost.

You might have noticed that I have days when things are right as rain, and days when life seems very foggy. Today is a very good day. Clear as glass. But I am becoming more forgetful, and it is possible that one day I might not know where I am or who I am or, even more important, who you are. So I wanted to say a nice, clearheaded thank-you while I still do have my wits about me, or at least some of them.

You are simply the best young woman in the whole world. Never forget that. The real me, inside here, remembers you well . . . as my little Mrs. Miracle.

Fondly,
Ella

One tear, then two, leaked from the corner of Mim's eyes and splattered on the envelope. She brushed them off and felt something else in the envelope. She pulled out four newspaper cuttings of Mrs. Miracle columns, from the last month, ever since Mim stopped nicking the columns from the Sisters' House.

It seemed to Bethany that she had always been worried about something. Now suddenly, her worries had evaporated into bright air.

Could people change? Bethany thought so.

She felt like a different person. She had come to Stoney Ridge to help her family get settled and she ended up having her heart settle. She prayed now, often. When she began to pray it felt awkward, forced, like those stumbling, start-and-stop conversations you have when meeting someone for the first time, full of uncomfortable silences as she racked her brain for the right way of saying things, just so.

Then one day, while she was kneading wheatberry bread dough, she started praying the way Geena prayed. Like she was talking to someone she admired and respected, yet knew well and felt comfortable around. She prayed for Tobe and Rose, her siblings, Galen, Naomi, Jimmy, and for all her doubts and worries, as well as all things she was grateful for. She had even started praying for her enemy, Jake Hertzler. *Shootfire!* Lord knew he needed prayers most of all.

Somehow, as she was praying, pushing and pulling and stretching the lumpy dough, warming it as she kneaded, back and forth, over and under, the stiffness melted away. Words flowed from her, easily, in a way that matched the way she was kneading: simple, rhythmic, forgetting to be worried about the outcome, focused only on the dough, waiting for that moment of elasticity when she knew the yeast and salt and water and flour were no longer separate ingredients but fully blended and the dough was smooth and springy. At that moment she pulled her gaze back to discover the bigger picture, to see what had developed through the kneading of the dough and the sheer honesty of her prayers—and she liked what she saw. She poked the bread and the hole sprang back. Good to go.

As the bread was rising in the Eagle Hill kitchen, she walked down the road to pay a visit to Edith Fisher.

When Edith opened the door, she stiffened. "Jimmy isn't here."

"I know that," Bethany said. "He's over at Galen's. I came to see you."

Edith opened the door and led Bethany to the living room. They sat on opposite sides of the room, very awkward. "I assume this is about your mother." Edith shifted her weight, putting a strain on the chair, whose joints squeaked in protest.

"Not really. It's about your father."

Edith Fisher's mouth went hard. Bethany hated to say bitter, but that's how she seemed, all tight and vinegary and hard. She had the coldest, stoniest look on her face she'd ever seen on a woman. For that matter, a man, either.

"Jimmy told me about your father. That he was mentally ill."

The color drained from Edith's face. "I suppose you told him what I did for your mother." Her lips clamped in a thin, silent line.

Bethany shook her head. "No. That's your secret,

Edith. All he knows is that my mother had a sickness. He needed to know that much, but only that much."

Edith relaxed a little. She rose and walked over to the window. "My papa was a wonderful man. He used to call me his 'little ray of sunshine.'"

Bethany couldn't imagine Edith Fisher as a little anything.

She chewed on her lip for a moment, staring ahead. "He loved to travel. He used to send me postcards from places. Years later, I found out that he was sending them to me from a home for the mentally ill."

Bethany rose from the chair. "The same one where my mother is?"

"Yes." She turned to face Bethany. "That's how I knew what the future looked like for your mama. They had the same sickness. And that's why I don't want you and my Jimmy together. Too risky. The chance of your children getting the sickness is too high."

Well, Bethany knew that wasn't necessarily true. The doctor had given her all kinds of information about schizophrenia. But she doubted she could convince Edith of that and she decided she wouldn't bother. "It's too late. Your boy Jimmy is in love with me. And I love him." The words came into her mind out of the blue, without any thought on her part, as if she had practiced a speech, but she hadn't at all.

"Edith, there are so many unexpected things that happen in this life. You know that better than anybody. Goodness, you just started to live a new life with a new husband, and poof! It's over." She crossed the room to face Edith. "You can be happy about us or you can be miserable about us, but it won't change how we feel about each other."

Edith turned back to the window and crossed her arms over her chest. "I know that. Jimmy told me."

"He did?"

"His eyes flashed with a hard, dark expression I've only seen once or twice in him. When he looks like that, I know he's made up his mind and nothing on earth is going to get him to change it."

Bethany's eyes prickled with tears. Jimmy was so many things that were fine, but the fact that he had stood up to his mother about Bethany was the moment she realized he loved her, truly loved her.

Edith did a sharp about-face. "You are one bold girl."

She nodded. "That's true."

Bethany clasped Edith's hands. "I don't remember much about my mother—nothing specific. But I do remember you, Edith. The bathtub—I remember you holding me, telling me not to be afraid. You wore a blue dress. I do remember that." She squeezed her hands. "Thank you for that. Thank you for all that."

Edith's mask cracked slightly but her lips didn't move one tiny bit. It was her eyes that gave her away. They glistened with tears.

As Bethany walked home in the afternoon sun, she thought again about her mother, walking down this same road when she was Bethany's age. She said a prayer for her mother, like the counselor had suggested she do whenever she started to think about her. Then she took a deep, deep breath, in and out, in and out. Then she waited and, slowly, she grinned. There was no hint of a panic attack.

Since school had started, Mim had stopped taking early morning walks with her mom. There were too many chores to do before school and she was staying up later than usual to keep up with the demand for Mrs. Miracle's advice. But after two more days of Danny acting so high and mighty in his new role as temporary teacher, she knew she had to talk to her mother.

When her alarm went off at 4:30 a.m., she woke with a start and nearly changed her mind. Another hour of sleep sounded sweetly tempting. But then she thought of yesterday, when Danny organized a spelling bee for the schoolhouse and paired Mim with a sixth grader named Arthur Zook. Nobody ever wanted to be paired with Arthur Zook. It wasn't fair—most eighth graders were paired with students from much younger grades, so they could be bossed around. Arthur wouldn't listen to anybody and mixed everything up. Sure enough, despite the fact that Mim told him exactly how to spell the word *isosceles*, Arthur spelled out "e-y-e-s-a-u-c-a-l-e-e-z."

They were the first pair—the very first!—to be sent back to their desks. Mim glared at Danny for the rest of the afternoon, but he never paid her any mind. He virtually ignored her. She was nothing more to him than another student. Less so, she thought at times. He didn't always call on her when her hand was raised in the air. And once, when he was called outside by a farmer one afternoon, he asked seventh grader Betsy Miller to watch over the class. A measly seventh grader! Worst of all, he had given Mim a C+ on a book review she had written, with a note that she could do better. She hated him! And she loved him.

Her mom was surprised to see her downstairs, waiting by the door. "Mim, what are you doing up so early?"

Mim shrugged. "Just happened to be awake." She stifled a yawn. "Thought I'd go out with you today."

"Well, I'm glad to have your company. I've been missing our talks since school started."

Mim followed her mom outside and onto the trail that led up the hill behind the house. The full moon, lying low, cast large shadows along the path. Her mom slowed to walk alongside her. "How's school going this term?"

"So-so."

"Must feel a little strange to have Danny as the teacher."

"It's . . . awful."

Her mother nodded.

"It's just that . . . he's trying to act like he's all . . . grown up."

"Imagine how hard it would be—to suddenly be a teacher to the very students you played softball with a few months back."

Mim hadn't thought about Danny's point of view.

"I know he didn't want to take that substitute teaching job. His mother told me the school board paid quite a few visits to their farm over the last few weeks. Finally, Bishop Elmo had to get involved."

Mim didn't know that. She thought Danny would have jumped at the chance to teach. He was a natural teacher. "It's just that . . . I thought we were friends. And now he acts . . ."

"Like there's a big wall between you?"

Mim nodded. They had reached the top of the ridge and were able to look down on both sides. Eagle Hill shared a border along the ridgeline with the Riehls' farm. It was impossible to get to the Riehls' farm from the hill, though—their side was a steep decline. As she walked to the edge, she could make out the creek that bordered the Riehls' farm. And if she squinted, she thought she could see someone carrying a lantern light from the house to the barn. Maybe that was Danny, doing early morning chores before he left for a day at the schoolhouse. "He told me to call him Teacher Danny."

"So stargazing is on hold?"

Mim took in a sharp breath. She had never told anyone—not *anyone*—that she stargazed with Danny. "You knew?"

Her mom put her arm around Mim. "I knew. And I also know you're fond of each other."

Mim's cheeks burned with embarrassment. She had tried so hard to hide her feelings. "Is it that obvious?"

"No, not really. Certainly not to others. But I'm your mother. Moms pick up on those kinds of things." She smiled. "You have fine taste in men, Mim. But you always did have an abundance of common sense."

Mim dropped her head. "Everything's changed. Danny's changed. I don't think he likes me anymore."

Her mom was quiet for a long time. "You need to take a long view. This is just a short period—until the school board finds another teacher."

Mim knew that wasn't going to happen anytime soon. And she could tell Danny loved teaching.

"I know it's hard to do when you're a teenager, I know

everything seems so important and so serious, but there's a much bigger picture to consider."

"What's the bigger picture?"

"Right now, Danny has a job to do. It's not an easy one, but he took it on. Instead of feeling overly concerned about yourself, or about how this job is affecting your friendship with Danny, think about Danny. Think about how to support him. Encourage the other children to respect him."

Mim didn't. Just yesterday, during noon recess while Danny was inside, Arthur Zook mimicked him. He pushed his glasses up on the bridge of his nose the way Danny did—and Mim joined in the laughter. She should have been a better friend to Danny. He was a good teacher, a fine teacher, even if he did act all high and mighty.

"Mim, you have a job to do too."

Oh no. Had her mom found out about Mrs. Miracle? She didn't subscribe to the *Stoney Ridge Times*. Hardly any of the Amish read the local newspaper. She thought her hidden identity would be safe. Had Bethany told? Had Ella?

"You're helping Bethany with the community garden. You're finishing your last year of school. The sisters want to pay you to be a Saturday companion to Ella. You have plenty of things on your own plate."

Relief flooded Mim. Mrs. Miracle's secret identity was still safe. So far, so good.

"Time is your friend, Mim. You're only fourteen. Danny's only sixteen. If you're meant for each other, nothing will get in the way of that."

"But . . . what if we're not?" That was the question, deep down, that plagued her.

"Then that means there's someone God has in mind who is better for you too. Not just Danny."

Harold the Rooster let out his first crow and her mom laughed. "That's our signal. Time to head back down the hill and start the day." Just then, the eagle pair soared over their heads. "I thought they might leave us, after their baby died last spring. But they've stayed. Maybe next year they'll have another baby. Maybe two." She looked at Mim. "Life can get good again."

She started down the trail and Mim waited a moment to watch the eagles circle low over the creek, hunting for breakfast. Then, feeling like she had dropped a heavy stone, she ran to catch up with her mom.

23

Ladies, the quilt's waiting for you," Edith Fisher announced as everyone took their places and began to stitch the green sashing. They all murmured their approval at the intricate Star of Bethlehem pattern, made up of blues and yellows and greens.

"It's pretty. Awful pretty," Edith Fisher said.

Naomi stopped sewing and looked at her. So did Bethany. Edith Fisher had never in her life said anything was pretty.

"Well, it is," she sniffed.

"Did you all hear that the lady preacher who was staying at Eagle Hill took the job as housemother at the Group Home?" Fannie said.

"Where'd you hear that?" Edith said as Naomi and Bethany shared a secret smile. Not only did they already know that piece of information, but Geena had already roped Bethany into volunteering to teach cooking classes for the wayward girls from the Group Home. Next summer, Geena wanted the girls to help out at the soup kitchen. She had even given the soup kitchen a name: The Second Chance Café.

"I heard it from her this very morning," Fannie said, looking pleased she knew something before Edith did. "I saw Geena Spencer in the Sweet Tooth Bakery wolfing down a cinnamon roll."

"Well, that's just dandy," Edith Fisher said. "Teach all those young innocents how to be women's libbers." Now she was her old self again.

Ella was following things better that afternoon than she had in a long time. "I heard that folks throw a cat on top of the quilt as soon as the last stitch is in. If the cat jumps into your lap, then you're the next to get married."

Fannie snorted. "*Now* you remember the secret to catching a beau, Ella. Should've told us that sixty years ago." The women all got a big laugh out of that and started vying to have the cat fall in their lap. All but Naomi.

She leaned close to Bethany and whispered, "I wish the sisters would remember that I'm not in my eighties."

Bethany grinned. "I have an announcement to make," she said. Her eyes moved around the ring of faces, starting with Sylvia and ending with Edith. The room was so quiet, they could hear Naomi's needle go through the quilt. The needle squeaked as she pushed it through the cotton with her thimble.

"I'd like to visit my mother," Bethany said. "On the rotation schedule. I'd like to go with you. Each month. She's my mother, even if she's sick. I want to help take care of her. The caregiver said my mother's best days were when the quilting ladies paid her a visit."

For a long moment, no one said a word.

"Me too," Naomi piped up. "I'd like to go too."

More silence. And then Sylvia smiled. "Of course. Of course." She looked at Edith. "That's a fine plan, isn't it, Edith? It's the best plan of all."

Everyone looked to Edith. "I suppose."

"Then count on me," Bethany said, and her heart was suddenly too full for words as she let her gaze roam lovingly over these women: the ancient sisters whose hearts were so large; Jimmy's mother Edith, who wasn't nearly as tough as she liked others to think; Naomi, her loyal and kind friend. It was a wonderful place to be, nestled in the heart of these good women.

They sewed quietly for a long time, no longer feeling a need to talk, until at last, Edith Fisher stuck her needle into the quilt and took off her thimble. "Somebody tell me where's the time gone. I forgot all about refreshments." She placed her hands on the side of her chair and hefted herself up. "I'll put the teakettle on. Tea always hits the spot after an afternoon's sewing. Did I tell you I've got shortbread?"

She took a few heavy steps toward the kitchen before stopping to place her hand on the back of Bethany's chair and leaning over to examine the quilt in front of her. "Well, lands sake, those are real nice stitches. You're coming along just fine."

She looked at Edith and smiled, and, in her own stiff way, Edith smiled back.

Summer had a few days left to run, but here and there, spots of yellow and pale orange on the trees made it clear that fall was fast approaching. A gust of wind in the branches made a rustling sound, as if the leaves were made of paper. The sun shone bright and clear in a sky of brilliant blue.

Bethany was on her way to Eagle Hill after another session of cleaning out the Sisters' House. Today, she thought she might just be making headway in the de-clutter process. A person could walk through the living room now without having to swerve around stacks of books or bags of quilt scraps. The sisters were still a long way from being ready to host church, but it was on the horizon. The far, far distant horizon. Especially now that the sisters had asked Bethany to supervise the Grange Hall Second Chance Café and she had said yes.

Shootfire! How did that happen, anyhow? One minute, she was lugging the little red wagons over to the Grange Hall just to help the sisters. The next thing she knew, the sisters smiled their sweetest smiles at her and suddenly she was in charge of the soup kitchen. But how could she say no? What would happen to all those down-and-outers if something happened to the sisters? They weren't spring chickens, after all. A slow grin lifted the corners of her lips. Those sisters could talk the birds right out of the trees.

Bethany had one foot on the porch step of Eagle Hill when she stopped, spun around, and strode over to Naomi's. She wanted to see how Naomi was faring after a fierce headache that kept her sequestered in the basement all weekend.

As Bethany walked through the privet hole, she noticed Galen standing by the far edge of the barn, talking to someone, slapping shoulders the way men do when they're glad to see each other. She stilled, realizing it was Jimmy to whom Galen was talking.

She hung by the privet, watching the two from afar. She thought of the first time she had seen Jimmy, at the farmers' market, and he was just a stranger, handsome and amusing, eyes with a fiery sparkle that caught girls under his spell. Not Bethany, of course, but most other girls. He was still a boy, she had thought then, in a man's body. But Jimmy seemed different somehow, taller and older than just a week ago when he had come to talk to her at Eagle Hill.

She could hear the rumble of his laugh from where she stood. She loved that laugh of his, so kind and warm-hearted. When he laughed, he reminded her of a feisty horse you couldn't help but be fond of, full of life and spirit. With a start, she realized she had never felt happier than she did at that moment. No, wait. It wasn't happiness she felt. It was joy. Something deep down that couldn't be stolen.

Just then Jimmy caught sight of Bethany and snapped to attention. Galen noticed and politely absented himself, disappearing into the barn.

She waited for Jimmy to stride across the yard to come to her, as recommended by *A Young Woman's Guide to Virtue*. A girl must never chase after a boy.

Jimmy did cross the yard, but he stopped a few yards away from her. Merriment sparkled in those blue, blue eyes. "Something on your mind?"

"Why yes, there is." A voice that she was surprised to realize was hers said, "Jimmy Fisher, I love you." Her heart beat faster. "That's all I have to say. I honestly and truly love you."

Jimmy looked at her intently for a long moment beneath his hat brim, then his blue eyes twinkled. "I know. I knew it all along. But I'm glad you finally got around to figuring it out for yourself." A slow smile, homey and unhurried and sweet, like syrup over pancakes on a Sunday morning, spread across his face.

Naomi was right. No one had ever looked at her the way Jimmy did. It was the look of a man in love.

He opened his arms. "Come here."

She walked toward him and he met her halfway, their lips meeting at the same time. It felt like home to be in his embrace, familiar and safe.

Rose's Blueberry Buckle

¾ cup	sugar
¼ cup	soft shortening
1 large	egg
½ cup	milk
2 cups	sifted all-purpose flour
½ teaspoon	salt
2 teaspoons	baking powder
2 cups	blueberries (fresh or frozen)

Preheat oven to 375 degrees. Mix sugar and shortening, then add in egg. Stir in milk. Sift together and stir in flour, baking powder, and salt. Carefully blend in berries. Grease and flour a 9" square pan. Spoon batter into pan. Put on crumb topping before baking. Bake 45–50 minutes, depending on your oven.

Crumb topping:

½ cup	sugar
½ cup	flour
½ teaspoon	cinnamon
¼ cup	soft butter

Blend together with fingers and drop mixture on top of batter, spreading evenly.

Discussion Questions

1. Finding a trunkful of human bones in the basement of the Sisters' House might seem amusing, but it actually kicked off a theme of "skeletons in the closet." Has there been a time in your life when you were faced with some unfinished business from your past? (By the way—finding a trunkful of human bones in an attic of an Amish farmhouse was a true story!).
2. Which character did you identify with the most? Why?
3. How were the concerns different for each of the characters: Bethany Schrock? Mim Schrock? Geena Spencer? Jimmy Fisher? Naomi King?
4. Sylvia, the youngest of the ancient sisters, gave this advice to Bethany: "You mustn't blame yourself or look back—not any longer than it takes to learn what you must learn. After that, let it go. The past is past. But you're still here," she whispered urgently and exerted a gentle pressure on Bethany's

arms. "And I'm glad. You be glad too." When might you have needed such advice?

5. How did Bethany's view of herself change throughout the story? What contributed to that change?
6. All families face strife from time to time, just as Jimmy and his mother did. What were your thoughts when Jimmy decided to set aside his passion for horse training and return to the Fisher Hatchery to help his mother?
7. In spite of her headaches, Naomi is peaceful in her spirit. In what ways, surrounded by a troubled world, can we cultivate a spirit of peace?
8. Did you pick up on any clues that Stuck, who wrote letters to Mrs. Miracle, was Rusty? How did Mrs. Miracle affect Stuck/Rusty?
9. A person cannot change his or her past actions, but can they make up for the hurt they've caused by helping others? Does the good that Edith Fisher did for Bethany's mother make up for the years of keeping her whereabouts a secret?
10. What did Ella's lost thimble symbolize? How were other characters searching for something from the past?
11. How did reality measure up when Bethany met her mother?
12. Bethany obviously feels respect for Geena. How does Geena share the same high opinion for Bethany?
13. Another theme in this book is coming to grips with one's past so one can move forward. Bethany

longed to find purpose, Geena was seeking purpose, even Mim was looking for purpose with her secret identity of Mrs. Miracle. How did all three find purpose through serving others?

Acknowledgments

As the saying goes, writing is a lonely business. It would be impossible to get books out into the world without a solid network of help and support. My circle is rich, and they deserve the small moments of attention here.

I could never get anywhere without the saintly team at Revell, welcoming the characters of Stoney Ridge with open arms. And deepest thanks to my editor Andrea Doering, for helping me find my best work, over and over again, and challenging me to be better than I think I can be.

Special thanks to my agent, Joyce Hart of The Hartline Literary Agency.

The Grange Hall soup kitchen is based on a true story. There is a woman in the San Francisco Bay Area, Mother Williams, who started a once-a-week soup kitchen while in her early eighties. She is nearly ninety now and still going strong. A remarkable and inspiring woman. It took five sisters in this story to match the energy and determination of one Mother Williams! Grateful to you, Becky Blakey, for filling in some details.

And last on the page, but not in my heart, thanks to my readers. The circle is not complete without you, so thank you from the bottom of my heart. I love hearing from you and listening to your stories. Find me online at www.suzanne woodsfisher.com or send me an e-mail at Suzanne@suzanne woodsfisher.com.

Suzanne Woods Fisher is an award-winning, bestselling author of more than two dozen novels, including *Anna's Crossing*, *The Newcomer*, and *The Return* in the Amish Beginnings series, The Bishop's Family series, and The Inn at Eagle Hill series, as well as nonfiction books about the Amish, including *Amish Peace* and *The Heart of the Amish*. She lives in California. Learn more at www.suzannewoodsfisher.com and follow Suzanne on Twitter @suzannewfisher.

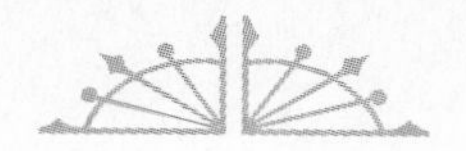

The Inn at Eagle Hill is a place of ***unconditional love*** and ***unexpected blessings***

a division of Baker Publishing Group
www.RevellBooks.com

Available wherever books and ebooks are sold.

Meet Suzanne online at

Suzanne Woods Fisher

suzannewfisher

www.SuzanneWoodsFisher.com